The Mixing Bowl

DONNA LYNN LITO

WEBM 4Press

979-8-9902972-9-6
979-8-9902972-4-1

Donnalynnlito@gmail.com

WEBM 4Press

First edition 2024

To my daughter Tootsie~
You make life sweeter.

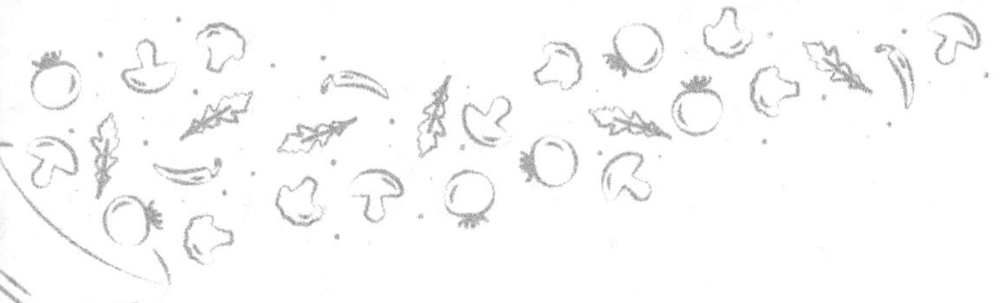

PART I

Peach Cobbler

Ingredients

- 1 cup of flour
- 1 cup of sugar
- ½ cup of milk
- ¼ cup of melted butter
- 1 cup of canned peaches

Directions

Mix together flour and sugar. Add butter and milk. Pour mixture into baking dish.

Pour fruit over this mixture and bake until the top is brown at 325 degrees.

Original recipe by Eva Wilson
Shared by Sheila Wilson Streckert Summerville, S.C.

CHAPTER ONE

THE SUN WAS BEGINNING to poke its brilliant head out from the trees surrounding the small South Carolina town. The Pines were an essential part of the community, which locals took pride in preserving. Each summer, folks from all over the country traveled to the coastal town to indulge in the Palmetto State's fine cuisine, lush landscape, and Southern hospitality.

Visitors basked in the sun, enjoyed the warm beaches, and found surprising menu items scattered throughout the state. One favorite and misleading dish was Frogmore stew; despite the name, no frogs were included. Instead, the rich flavor of spices, fresh seafood, plump potatoes, and corn on the cob would delight newcomers repeatedly. Not only did Southern hospitality appeal to vacationers, but the array of Southern cuisine, homemade ice cream, and strolling the streets of small towns also made South Carolina a vacation spot for many. After appeasing their appetites, visitors would pacify their sweet tooth at the town's oldest and most beloved bakery—a place that would one day hold a lifetime of memories for the Loring Family.

Throughout her life, Isabel had been keenly aware that things were not as they seemed. Life had proven that often, people would see whatever they wanted to see. Perspective was a funny thing; each viewpoint oddly different from another could make any reality questionable.

For Isabel, being underestimated was nothing new. At first glance, one might mistake her for a typical Southern Belle. Her long hair, round face, and bright smile could easily lead any observer to think she was easy to please. However, this couldn't be further from the truth.

She stared at the mirror, tucking her honey-blonde hair behind her ear. While she appeared slim and unassuming on the outside, inside, she was fierce. Her tenacity had begun in childhood when many kids teased her for wearing ragged clothes and having unkempt hair.

Determined to show others she was not her financial status, she started collecting used clothes and making unique blankets from the leftover fabrics. If nothing else, Isabel was resourceful.

She sold the blankets to local vendors for extra cash.

Whenever she couldn't sell the fabrics, she found other ways to earn money to help with the family's accruing debt, her mother teaching her to hem pants and sew buttons on shirts.

"Knowing how to sew will help pay the bills," her mother would lecture. As much as Isabel groaned about it, her mother was right that it did bring extra money. But the truth was, Isabel hated to sew. It was tedious and cumbersome, and she longed to do something faster-paced.

By the time she was barely a teenager, she discovered her passion for cooking after signing up for a baking class at school. While she despised the repetitive task of hemming trousers and steaming pleated skirts, she cherished the idea of creating food for others to enjoy.

Isabel was creative and a risk-taker, and sewing was predictable and boring.

She saw cooking as an art and embraced the challenge in the kitchen, feeling a part of her come alive under the pressure and urgency to perfect the recipe.

At the time, young girls understood their role in the South, and that was to find a husband and become mothers. However, this made Isabel anxious, so she did everything she could to be different from the other girls. Isabel was brave and bold, some would even say, a bit too much for others to handle.

While most young women her age were busy searching for husbands, Isabel focused on discovering new recipes. Taking the plunge into her authentic self and passion for cooking was intimidating, but she knew she could always return to being a seamstress if it didn't work out. It wasn't long before she completely traded her needle and thread for a cutting board and knife.

As much as Isabel wanted to start working at local restaurants, her father would have no part in it, worrying she would be taken advantage of by local men or, even worse, killed.

He had heard stories of young women who met such fates and didn't want his daughter getting caught up in any trouble. As it was, he was in a vulnerable state.

He had recently lost his wife to heart failure, and the thought of another loss was too much for him to consider. George, who had once been a brazen man working on the farms, had soon become quiet and angry after his wife's death. Isabel couldn't remember the last time she had heard his laugh, and he slowly became more withdrawn as time passed.

By the time she was fourteen, Isabel was left motherless and found herself caring for her father, who lived with a broken heart and a fondness for alcohol—being responsible for keeping her father away from drinking left Isabel with little opportunity to be like the other kids at school. Instead, she channeled her determination into becoming the best she could, hoping to one day work at a restaurant far from the small town of Grover Creek.

She tried and retried recipes, saving for ingredients the little money she earned by selling blankets. Not only was this her passion, but she also wanted to bring joy back to her father's life through his tastebuds. Food brought people together, and she hoped it would sway her father to gain some excitement. However, despite all her efforts, he rarely ate and spent his time alone.

Isabel was grateful for the small pay she received and worked hard, even competing in local pie contests. Her mother had been a good cook but only did it for the family's enjoyment. She would never dare to suggest getting paid for something she deemed as her duty.

Isabel was as traumatized by her mother's sudden death from a heart attack as her father was.

Her mother had appeared healthy and vibrant, and the thought that her heart would stop working properly was Isabel's first understanding that things were not always as they seemed.

The passing was so sudden that it took Isabel's young mind months to come to terms with the fact she was really gone. Her daddy, George, busied himself day and night in his garage after his wife's passing, barely able to look at Isabel because the resemblance was strong.

On the occasions when he did look at her, he would immediately take to the bottle, soon passing out. Isabel knew that seeing her reminded him of her mother.

So, she learned to stay out of view to avoid more heartache for her father.

The lack of interaction with her father often left her alone.

To occupy herself, she would remember her mother's sweet treats and try to reproduce each one, making her feel closer to her mother, whom she missed dearly.

As the years passed, and after years of trying—and failing—to recreate her mother's perfectly tart lime pie, Isabel was proudly ready to show off her talents. Now that she had perfected the complicated recipe, it was time to enter as many competitions as possible across the Lowcountry.

Despite her best efforts and to her disappointment, she didn't win. Nevertheless, she kept traveling by bus to compete at farmers' markets, fairs, and Christian conventions. Although the prize money wasn't as high as in the major cities, Isabel was motivated to compete more for the thrill of winning than for financial gain. She yearned for validation. Perhaps it was the loss of her mother or the neglect from her father, but Isabel found confidence through the perceptions of those sampling her treats. She would never scoff at money; she could use every penny she could get her hands on, but the pleasure of competing was all about recognition.

The competition was always fierce, and a slightly older woman named Nancy would usually win, leaving Isabel collecting yet another second-place trophy. This only made her more determined to continue perfecting her skills, though each time she ran into Nancy, she secretly hoped her pie would fly off the sizeable porcelain cake stand and find itself on the floor.

Nancy didn't care that Isabel was young enough to be her daughter; instead, she viewed her as a child with a hobby, which only outraged Isabel even more.

"Well, Hello, Nancy. Bless your heart, is that another lime pie? I thought you would try a new recipe like that apricot cobbler you raved about the last time I saw you in Summerville. The town sure did put on quite an event."

"Iris, hello." The woman's voice was dismissive with a flair of condescending tones.

"It's Isabel." Isabel's voice was tense, insulted she had already corrected her four times.

"Oh, right. My apologies. I thought about trying the new cobbler, but I kept winning with my lime pie every time, so I decided to stick with it. Though, I'm running out of room for all the trophies," Nancy said with a laugh.

Feeling her cheeks flush, Isabel took a deep breath. "Well, as always, best of luck to you. I will be seeing you around."

"You certainly will," Nancy said as she waved her hand, walking away.

Isabel looked down at her pie. Was the whipped cream thick enough?

Had she remembered to squeeze a little extra lime into the batter and add a touch more sugar? Suddenly, she felt anxious, and her armpits dampened.

Dammit, the last thing a Southern woman needs when she's trying to portray elegance is sweat marks under her armpits, she thought.

Isabel took deep breaths, trying to remain calm, but she had already been close to tears.

If she didn't start winning some competition money, she could not justify taking the long drive around South Carolina in the summer.

"Something good's gotta happen. If only Mama were still alive, she'd know how to beat the pants off Nancy."

At times like these, Isabel longed to have her mother back to guide her about life.

Worse, after her mother's death, her name had never been mentioned again, which only added to her loneliness. Her daddy thought it too hard to talk about her and had taken down every picture around the house. Once, when Isabel felt particularly brave, she asked if he missed Mama. George's eyes filled with tears and rage before hollering, "Your mama is gone now. Get over it. She ain't never coming back, so there is no use wishing for something impossible."

Defeated, Isabel walked out of the house and down to the lake half a mile away.

Her eyes stung, and her breath was heavy.

Trying not to cry, she kicked rocks and threw sticks into the lake.

Specks of dirt were hitting her face as she stomped on the dirt road, cussing under her breath.

"Mama, if you can hear me, I miss you and want more than anything for you to return."

The silence was deafening as the warm wind hit Isabel's tiny face.

Wiping tears, she promised, "One day, Mama, I am going to open a bakery and make your recipes the most famous in South Carolina."

As the years went on, George only became more withdrawn and spent much of his time in the garage, drinking until bedtime.

He supported Isabel's passion for cooking, though he thought her ambitions were to be a good wife, not a career chef. "You are going to make some man a very happy husband, especially with how you cook," he would say on the rare occasion he came in before dark.

"Actually, I was thinking of getting a job."

"A job?" he said.

"Yes, at a restaurant. You know it yourself, Daddy. I have talent. I want to work in a kitchen at a restaurant," she said slowly.

"A young girl belongs at home in our kitchen, helping out," he barked. "Too many men would happily take advantage of a young, innocent girl working in a paid kitchen; no, you belong here."

"Daddy, please, I really want to learn," Isabel pleaded.

"Learn here. And you can start by making me supper; I'm starved."

Isabel knew there was no use in arguing with her father.

What he said went, and it would be futile to argue. Quietly, she began preparing dinner and silently figuring out a way around her father's demands.

Chapter Two

It was over three years later, not long after her eighteenth birthday when she found her father lifeless on the garage floor. The coroner stated that an alcohol-induced stupor contributed to his death, which was hardly surprising. He had tripped over his tools and slammed his head against the floor. It had been hours before Isabel checked on him, only to discover him lying in a pool of blood, dead. She felt immense guilt for focusing more on the focaccia bread baking in the oven than on her father that day, yet she couldn't help feeling anger toward him for not taking better care of himself.

Due to his reckless behavior, Isabel was now on her own and had no choice but to find work, or she would starve. She supposed she could have found someone to marry her, but there were few suitors, and Isabel had never sought one in any case. Now, though, she was free to take a job if she wished.

She could easily have returned to sewing to pay her way, but her heart did not lie there.

No, despite all odds and the opinions of many that women's roles were to be in the kitchen, not running one, Isabel was determined to continue working on her craft.

She knew it would be challenging, and she would face affront from egotistical men, but that hadn't ever prevented her from pursuing her goal so far.

After George's death, others assumed she would marry the first man who paid attention to her. However, Isabel had no interest in marriage despite the not-so-quiet whispers at the market. Those hadn't bothered Isabel one bit, though the town gossip would say otherwise. In fact, out of spite, Isabel was vowing never to wed at all and thus teach everyone to mind their own business.

"That poor girl, still not married," she overheard a woman in her early thirties declare from afar.

Her hair was in a tight bun, and her belly protruded; three small children ran around the shopping cart recklessly. The older woman with whom she had been talking nodded, not realizing that Isabel was standing beside the two as they shared gossip about the town spinster.

"Ahhh, it is such a pity that I am not bogged down with all these monstrous children and that I'm not standing talking nonsense about other people in the aisle of a supermarket on a Friday afternoon. Poor me," Isabel said sarcastically. She waved her hands for theatrics.

"Oh honey, bless your heart. I didn't realize you were standing there. We don't mean anything by it, dear. It's just that we are concerned for you—"

Isabel cut her off. "Well, don't be. Be more concerned that one of your wretched kids just shoved a grape up his nose."

The mother gasped, hurrying away to remove the grape from the child's nostril.

Isabel laughed, shaking her head and smiling. "This town ... I'll show them."

Despite her reluctance to marry, Isabel occasionally entertained thoughts of what being a wife and mother would be like. Women obtained a certain security and respect through a man's last name. She'd had a few relationships throughout the years, but none had kept her attention.

Mostly, the boys around would see her as a challenge, but once they realized they could never take advantage of her, they would retreat to a girl more eager to please.

Isabel hoped to find someone who matched her energy, but she was only interested in a man who was secure in himself and not intimidated by her goals. If she were to take a man at all, she wanted one who wouldn't try to minimize her talents but would celebrate them alongside her.

It would be a tall order to find a Southern man willing to allow her to be herself.

It was a time when Eleanor Roosevelt had changed how Isabel thought about herself and her future. Eleanor spoke of courage, responsibility, and hard work and was a champion for the American workers, especially women, and the barriers they faced. Using her icons as her guide, Isabel was a kindred spirit who wanted to invoke change in the South. Mostly, though, she enjoyed spending her time in the kitchen and serving others as a career, not an obligation.

Fascinated by culinary arts, she would spend hour upon hour practicing her craft, from soufflé to grits. The young, fiery chef was like no other, especially in the South when the expectation was nothing greater than to provide a home for a husband. She didn't even mind much that she didn't follow unwritten rules or that others judged her for living exactly how she wanted.

She suspected many were jealous of her or confused by her free spirit, so she chose to ignore the whispers in the streets and the side eye of demeaning strangers.

All the time, she felt the stares, and only once did she address a woman because of it. This particular distasteful woman had more than an air of arrogance about her, displaying open disdain for Isabel without regard.

They had been waiting at the meat market counter when the woman in her late twenties was dressed in a plaid skirt cut in front of Isabel.

She would have allowed this to occur but was taken aback when the woman—just as she brushed past—had the audacity to mumble, "Some of us women have responsibilities."

Confused, Isabel said, "Excuse me, ma'am. Were you just talking to me?"

The woman with a short bob cut, red lipstick, and mouth agape just stared, ignoring Isabel's inquiry, and continued ordering a pound of beef from the stocky butcher behind the counter,

Isabel's voice grew louder. "Did you hear me? I was here first, and you just cut me in line."

The butcher, seemingly uncomfortable, shifted the meat around with a long spoon. "I don't know who was in the line first, but can I help either of you ladies?"

"Yes, you can help me since I was here first," insisted Isabel, enunciating the *first* sharply.

"You can't possibly let her go before me, Jack," huffed the woman. "I am a mother and a wife, with responsibilities, may I add. I need to get home before my husband gets cross that dinner is late."

Isabel turned to face the woman. "Well, your first mistake is worrying about what your husband thinks. If you ask me, he should appreciate you making dinner at all," she said.

"How dare you? What do you know about being a real woman? Aren't you the one who works in a kitchen with many men? Have you no respect? You must apologize to me. I am a mother and wife, and I demand you speak well to me." The exasperated woman rolled her eyes. "Whatever has happened to this society?"

"I ain't doing no such thing. God doesn't like ugly. Y'all sure are acting ugly for a woman pretending to be such an important lady," said Isabel.

"And if you had a family, Miss, you would understand the importance of getting home to provide a hot meal instead of running around like a man," barked the lady barely older than herself, holding her ground beef as the butcher stared blankly.

The lady gathered her things, paid the butcher, and left the store, slamming the door behind.

Not often would people be so blatant about their dismay at Isabel's living preferences, but when they were, Isabel stood firm with confidence about her place in the world.

She knew she was different, but it caused her no insecurities whatsoever. One thing she was serious about was the legacy she would leave behind. She was keenly aware that the world around her was changing, and she was determined to be a participant in the evolution.

Though she was serious about paving the way for other women to work outside the home, she enjoyed life. While other women held jobs working in the mills, she had little interest in being like any of them. Isabel set out to be different, and different she was.

Her demeanor was anything other than a typical Southern Belle who occupied the streets of South Carolina. Her hair was never meticulously done, nor did pearl beads occupy her slim neck.

Isabel maintained a natural beauty of which she was largely unaware and did not care much about. Instead, she enjoyed her assertive personality and couldn't hold her tongue.

She pushed boundaries, knowing that a different life could be waiting if only women held more power. She rejoiced in Rosie the Riveter, a national icon whom Isabel admired.

She, too, wanted to make a difference and hoped that in the South, people would look to her for inspiration to be the backbone of women of her time.

There was still a patriarchy, and though less discussed, the division was apparent for women, especially for those who wanted more from life than motherhood. Isabel admired the women around her who cared for their homes and children, who were nurturing and loving, and who were willing to give away and sacrifice themselves for the greater good of societal expectations.

But being more of a rebel herself, she despised the box that her gender provided, deciding from an early age that she would do the opposite.

Even in the schoolyard, while the girls had been busy braiding one another's hair, Isabel had always insisted on playing kickball with the boys. When they refused to let her play, she would insist until they relented and put her on a team, though she was always picked last.

Some other girls also wanted to play but had been taught to keep clean and not interrupt the boy's playtime. Regretfully, they listened to the advice, not realizing they also held power.

They loved watching Isabel revolt against the idea that because of her gender, she couldn't play the boys' games. This would be the start of Isabel's lifelong fight to go against the grain.

She was admired, feared, and outcast all at the same time.

Mostly, she simply ignored it all and did what made her happy.

Being on her feet all day was tiresome, but the thrill she got when she perfected a recipe made the arduous work worth the long days. Isabel was unique, tenacious, and independent, and besides all this, she was also tall at five foot seven, her long, lanky legs giving the appearance of someone taller. Her appearance and confidence intimidated men and helped to make many of them intrigued by her unique mannerisms.

But at the same time, she was feminine with a vital air of entitlement, always demanding equality. Few women looked, spoke, or held themselves in the same manner, and so she became a mystery of sorts. With no regard for subservient behavior, like Eleanor Roosevelt, she stood firm in her beliefs and was unwilling to negotiate in her passion to pursue a chosen career.

Isabel possessed a rare talent for balancing femininity and boldness equally.

She would greet men with the same enthusiasm as they greeted one another, so she could often be found chugging a beer at the bar alongside many of them after a long day's work.

While she enjoyed cooking, baking, and delighting people's palates, she was also quite brazen in proclaiming she possessed no interest in doing that inside the home.

No, Isabel wanted to introduce the town to her God-given talent, get her deserved accolades, and even be paid for it. Isabel was not even bashful about her desire to gain financially from her work, fighting to be paid the same as her male counterparts.

Of course, she never achieved that goal, but she fussed so frequently that employers would agree to her fee just to prevent her from causing a publicly embarrassing scene.

CHAPTER THREE

Isabel didn't rise overnight. She began her career working in a small diner on the backroads of town. Although the "Dig-In Diner" wasn't on the main road, it was popular for its delicious food, inviting atmosphere, and hometown charm. The term 'diner' seemed more casual than the menu implied. While they offered their share of fried eggs, pancakes, and comfort food, a selection of top-notch items kept customers coming back for more.

You never knew what latest item would appear on the menu, which kept it exciting and fresh. It included fish and meat specials with homemade desserts, bringing crowds from the coast to try out the constantly changing menu items and to hear about the eccentric female chef.

When Isabel heard that folks up north put corn in their shrimp and grits, she would scoff, "Southern cookin' is real cookin'. Dangit, there is never corn in that dish. Long-cookin' grits deserve only cheesy goodness. I'm going to have to learn you all how to cook some proper Southern food, y'all." Her belief in old-time traditional Southern cooking was fierce, and she would protect the culture to its end.

Through word of mouth, even damn Yankees from the North drove South to find out what the rave was all about. The hype did not disappoint.

The food was some of the best Southern cuisine available, the service was friendly, and the atmosphere was far more unique than expected. It had a rustic feel, oozing with charm.

At first glance, the building stood tall and unassuming. Inside, light blue walls, warm linens, and glistening chandeliers greeted eager customers. Pictures of celebrities hung on the walls, and signs said, "If it ain't Southern, it ain't good."

Like Isabel, the restaurant was an array of contradictions, but somehow, it worked, and people reveled in its eccentricity. Perhaps that was why Isabel felt so at home at her job.

She couldn't imagine working anywhere else.

Working as a prep cook had its set of challenges. She knew she should run the kitchen and have more authority, but in the end, no one would respect a chef who didn't work her way up the ranks. The hours were long, the pay modest, and the experience insightful. She did the chopping, seasoning, marinating and was quick and efficient. Later, she started making big batches of soup, baking loaves of bread, and making sauces. Isabel watched the more experienced cooks, noting how they prepared the food, what ingredients they included, and their processes.

She observed how they worked and took great care to devour any knowledge given. She wasn't afraid to ask questions or make mistakes, but always careful never to do either twice.

Randy, the head Chef, noticed Isabel's interest in the kitchen and gave her more responsibilities. Isabel was exhilarated by it, only working even harder for his approval.

She started with sauteing vegetables, and slowly, he trusted her with more intricate dishes like the stews and fish.

Within three years, Isabel was working side by side with Randy, and together, they had the kitchen working in sync and smoothly, even during their busiest hours. She was grateful that Randy took her under his wing and encouraged her to try more complex dishes. He was patient and kind but had little time for inefficiency and laziness. Randy didn't get angry when Isabel added too much salt to the stew; he only made her start again, this time being more careful.

"There is no shame in starting over. It only upsets me if you quit or take the easy way out. The kitchen is hot in more ways than one," he said, taking a long sip of sweet tea. "To be honest, the best thing I can teach you is not how to marinate steak or season fish; it's to take pride in your work, show integrity, practice patience, and always learn from your mistakes."

Isabel nodded in agreement, though not entirely sure about what.

Isabel tasted the stew, this time satisfied with its flavor. Adding too much salt the first time had spoiled the flavors, but this time, there was a perfect balance of flavors and spice.

"I doubt you will ever make the same mistake twice," said Randy.

He took a spoonful. "That there is some good stew."

"Thank you, Randy. I appreciate you," Isabel said. It was not lost on Isabel how fortunate she was to work side by side with a man with in-depth knowledge and the grace to share it.

Before Isabel could say more, Randy snapped, "Now get back to work."

The two continued to work side by side for years, creating flavorful dishes unavailable elsewhere.

In late December of that year, Randy showed up late for work. He looked tired and worried and didn't have the same energy. "Are you okay?" asked Isabel.

"Not really. My wife, she's sick," Randy said. His big brown eyes had tears as he shook his head in disbelief. "She's my everything," he said as he chopped parsley. "I can't imagine what I'll do if she ain't goin' to survive."

Isabel looked at the flame on the stove, unsure what to say. She slid over a cream sauce for tasting and nodded to Randy, who turned his face to hide his tears.

CHAPTER FOUR

A YEAR LATER, ISABEL was surprised not to find Randy in the kitchen when she arrived at work and soon saddened to hear he would be cutting down his hours at the restaurant to care for his wife.

She would miss working alongside him and still had a lot to learn.

This new arrangement left Isabel in charge, which was both exciting and intimidating. She wanted to make Randy proud and hoped she was up for the task.

It was not that she doubted her abilities, but the responsibility would be solely on her shoulders. She was confident that she could handle the tasks, but gaining the confidence of the staff might be a challenge. As it was, it was unheard of for a young Southern woman to have that level of power in the workforce. Although she invoked confidence, skill, and a mastery of cuisine, still, she often heard the whispers of some of the men making sexist remarks.

It took time, but eventually, the staff gained respect for her, and all awaited Randy's return.

The arrangement was supposed to be temporary, which made it easier for the staff to tolerate Isabel as their boss. However, when Randy's wife took a turn for the worse, he began to come in even less frequently. Eventually, he stopped working altogether to care for his wife full-time.

"Kid, you have talent. Keep this up, and you may be the first woman in South Carolina to take over the entire state." He chuckled. "We have seen this business triple since you started here, and with you in charge, I have complete faith you can handle it."

Isabel fought back tears. She wasn't accustomed to compliments, but they touched her, especially those from Randy. He had always been hard on her, pushing her to be better.

At first, she'd assumed it was because she was a woman, but as their relationship grew, she understood he saw her talent far more than he ever noticed her gender.

"Thank you. I'll do my best to make you proud."

"You already have, Chef."

This was the first time she'd been referred to as a chef, the highest compliment in the culinary world. You aren't a chef by any standard until the top chef refers to you as one.

The word chef rang in her ear, her heart fluttering excitedly at the words she had worked so hard to obtain. Chef Isabel. She liked the sound of it.

She felt her face flush as she stood up taller.

"You have worked hard and proved yourself. Keep making me proud. Even better, make yourself proud. Show this damn town what you are made of."

Randy took off his apron for the last time.

He patted her on the shoulder as he glanced around the kitchen in which he'd spent most of his life.

With a wink and a smile, he left Isabel alone to manage the afternoon crowd for the first time.

Isabel went quickly to work.

There was much to be done before Gary, the sous chef, arrived, and she wanted to make a good impression on the first day of being in charge. Randy's permanent elimination from the kitchen caused anxiety among the staff, and Isabel needed to calm their concerns and prove everything would still run smoothly. It was her job now to ensure both order and confidence.

She studied the specials list for the day, ensuring the ingredients were plentiful and ready to be prepared. She made a note to add catfish stew to the specialties for next week and to add a twist to the recipe. The local fish supplier mentioned he had fresh catfish coming in, and this Southern classic was sure to delight. She rearranged a couple of the stations, noting how it would be more efficient to have the prep line more organized, also making the service line two feet wider for easier access. By the time the rest of the staff arrived, the kitchen was in the order Isabel had always imagined but would never be so bold to tell Randy.

She confidently greeted the staff, "Hello folks, today will be a good day. We all will miss Randy, but the show must go on. Let's make him proud."

Some of the older men were not as talkative as usual. Isabel could have sworn she saw one roll his eyes. She ignored the obvious tension.

"Okay then, here is the expectation for the evening. We have eleven reservations and our regular crowd, so we need to stay focused.

I've arranged the prep line differently, so please note that and make adjustments."

She then instructed the dishwashers, "Please fill the soap buckets and clean the dishes within twelve minutes. I've been timing the turnover time, and it's been too slow in the past."

She didn't hesitate as she watched the men look around at one another.

"Lastly, I have expanded the serving station so the waitstaff can get in and out quickly. Please leave this space open for them at all times, y'all."

Isabel kept her voice strong and confident, ensuring she wasn't talking too fast.

As the crew listened attentively, she continued with authority.

"Oh, and one last thing," she said, staring at Gary. "If I hear one word disparaging me or anyone else in this kitchen, I will fire your ass on the spot."

Gary, who was known to lead the charge against a woman running the kitchen, lowered his head as the other men looked around awkwardly.

"You are dismissed. Now get to work. We have a busy night ahead of us."

Her heart was racing, and she almost expected someone to challenge her decisions, but to her surprise, when she was finished speaking, they nodded and went to work.

She entered the office, sighed in relief, and wiped the pearls of sweat off her brow.

Then, she went back into the kitchen and got to work with the rest of the crew. After that day, Gary nor any other help did not question her ability or authority, and the staff worked in sync.

The owner of Dig-In Diner, Johnny, was tall and attractive, but his messy brown hair and kind eyes made him seem less intimidating. He had attended college to learn business and hospitality and never let his employees forget it. He was proud of his achievements, and though approachable, everyone knew he was their boss. He'd worked hard for his education, claiming to have fought tooth and nail to get scholarships to afford the tuition.

Unlike many wealthy generational Carolinians, Johnny had worked hard to gain access to the elite, making him both relatable and knowledgeable. Isabel appreciated that Johnny was a blue-collar worker with an education and was willing to teach others what he had learned.

"At university," he would lecture, "We learned the intricate part of business ownership, so if you don't mind, I will make the final decisions."

It amused the staff how much input he wanted about how the restaurant ran, but in the end, he would still do exactly as he pleased. It seemed futile to hold meetings about changing the napkins to blue only to keep the red ones Johnny had initially settled on.

Most kitchen helpers learned from hands-on experience and were often more qualified than educated business owners to make decisions.

However, Johnny had a say over many of the decisions and would butt heads with the staff, even if only for theatrics, to show the staff who was boss.

As a woman, she had few opportunities to attend college, so Isabel had to work twice as hard to prove herself. She learned everything she knew by paying attention, asking questions, and trial and error, never letting a lack of education or her perceived weaker gender deter her from absorbing the knowledge she needed to achieve her goals.

Fortunately, Johnny was generous with his expertise and admired Isabel for sticking in an arena of men who often made life difficult. Johnny managed the finances but stayed out of the kitchen. He was pleased with Isabel in her new role, though he never offered her a title or pay raise.

"I must admit, Isabel, you have exceeded my expectations in every way."

"I appreciate that," Isabel said casually after the restaurant closed for the night.

"What are your plans moving forward?"

"I don't have any just yet," Isabel lied.

Johnny laughed, knowing that a woman like Isabel always had a plan.

She never mentioned it out loud, but her ultimate plan was to take over the business and make it her own. When her insomnia crept in, she would rise again and write out business plans, sketch pictures of her venue, and write down local banks where she could attempt to get a loan.

She knew it would be difficult without being the wife to some local man but was hoping her reputation would convince the bankers to give her a loan.

Though this dream was still a long way away, she wanted nothing more than to serve customers the food she created, even ones who were demanding and sometimes unreasonable.

A few girls younger than Isabel worked as waitresses at the diner. She recognized them from when she'd attended the local high school. They had a bright presence and were always kind to her but never tried to engage. They were neatly dressed, with rosy cheeks, high ponytails, and painted lips. She envied their beauty and ability to mesh with the locals, watching from the kitchen as they greeted customers with genuine delight and walked easily carrying heavy food trays. Though Isabel didn't want to be a pretty face when presenting food, she appreciated the need for these young women to represent the restaurant in a positive light.

Isabel enjoyed the sweat dripping down her dirty clothes whenever she was behind the hot flames making the food. She was always far more interested in being the person in the kitchen, sweating and swearing to make the magic happen. It was best that someone with a more polite demeanor presented the food afterward; the girls from her old high school were the perfect fit.

The young women were obedient, friendly, charming, and raised in good Southern homes where women knew their place. The frontline was the image of the restaurant, whereas, at least in Isabel's opinion, the real magic all happened in the kitchen.

Organized chaos, high demand for the staff, and unforgiving time constraints were all part of the process, and Isabel thrived on it. The key was to be efficient, effective, and consistent while maintaining order. Isabel was a natural, and taking charge came as second nature.

If other chefs would get overwhelmed and frustrated by the demands of a customer's specific requests, Isabel would shout, "Get it together, y'all. We're here to perform and deliver. Make it happen." She would do an impromptu jig to release the building tension.

Her zany ways mildly amused all the staff.

Isabel was filled with life, but above all, she persistently focused on being the best.

As a woman, she had something to prove, and often, she found her tenacity mistaken for arrogance. However, her upbeat attitude and quirky mannerisms kept everyone on their feet.

From singing, quoting the Bible, and acting out Shakespeare while searing salmon, working in Isabel's presence was a delight. She demanded high quality but led by example with a strong work ethic and a love for food. Isabel was doing what she loved and made no apologies for it.

Sure, not everyone loved her style, but over time, they gained a deep respect for her.

As efficient as Isabel was in the kitchen, she struggled if forced onto the floor to serve customers, unlike one of her former schoolmates, Chrissy Namble.

Chrissy was a vibrant redhead with piercing blue eyes and an eager smile. She gushed to greet customers, filled their waters, and checked to ensure they were satisfied with service and food.

She was a natural; customers asked after her by name and returned for her excellent service.

When Isabel was just starting out at the restaurant, she reluctantly worked her first shift as a waitress; Chrissy had called in sick with a stomach virus, and none of the men in the kitchen would step up to take the job.

She barely made it to the end of the day. Carrying the large trays of food, nodding politely as the customers demanded more water and different condiments, and complaining about the restaurant's temperature was just not Isabel's way. While she was pleasant and likable, she would be out of her element if she weren't in the kitchen. She knew from the start where she belonged, and it was, without a doubt, preparing food and not serving it.

Working in the kitchen was difficult, but she found a new respect for the waitstaff, knowing their patience for customer service far exceeded her abilities. Yet despite her lack of desire to leave the kitchen, Isabel forced herself to learn all the elements of running a restaurant.

She would ask questions about pricing, inventory, and health regulations, yearning to learn everything she could, even without a formal education. How she learned it all didn't matter much, but she knew the more experience she gained, the better off she became for it.

As a child, Isabel had excelled in science, and experimenting with flavors reminded her of the times in elementary school when she'd been far more enamored with science and math than many other girls. "Cooking is, after all, a science, but with more flare," Isabel reasoned.

Being in the kitchen and creating new recipes excited Isabel. She had a natural knack for high pressure and for making quick decisions. Despite detailed planning, there were times when she would run out of ingredients for the evening's unique menus and needed to improvise.

Once, Eartha Kitt came into the restaurant with three of her business managers.

They had driven over an hour and wanted to try the halibut that one of the dancers of her hit show had bragged about. The guests were ravenous, all looking forward to trying the dish and eager to learn what the fuss was about. To Isabel's horror, she was just about out of the halibut.

"Fuck. What am I supposed to do now? I can't tell Eartha Kitt I can't feed her this dish after them traveling all the way here. Think,

think, think," Isabel demanded of herself. "Cooking is improvising and creating. So, make your magic happen."

If she were to screw up one of the hottest celebrities' dinners, it would give the men something else to insult her about. She was on the verge of tears but knew better than to show emotion, especially when the heat was turned up. It would be viewed as weak, and the early disrespect from the kitchen staff could potentially be an issue again.

She recalled the earlier days working in the kitchen when Gary would mumble, "Go cry in *your* kitchen," when Isabel fumbled or hesitated, unsure. Her nerves were beginning to fray as dinner orders began to pile up. As the unofficial head chef, she needed to find a solution.

Though Isabel ran the kitchen and the staff, she was never awarded extra pay or the title of head chef. Men's egos would have had a tough time with it; Johnny didn't want to start any trouble.

Months back, when Isabel had once spoken up, noting the pay discrepancy between her and her male counterparts, Johnny had immediately claimed she was starting trouble.

"I ain't starting no trouble. I just expect what is due to me. To get the accolades and pay I deserve."

"Now, don't be like that. You are lucky even to have this kind of job," said Johnny.

"Now, am I? I quite think you're lucky I keep this job, Johnny Woolrich. What if I walk out of here right now? How do you think the dinner crew will handle it? Think Gary's up for the job?"

Johnny didn't move, knowing not to test her bluff. "I didn't mean it like that. We all know you are the best. It's just that ..." He hesitated. "Men are men, Isabel. I don't make the rules. They don't want some woman telling them what to do."

"Too bad," interrupted Isabel, her expression hardening. "I am made for this. You know it, I know it, and damn it, the entire state of South Carolina knows it. I refuse to sit back and be disrespected. That may work on some of the meek girls of the South, but Johnny boy, that shit won't work with me, and you know that too."

After a labored silence, she grabbed her jacket and headed toward the door.

Before she left, she called back, snickering, "I'm sure I'll see you in a couple of hours, begging for me to return." She slammed the door behind her, walking away briskly.

Isabel and Johnny both knew she was right.

The restaurant would have a hard time functioning without her direction. Johnny knew the kitchen needed Isabel. He also knew Isabel needed her job since he was the only man in town willing to hire a woman, especially in that capacity. It was a dance they played with one another, knowing each depended on the other, neither willing to admit it.

"Isabel, don't. Can't we talk about this?" he called out.

It was too late. Isabel was stomping down the path to her car. It would be a long night without her, so Johnny did what he always did. He poured himself a bourbon.

Isabel drove home feeling empowered, but three hours and two whiskies later, she longed to return to work. It was all she knew how to do. It had been years since she'd taken a day off to rest, and she was already anxious about the dinner crowd and angry at herself for letting Johnny get the best of her. *I should have ignored the old fool,* she thought. *I know better than to expect more from the men in the town.* She gulped down the last drink.

By the time the restaurant closed, Johnny was indeed right there at her door, begging her to return and promising her a raise and the understanding that she was, in fact, the head chef.

"I was wrong. You are one hell of a cook."

"A cook?" Isabel stammered.

"Okay, okay, a chef. I need you back. I want you back. I apologize. It was a lapse of judgment. I have been under much pressure, and sometimes, things don't come out right."

"Fine, I'll come back under two conditions. First, you only refer to me as Chef from this point on."

Johnny nodded in agreement.

"And two, I get a raise and earn more money than the other kitchen help."

"Isabel. I mean, Chef, those men have families to support. They deserve to make the money."

Johnny watched as Isabel steadied herself, knowing he would lose this argument.

"Okay, you got it. But I don't want you to tell the others about this raise, or they will come at me with demands."

"Deal," Isabel said, satisfied.

Despite playing hardball with Johnny, she understood that even her tenacity was limited in South Carolina. Outwardly, she was confident and bold, but she was no fool. She backed down when necessary, knowing men with power could and would make it impossible for someone like Isabel if she overstepped the invisible line of feminine entitlement. She walked a thin line, knowing the town's men had the power to ensure she would never work again.

***

As the memory faded, Isabel jolted back to the present, dealing with the issue at hand.

She continued searching through the refrigerator, desperate for a solution. The last thing she needed was Johnny down her back for screwing up. She liked that she was diligent and hard-working, leaving little room for criticism. The worst anyone in the kitchen could say about her was that she was confident and a woman, neither of which she apologized for.

Also, the food industry being fickle could cause a lot of problems. Celebrities could single-handedly ruin an establishment's reputation, and Isabel did not want that on her watch.

Unfortunately, she only had enough halibut for three people and didn't want to disappoint the one guest. Running out of their special early in the dinner rush would be a bad look.

What the fuck am I going to do?

But there was nothing she could do since her fish supplier had got stuck on the side of the road with a flat tire, and there was no way to get the fish safely to the restaurant on time without the risk of spoilage. Food poisoning would be far worse than running out of halibut, but still, there had to be a resolution. "Of all the days for this to happen," she huffed.

She felt her heart thump in her chest and heard Randy's voice echoing, "Remember the importance of overcoming obstacles, and there will always be obstacles in the kitchen." Isabel patted her apron as she paced the kitchen. She ran through other recipes she had memorized throughout the years as an alternative, searching for an acceptable substitution.

"Aha," she said with a smile when she noticed the shrimp on the second shelf.

She cut the halibut into smaller portions, added four ounces of shrimp to each, and topped it off with a creamy lobster sauce. The patrons had no idea of the sudden change of recipe, and despite the chaos in the kitchen that night, they were none the wiser.

"A good chef knows how to cook. A great chef knows how to adapt."

Her efforts paid off when, the following day, Ms. Kitt spoke to news reporters raving about the cuisine at Dig-In Diner, even calling out Chef Isabel by name. The publicity only furthered the popularity of the restaurant. Isabel swam in the accolades of the public, while Johnny enjoyed the financial reward.

CHAPTER FIVE

THERE WAS A PARTICULAR customer who caught Isabel's eye. She stood to attention when a gaggle of businessmen would grab lunch, argue over politics, and always leave a generous tip. The men dressed sharply in suits, hair slicked back, and their shoes shined. One gentleman, in particular, would show up daily with the lunch crowd, even if not accompanied by the others. Liam Kaats was the most powerful banker in town. He had kind eyes, but if pushed, could be problematic.

Liam came from a long line of bankers, and his generational wealth was enormous.

He was known as a brazen businessman with a big heart for most, except for Johnny.

It had been rumored there had been a long-standing feud between the two. No one quite knew the whole story, but everyone in town knew these two men hated one another.

As the years passed, Liam continued appearing at the diner, always causing a fuss and making Johnny intentionally agitated. He had no reason to frequent the local diner other than to get under his skin but did so to make a point.

It always sent Johnny into a bad mood and to the bottom of a bottle of bourbon.

On those days, the staff stayed quiet as Johnny locked himself in his office, throwing things at the wall. Johnny's discomfort was so obvious to Isabel on the days when Liam frequented the restaurant. Yet, there was something about Liam that intrigued her. She would catch him staring at her through the glass window in the kitchen. She ignored him mostly, but sometimes, when their eyes met, she felt a rush that she had never felt before. She would then quickly busy herself and get caught up in the day's work, forgetting Liam was even there.

Without a doubt, he noticed the mutual attraction and took a liking to her spunk.

He was entertained by her wit and admired her confidence.

Of course, he would demand to talk to the chef, knowing it was Isabel in the kitchen, even when she would tell Chrissy she was too busy for conversation.

"But it's Mr. Kaats. He doesn't care that you're busy. He wants to talk with you right now."

Isabel would huff, "I don't have time to chit-chat with some big shot. My time is just as important as his," she would grumble.

However, she would braid her hair, pat her apron, and do as she was told in fear that he would pull the loan from the diner, resulting in her losing her job.

"Good morning, Miss Isabel. It is Miss, right?"

"Yes, sir. I am married to my recipes, not a man, and that's good enough for me."

"I see." Liam smiled. "So, what do you have on special today, Miss Isabel?" He emphasized *Miss* with a lingering s sound.

"I am sure your waitress could tell you all about the specials, Mr. Kaats," Isabel said, staring at the shiny gold on his ring finger.

He fidgeted with his finger, looking down, and lifted his eyes to meet hers again.

"But I would like to hear them from you. I find they always sound better when described by the person making it."

Isabel glanced at the clock on the wall.

She only had forty-five minutes to start preparing for the early dinner crowd.

Rapidly, she shot off some of the specials she had been preparing all morning.

"To start, we have fried green tomatoes with Gulf Coast spicy shrimp remoulade. We also have our secret recipe, mac and cheese with country ham, cheddar, toasted cornbread crumbs, and scallions available. As an entree, if I may suggest my favorite, glazed teriyaki salmon with sweet tea drizzle and sweet potato purée, field pea & corn succotash."

Liam thought for a moment.

"I trust your judgment. Bring me what you think will delight me most, sugar." Isabel let the word sugar linger before Liam felt the discomfort. "I mean Miss Isabel."

The exchange was condescending and exhausting, though it was not lost on Isabel that she needed to plaster on a weak smile and do what the man had ordered.

Isabel rushed into the kitchen, preparing the meal for Mr. Kaats, hoping to get him out of the restaurant as soon as possible.

The staff was on edge when he came in, afraid that one mishap would jeopardize the entire place. It was difficult enough to find work, and no one wanted to take the chance of losing one of the most profitable restaurants in town. The staff knew to appease Mr. Kaats, and for the good of each other, they all did what was expected to make him happy, even Isabel.

Liam understood the power he possessed but wasn't unkind.

Although reluctant to succumb to his demands, Isabel knew his importance. However, she always got the sense that he was rather lonely and wanted to connect with regular folk, but it was clear he wasn't sure how. Being raised surrounded by money and prestige, it was challenging for Liam to understand working people, though he was curious about how other people lived and was interested in them and their lives outside of work. Unlike some of his constituents, Liam appreciated hard-working people and showed respect to those who served him. Though he was no fool, he sometimes used his clout to intimidate, making it known that he was more than just any businessman and demanded respect and attention. Liam would not tolerate the answer of no. He was friendly, confident, and had a presence that demanded attention. Although difficult at times, he was kind to Isabel.

He would ask her about new recipes, and she felt a strong connection in return. Although she tried to ignore her attraction to him, understanding that the wealthiest man in town would have no interest in her, she still found herself thinking about him.

"Please, Isabel, come sit with me," he would gesture when he visited.

"Oh, I mustn't. I have a lot of work to do in the kitchen."

His piercing green eyes looked right through her. He smiled softly.

"Please, Isabel. I enjoy your company. Everyone in the town wants something from me. You just want to feed me. It's refreshing."

Isabel sat with Liam as he discussed his garden. Something so luxurious seemed far-fetched to her, and she could only imagine the fragrance the variety of flowers produced.

"It sounds wonderful," she gushed.

"It is. You should come see it sometime." Immediately, Liam regretted the offer, and his cheeks reddened. "Oh, Isabel, I'm sorry. I didn't mean to make you uncomfortable. I just thought you would enjoy seeing it. It is spectacular."

"I'm sure it is," she retorted. "Anyway, I need to get back to work. I have a lot to do before the dinner rush comes in."

Isabel hurried back to the kitchen.

Liam was flirting with her, and if she was honest, she enjoyed his company. But there was a Mrs. Kaats for sure, so Isabel quickly dismissed any attraction she momentarily felt.

He became more of a friend to her with each visit, though she kept it professional. Most didn't know that he was witty and caring. "I had the wrong impression of you," admitted Isabel.

"Most do. People assume that because my family has money, I am a certain way. While I can't speak for my ancestors, I treat people respectfully and kindly."

Liam was pensive before indulging in another bite of a fried green tomato. "These really are something. You gotta give me your recipe to try it at home."

"You cook?" Isabel's eyes widened.

"You are surprised?"

"Well, I guess." She stopped speaking and looked out the window.

"So, you thought I would never cook for myself because I have money. So, you assumed too!"

Isabel was embarrassed. "Okay, no more assuming. I will take your word for it."

"Better yet, let me go in your kitchen and help cook one evening," said Liam.

"What? I couldn't. Johnny would never allow it."

"Let me worry about Johnny," replied Liam, taking the last swig of his cola before leaving.

The following evening, Liam came in two hours before the dinner crowd.

He was dressed in a light button-down shirt, loose pants, and tennis shoes.

Isabel had only seen him dressed in a full suit and was surprised by his transformation. He seemed relaxed as he made his way to the prepping area.

"So, what are you making?"

"For tonight's special, we will serve grilled flounder with seasonal vegetables topped with a white wine sauce."

"Sounds good."

Isabel left Liam to prepare the fish while she managed to stay focused on the remaining specials. By the night's end, the fish dish Liam had prepared was sold out completely.

"I have to say I'm impressed."

"I saved you a plate. I noticed you snuck a bite earlier before it went to the customers, but I had to have you taste the entire plate," Liam said proudly.

Isabel took a heaping scoop, savoring the flavors. "Liam, this is really delicious. How did you learn how to cook like this?"

"To be honest, I always wanted to open a restaurant. I love to cook and would do it for fun. When my daddy would catch me in the kitchen cooking, he would scold me and tell me to stop doing women's work. Eventually, I lost interest in it and did what I was told."

"Which was?"

"To go into the family fortune of banking. Made loads of money, joined a country club, and kept the family name intact. That was pretty much a given."

Liam was quiet as Isabel took another forkful of fish. "Sometimes, I wonder what life would be like if I were just a regular person."

"I wonder what life would be like being you," Isabel joked.

Liam looked hurt by her off-hand comment before saying, "Anyway, thanks for letting me cook with you tonight." He took off his apron and laid it on the counter. Isabel was busy prepping the dishes for the following day when she noticed Liam staring at her.

"Oh, sorry. Did you need something else?"

"No," he said quickly. "It's just that I have never met a woman like you, Isabel. I had a real nice time tonight."

"Thank you. I'm glad I could make your dream of being a chef for a day come true."

Isabel went back to work, intentionally not making eye contact with Liam. He left out the back door, and soon, she watched his tires roll down the driveway.

Johnny came in to lock up. "Did Liam leave yet?"

"Oh yes, he left about twenty minutes ago."

"Good."

"What's with that guy?" she asked. "I would never think he would want to spend his evening in a hot kitchen serving others."

"He will do anything to get under my skin. He has issues." Johnny didn't elaborate further, and Isabel continued slicing up chicken. "Isabel, be careful with him. He may seem charming but will turn on you in a heartbeat."

Isabel nodded and watched as Johnny entered his office to pour himself a drink.

Chapter Six

The lease for Dig-In Diner was nearly up when Liam walked into the restaurant for a meeting with Johnny. Behind closed doors, raised voices and fists slamming against the desk echoed from the kitchen. Isabel attempted to ignore it, hoping it was just a negotiation tactic that Liam employed. It was known that Liam could be shrewd but also helpful if you were on his good side. By nature, he was an erratic man who was difficult to read, transforming from a warm smile and friendly demeanor to dark eyes and a furrowed brow. Liam was a man accustomed to getting his way, and at the first sign of compromise, he would become angered.

As Isabel entered the refrigerator to grab the lobster tails for the night's special, she overheard Liam's stern voice, deep with conviction. It was intimidating.

"We both know, Johnny, you could face harsh consequences if this doesn't go my way. In fact, I was recently chatting with Judge Myers at the country club, and he mentioned criminal charges for falsifying tax documents."

Johnny roared, "You son of a bitch. You set me up. I didn't break no laws. You falsified the documents."

"Now, now, Johnny boy. You wouldn't want assault added to the list of charges against you, would you?"

Johnny slammed a fist into the wall, causing a painting gifted by a local artist to crash to the floor. "Fuck you, Liam. You are nothing but a thug in a suit. You are a piece of shit."

"This could all be avoided, Johnny. You know what I want. It isn't even a big ask. I am sure you could hire plenty of other talent in this town. I want to enjoy the food your guests enjoy regularly. And she isn't half bad to look at either."

"You can hire any woman in the state of South Carolina. Why her?"

"Because you want her."

"Haven't you taken enough from me and my mama? But I get it. I am the family's dirty little secret—your daddy's bastard son. My mama paid dearly for that. Bless her heart. She is long gone now, Liam. Can't you just leave the past where it belongs?"

"How fucking dare you, Johnny. Your whore of a mother went off and got herself pregnant to tear my family apart and steal our money, and you want me to show mercy?" Liam retorted.

"That's not what happened, and you know it. My mama loved your daddy, and he took advantage of her."

"Don't you dare rewrite history! Your mother seduced my happily married father to get our fortune. When Mama found out, her heart broke, and it nearly tore our family apart."

"Ahh, not this again. You have been carrying on with this for decades now, Liam. We were just kids ourselves. We had nothing to do with what the adults decided. We could have grown up as brothers once you found out the truth. Instead, you shunned me and went out of your way to antagonize and be cruel to me. For what, Liam? What did it get you?"

Liam's face flushed. "You and your whore mother ruined my family. It's my job to see that you pay for your mother's sin."

"No, Liam, our parents' decisions. They both had an affair. You have spent years blaming this on my mama as though your daddy was some innocent bystander. Everyone in town knows that's not true. But your daddy never recognized me as his son, never once checked up on me or Mama, even when he knew we were suffering. What kind of man does that to his own son?"

The only sound in the room was both men breathing heavily.

"In any event, my bastard half-brother, you have a decision to make."

"I don't reckon it's a decision at all. It sounds more like a demand," quipped Johnny.

"Take it as you wish. But you have until the end of the week."

Isabel heard a loud slam, putting her hand to her mouth as she listened by the door.

She needed clarification about what the men had discussed and how it involved her. She couldn't imagine who else they could have been talking about, but none of it made sense.

She had heard the rumors of them being half-brothers but never really connected the dots. Well, that explained why there was so much tension between the two and why Liam would frequent the restaurant. It had always seemed it was to taunt Johnny.

Usually, Johnny would hurry out, claiming he had errands to run when he saw Liam's white Cadillac pull in and take up half the front parking spaces.

Moments later, Liam moved to exit the office, walking past Isabel.

But before leaving, he turned around when he knew Johnny was in earshot.

"Ahh, Isabel. It's nice to see you. I am sure we'll be seeing one another soon."

"Get the fuck out of here," snarled Johnny.

Liam's car screeched out of the parking lot, leaving a billow of smoke behind.

"What was that all about?" asked Isabel.

Johnny's eyes softened. "Don't you worry. I will take care of him."

Isabel hadn't intended to pry, but a few weeks earlier, she'd also overheard two older gentlemen gossiping about the long rift between the brothers. This surprised Isabel, and she assumed it wasn't true. Now, though, it seemed to make sense.

"Johnny, is Liam Kaats, your brother?" Isabel asked slowly.

"Not in any way that matters," snapped Johnny.

Johnny walked away, his shoulder slumped, and he shook his head in disbelief.

Isabel pressed for more information, hoping Johnny would share more, but he returned to his office and put his hands over his head.

What does this all mean, Isabel wondered. *Who were they talking about?* She tried to make sense of the conversation and replayed it in her mind but was perplexed.

Isabel had no more time to lament and began preparing for the week's special. She loved her position as head chef and was getting incredible reviews.

The business was at an all-time high, and Isabel's confidence was soaring. The summer was soon approaching, and the restaurant would be busier than ever.

Vacationers from all over the East Coast would soon arrive, and though it would mean that the traffic would be miserable, the town would light up with excitement.

Over the past few years, farmers' markets, street fairs, and local musicians would gather in the town center, lines forming with excited families wanting to taste homemade ice cream, cotton candy, and specialty popcorn. Later, the crowd would wait over an hour to be seated at Dig-In Diner for authentic Southern cuisine. A sense of pride overwhelmed her, knowing she had worked for this position and prepared to make Dig-In Diner the most sought-after establishment in the South. She was becoming somewhat of a local celebrity, and restaurant goers would ask for her to come out of the kitchen so that they could meet the woman behind the cuisine.

Isabel often declined, being too busy to engage for long, but Johnny encouraged her to interact with them, which only made business boom even further.

"Hello, Chef, I just had to meet you," a lady in her late seventies gushed. "I have lived in this town all my life, and I have yet to taste Frogmore stew quite like this one."

"Thank you," Isabel said.

"And the gravy of the chicken fried steak," her husband interrupted. "What exactly is that made from?"

Before she could answer, Gary waved her back into the kitchen, signaling she was needed.

"Excuse me, I have to head back to the kitchen. Enjoy your meal, and please come again soon." Isabel hurried back into the kitchen to finish the evening's order. Once the kitchen had quieted down, she began cleaning up for the evening and preparing for tomorrow's hectic day.

The restaurant would be in full swing for the next three months, leaving Isabel no time to catch her breath. She was exhausted, and though the conversation she had overheard weeks prior between Johnny and Liam haunted her, she had dismissed it as a family issue.

Once fall hits, I will take a week's vacation to relax. Maybe head to Myrtle Beach and rent a hotel room at one of their resorts, she thought.

She had considered the beach town as a place to open up her own place in the future, but for now, she was still quite content with her position working for Johnny.

Isabel had been saving money for years now in hopes of gaining enough recognition and being able to venture out to open a new establishment. She would still have enough money for a short vacation, which she deserved after sixteen-hour days for months on end.

Isabel looked forward to that week away to gather her thoughts and relax.

It was what was getting her through these brutally long days.

At half past midnight, Isabel was about to lock up when she noticed Johnny's light still on in his office. She tapped lightly on the door and peered in to find him staring at the ceiling.

"Hey, boss. You doing okay?"

He let out a long sigh, not making eye contact.

"I have been better."

"Is it the business with Mr. Kaats a few weeks back? He sure does know how to get under your skin."

Johnny scoffed. "You think?" he said with a laugh.

"Don't let him bug you too much. The restaurant is doing just fine. We are busier than ever, and I will do my part to keep that up. I've been experimenting with new recipes and think next week's will blow the socks off our customers."

"Isabel, come in and sit down," Johnny interrupted. "We need to talk."

Isabel grew concerned when she noticed the dark circles under his eyes. "Johnny, you look like you haven't slept in days. What's going on?"

"I haven't. Listen, there's no way to get around this. I don't even know how to say it."

"Just say it. We'll work it out. Don't worry. We have been through plenty, and I'm sure this is just a setback."

"No, Isabel," he said, glancing at his hands. "There is no easy way to say this." His eyes filled with tears, and his voice shook. "You're fired."

Isabel had never seen Johnny show emotion.

He seemed so genuinely distraught by this.

Time stood still, and Isabel thought she would be sick. "What? What do you mean? Have I done something? Johnny, we're at the top of our game."

"No, no, no. It's nothing like that. It's just that Liam won't renew my lease unless you agree to work for him. I tried to explain that the livelihood of our restaurant depends on you. That people come here because of you."

"Why would he want me to come work for him? Why me? Why now?"

Isabel thought back to her attraction to him and was immediately revolted.

She wasn't a piece of property he could barter.

"Is this about him working with me a few months back in the kitchen? I swear, Johnny, I thought it was an innocent thing, and he wanted to show off his cooking skills."

"Nah, Isabel. I tried to warn you. There is another side of Liam that people don't know about until it's too late." Johnny took another sip from his glass, wiping his mouth with his hand. "Liam comes off as charming, but there is always a catch. If I don't cave into his demands, we will all be out of work."

"He can't do this. Let me talk to him," pleaded Isabel.

"Liam promised to double your pay if you work for him and says you will have free rein over the menu. His wife Mary is quite lovely; maybe you will be happier there. It certainly will be a less demanding job."

"But I don't want another job. I want this job. I've worked for years to get to this level, and I don't want to work for some wealthy family making dinners and fluffing pillows."

Isabel felt her voice rise, and though she tried to stay composed, she was unraveling.

"I know," Johnny said quietly. "I have no choice. I'm sorry."

"When does this take effect? We have a big party coming in tomorrow night, and I promised to make them special desserts."

"Immediately. Please gather your knife set and any other belongings, and I will see you out."

"Johnny, you can't do this. There has to be a way around that monster."

"I'm sorry, there is nothing else to do. You have talent, kid, real talent. Don't let this stop you from dreaming big. Keep saving money, and one day, get out there and show this world what they've been missing."

Johnny's words came out urgently, imploring Isabel not to let Liam discourage her from reaching her goals. He worried she would lose her fire and become just another woman in the world, bitter and regretful that a man's power had stolen her dreams.

Johnny reached over to embrace Isabel, but she quickly pulled away, lowering her head to hide the tears streaming down her cheeks.

"How could you do this to me?" she said in a whisper filled with rage.

"I didn't. That piece of shit Liam did."

Isabel quickly gathered her knife set, apron, favorite yellow mixing bowl, and some recipes she had recently written down. She looked around the kitchen one last time before storming out the door, leaving Johnny behind.

———

Her hands tightened on the wheel as she drove home, trying to reconcile what had transpired.

Her hands shook as she turned the key to her house, adrenaline rushing through her veins. She poured herself a whisky, swallowing it down in one gulp. She poured herself another and then another until the room spun. She sat down on the couch, numb, and started to cry.

The following day, her head pounded, and her stomach swirled with nausea.

She hadn't had a chance to eat the night before, and the alcohol wreaked havoc on her insides. By midday, she had stumbled out of bed, the room still spinning and her throat begging for fluid.

She guzzled three glasses of water before noticing the stark white envelope slipped under the side door. She carefully opened the letter with her name scribbled on the outer.

She knew who it was from even before unfolding the stationery.

Miss Isabel,

I am pleased you will be working for Mary and me at our home. I trust you will find the accommodations spectacular. As we have discussed, I am eager to show you my magnificent garden. We also have a beautiful ocean view and will provide your quarters in the guest house. We look forward to your arrival by early next week. That will be enough time to sort out your affairs. As Johnny has indicated, you will be paid handsomely for your services. If you need any supplies to be provided in the kitchen, please do not hesitate to reach out.

With much anticipation,

Liam & Mary Kaats.

Isabel threw the letter on the counter and began searching for the spare pack of cigarettes she had kept for the many days on which she needed to unwind. Not much of a smoker, she kept a hidden pack on the desk next to the kitchen for when she craved something to take the edge off.

She lit one, hoping it would calm her nerves, but it didn't help.

Who is Liam, really? she thought. He had been kind, witty, and engaging so many times when she'd encountered him. Hell, she'd even had feelings for him for a bit. She couldn't imagine the man she knew was the same monster now forcing her out of a beloved job for his own benefit.

She replayed the conversation from the night before.

"I'm not going to work for that fool," she said. *Liam Kaats can't make me be his housekeeper. I'll find another job somewhere else.*

Isabel was outraged. She paced the floors as she cursed the day she'd met Liam Kaats.

"He wants me to move into his house, too? I am not moving out of this house. I love it here."

Isabel looked out onto her porch, where she found solace after a long night at the restaurant. There she sat for a long while, thinking over her options, knowing there were few.

She considered running out of town but knew Liam would eventually track her down. So many thoughts were rushing through her mind. She thought again about what Johnny had said, too. *If I decline his offer, Liam will ensure no one hires me in the surrounding towns.*

What would she do?

What could she do?

Her head was pounding, and her heart was racing, trying to find a way out of this forced arrangement. This wasn't even a legal transaction.

She wasn't a piece of property that could be traded. Isabel felt used and worthless.

How could these men treat her so inhumanely?

Liam's vendetta had gone so far that he was willing to use Johnny's top employee to make him suffer.

Isabel didn't know the details of their relationship but understood it was a lose-lose situation.

CHAPTER SEVEN

As the sun set, Isabel still lay on the couch, drifting in and out of sleep. She felt deflated and had no energy to move, needing some time to figure out her next step. But first, she needed rest. From a distance, she heard the sound of relentless sirens screaming down the street. The urgency and vigor got Isabel's attention as she instinctively knew where they were headed.

She fumbled for shoes and car keys as she raced to Dig-In Diner, following the billow of smoke down the long, windy road. The thick air was overwhelming, but a slight breeze provided small relief from the South's relentless summer.

Isabel squinted to see a small crowd gathered around.

This was what Isabel had feared. The diner had gone up in flames, and all she could do was watch as the roof beams crashed into a fiery pile of ashes.

She pushed through the crowd until she reached a uniformed police officer taking notes and assessing the scene.

She recognized him as one of the officers who frequented the restaurant for lunch.

"Officer, what happened?" Isabel said breathlessly. Her eyes stung from the smoke, and her breaths came in ragged gasps—due to nearly bursting into tears.

The officer wrote down some notes as he spoke to another officer in the distance.

He turned to Isabel, looking curiously at her as if brought back from a deep, involving dream, before finally recognizing who she was and why she was there. "Oh, Isabel ... it is, right?"

"Yes, that's correct."

"We were going to come and find you once this got under control. You are the head chef here, aren't you? This your workplace? Or rather, *was* this your workplace?"

Not thinking, she replied, "Yes. I am head chef." Quickly, she corrected herself too. "I was."

"I'm sorry you had to find out this way. I'm sure you are terribly upset. But do you mind if I ask you a couple of questions?"

Isabel nodded agreeably.

"Did Johnny mention any trouble? "

"Trouble? What kind of trouble?"

"Financial, emotional, legal? Anything like that?"

Isabel hesitated. How much should she say? Where was Johnny anyway, she wondered.

Just then, an ambulance came rushing out with a white sheet draped over a body.

Isabel gasped. "Johnny," she said, rushing toward him. The officer held Isabel back. "I'm sorry. I was waiting to tell you. I wasn't sure if you knew. Again, I'm deeply sorry."

"No, no, no," sobbed Isabel. "I had no idea."

"It's an apparent arson-suicide," the officer said solemnly. "A serious crime, but there's nothing much we can do about it. Awfully sad. We're going to need you to answer some questions, I'm afraid. But later. There's still much to sort out."

Much to sort out was a grievous understatement, she thought, thinking of all the work she faced in putting her life back together. How she could do it, she didn't know.

Before Isabel could say more, Liam came from behind, squeezing her shoulder.

"I came just as soon as I could. I heard about the suicide note." He looked at the young officer. "I play golf with the Sheriff, and he tipped me off."

Liam shook his head in disbelief.

"What a shame! Johnny was at the top of his game. I don't know why he would choose to do such a thing. Kill himself and set his business on fire? It just doesn't make sense."

Liam was rambling but never letting his eyes lose contact with Isabel.

Isabel looked at Liam in horror, feeling his grip tighten and pinch against her back.

"Now, Miss Isabel, I don't want you to worry about a job. I will certainly employ you until you get on your feet. I know how hard it is to be a woman in the restaurant industry, and I will do what I can. It's the least I can do."

Isabel glared at Liam. The officer, sensing tension, looked at the pair inquisitively. "Do either of you know what would cause Johnny to go to such lengths? His was the hottest spot in town."

He seemed not to realize he had spoken a terrible pun. But no one was laughing.

Isabel looked down at her feet, but before she could speak, Liam said, "I know he had a lot of trouble with the bottle. I tried to get him off it many times, but you know how it is. Sometimes, the devil takes over, and only God could save him. That's why they call it the demon drink."

The officer shook his head in agreement as Isabel stood frozen. "Johnny enjoyed a drink like most but certainly had a bigger problem than that." The officer was called away to make a statement to the sergeant, leaving Liam and Isabel alone.

"Sure is a shame. Johnny couldn't handle the pressure, I guess." He was quiet, momentarily sizing Isabel up before adding, "I wouldn't want anything bad to happen to you."

"You did this, didn't you? You son of a bitch. It could only have been you. Any fool can see that."

"This isn't what it seems. And Johnny wasn't who you think."

"Bullshit," cried Isabel.

"Now lower your voice. I have done nothing wrong. However, as stated in my letter, I look forward to seeing you early next week. I think we will have a special arrangement, don't you?"

Isabel had ice in her eyes.

"Now darling, don't look at me like that. I'm not as bad as you may have decided I am. I'm actually quite a teddy bear if you don't cross me. And I don't think you will. Will you?"

There was a certain—threatening—look in his gaze.

Isabel wanted to scream the truth to the police who surrounded her.

She knew it was futile because they wouldn't believe her, or even worse, Liam would find a way to accuse her of setting the fire.

"You always wanted to open your own restaurant, isn't that so, Isabel? It sure would be a shame if the authorities suspected you had something to do with this. I and Judge Myer are very close friends, and I don't think he would go easy on a woman committing murder and arson."

Isabel felt herself go cold. He was right. He had the social influence, money, and will to do what he wanted in this town. She was trapped.

"I'll see you next week, Miss Isabel," Liam said as he returned to his Cadillac.

Isabel watched as he passed her with the arrogance of a fool.

"I have been fixin' for your fried chicken. You always did make the tastiest meals. I can't wait to be enjoying them regularly, personally cooked for me on the regular."

With that, Liam was gone, leaving Isabel dumbfounded.

She watched as the flames engulfed what was left of the building.

She stood stoic until the fire was out and the crowd dissipated.

Ashes blackened her face, and her clothes reeked of smoke. Her lungs hurt from spending too much time inhaling the fumes, and her mouth had a terrible dryness.

She was in a state of shock driving home, staring blankly before her as she tried to reconcile what she had witnessed. With her heart heavy and grief consuming her, she almost missed the road to her house. Pulling up her driveway, she stared at her home in disbelief that she would have to leave to live at the Kaats estate.

Now, with the restaurant gone, she considered running out of town and avoiding Liam altogether. It was unrealistic that he wouldn't come looking for her, but she wondered what he wanted. Long ago, she had felt the attraction between them, but once Johnny warned her about him, she'd backed off and assumed he had lost interest, too.

He came into the restaurant less, and before long, it was weeks before he would return.

Liam had now proved what he was capable of, and Johnny surely became involved in illegal activity. Isabel was no longer certain who to believe.

As she arrived home, she stared at the sky for answers and clarity.

She was too tired and emotionally bankrupt to make any decisions other than taking a shower.

Once inside her house, a calm arrived that only home could offer.

She undressed slowly, careful not to let the ash scatter around the floor. She deposited her clothes carefully in a garbage can before entering the much-needed water, letting the warm water run over her body as she lathered soap, scrubbing it with force to erase the black smoldering marks still left behind. She wanted to forget what she had just witnessed and forget the restaurant, but she mostly wanted to forget about Liam. She wondered, could she be so wrong about him? The tears stung her eyes. Or was she wrong about Johnny?

She was confused and didn't want to wind up tangled in two men's lies. For years, she suppressed any thoughts about Liam, trusting Johnny to be telling the truth.

Now, she was not so sure.

As she washed away the last of the black soot, she made a decision to never think of Liam as anything more than an employer. It would be impossible. He would be a constant reminder of all that had been lost, of Johnny's forsaken life that had ended so cruelly.

Before she could stop them, the myriads of tears finally released.

She lost herself in grief, allowing the terrible pain to consume her.

She hadn't cried this hard since her mama died, and the release of emotions exhausted her but also freed her from years of bottled sadness. Isabel had too tough an exterior.

How could she not? Now, alone in her bathroom with soap, soot, and dirt dripping from her body, she was the most vulnerable she had ever been. When her tears dried up and nothing was left inside, she dried herself off and fell fast asleep.

She had slept for over sixteen hours when a loud banging came to the door.

"Isabel. Open up. I know you're in there. No use hiding from me."

Groggy and dressed only in an old pair of shorts and a white T-shirt, Isabel went down the stairs to find Gary already standing in her living room.

"How did you get in?" she asked.

"You left the door open. Given what's happening in these parts, I suggest you start locking them."

"What do you want, Gary? I know about the restaurant already. And about Johnny's suicide note." Her voice was low as she said the word suicide.

"It just doesn't make no damn sense, Isabel. Why would Johnny go off and do something so stupid? He had everything going for him."

Gary's voice broke at the mention of Johnny. They had known each other since grade school, and although they led different lives, they were friends.

"I don't know," Isabel lied.

"So now what? Have you thought about what you'll do?" Gary looked concerned. Even with their differences, Gary had grown to care for Isabel, even becoming a friend.

"Actually, yes. I'm going to work for Liam and Mary Kaats. They kindly offered me a position as a housekeeper and cook." The words spit out of her mouth involuntarily.

She herself didn't know why she was agreeing to Liam's demands. Perhaps because she knew there were no other feasible options, or maybe she was tired of fighting so hard for a dream of owning her restaurant that may never come true.

"You? Working for someone? Isabel, you gotta be kidding. You won't make it the week. You are far too bossy not to be in charge."

Isabel ignored the friendly jab, which was meant to be a compliment. "Well, it's true. It will be a good change and easy money. Anyway, I could use more steadiness in my life. Working so hard for so many years has been hard on my body. Who wouldn't want a cushy job that pays more than the diner did?" Isabel didn't believe her words any more than Gary did. She had succumbed to Liam's demands out of fear, though she could never share that with him.

Gary shrugged. "For me, I'm heading out of town. I have some family in Myrtle Beach. Now's as good a time as any to reconnect and start something new."

He looked at Isabel, who was visibly exhausted.

His face softened. "Are you gonna be okay, kid?"

"Always," said Isabel.

Gary nodded, awkwardly embracing her. Well, if you ever find yourself in Myrtle Beach, look me up. Who knows—life is funny that way. Maybe we'll meet again."

Isabel smiled as Gary saw himself out. Once he was gone, she took a long exhale, clenching her fist at the unfairness of the situation. At least Gary had a plan, though. After Gary was long gone, she considered living in a tourist area. She considered his offer. "Hopefully, one day, Gary, we will meet again," she said under her breath as she took another swig of whisky.

CHAPTER EIGHT

EVERYTHING WAS HAPPENING TOO quickly for Isabel to comprehend. She was overwhelmed with emotion and fear of what life would be like for her come next week.

Despite her reluctance and anger, she decided to pack some personal items and do what was expected. She would report to the Kaats house, fully prepared to work early next week.

Surely, Liam would eventually tire of her, and she would be free to move on. Perhaps she could even meet Gary in Myrtle Beach and maybe work together again.

It took Isabel three days to fully commit to the plan, but she was ready to start a new adventure once she stopped feeling sorry for herself.

One thing she knew for sure was that life changed, and she needed to be open to it.

She would do what she had always done, rise to the occasion, and be the best in her new position despite inwardly being terribly miserable. For now, she would work for the Kaats, save her money, and figure out where to go next. One thing life as a chef taught her was to pivot, adapt, and regroup without letting anyone see her internally sweat. And that's what she intended to do. Despite her reservations, Isabel was intrigued by Liam's intentions.

As she drove away from her home and toward the estate, many thoughts raced through her mind. She was mainly angry but confident she could handle just about anything life threw at her. In her mind, this arrangement would be temporary, and within six months, Liam would grow bored of her, and she would be back to her life in her quaint house, looking for work elsewhere.

She had no reason to think otherwise.

The Kaats Estate was exquisite. Its long driveway, lush with greenery, led to a massive brick colonial house. Isabel didn't arrive at the Kaats Estate until Thursday, mostly out of rebellion but also because she needed the extra time to finish packing her house.

"Welcome. We are thrilled to have you," Mary gushed.

Liam stood by the doorway, eyeing Isabel as Mary awkwardly embraced her.

Isabel was staring directly at Liam.

"Hello, Ma'am. Thank you for having me. I think you will find great delight in my services."

Isabel remembered what Randy had said all those years ago: "Have integrity, provide your best work, and never let the customer see you sweat."

Those were great words of wisdom, and Isabel intended to do just that.

"Where shall I put my belongings?" asked Isabel.

"Honey, we've an entire guest house for you; you will find it most comfortable. I had the painters in to brighten up the place. But if you want a different color, of course, let me know."

"I'm sure it's fine," Isabel said flatly. She was not much for home decoration. She preferred comfort and was eager to get settled in her new surroundings. The large chandelier was impressive. She looked around the foyer, and rainbows appeared from the sunlight beaming in from the large windows. The wallpaper was blue-striped, making the room appear larger.

The stone fireplace was so grand that, at first glance, she would not notice the large painting of a meadow that hung above.

"Let's get you settled then," Liam said. "We are all excited to help you become acclimated with the estate. I am pleased this arrangement's worked out so well."

Isabel couldn't tell if he was being sincere or sarcastic. He had kindness in his eyes and a soft, genuine tone. But at the same time, she knew what he was capable of.

She had seen it firsthand but had difficulty reconciling that the man before her was the monster Johnny had warned her about.

Liam walked Isabel around the back of the house, down the cobblestone path to the guest house. It overlooked a large pool, lush garden, and patio with a firepit and lounge chairs.

"Feel free to use all of our amenities. I do want you to feel at home."

She cringed at the words "at home," knowing this would never be that.

As they entered the guest house, Isabel was struck by its beauty. It was light and airy, with a large kitchen.

'We brought in the best supplies we could find for you. These are for you when you want to cook for yourself. Our kitchen is stocked with similar cooking utensils to those in the restaurant."

He glanced away, not wanting to meet Isabel's eyes.

Liam continued, "If you want anything else, please let me know, and I will be certain you get it immediately." Isabel was impressed by the Kaats' thoughtfulness. She felt embarrassed by their generous gestures but was grateful for their consideration. "Look, I know this may not be ideal for you. However, my half-brother had many problems—things you know nothing about. I'm sure he made me sound like the monster and the one who took advantage. But Isabel, that wasn't the case. There was much more to the story that I didn't even want to get into. But let's just say Johnny wasn't as innocent as he may have led you to believe."

"You burnt down his restaurant," Isabel said without thought.

Liam glared at Isabel. Hurt ran across his face and then anger.

"I'm sure that is an easy story to believe. But that's not the entire truth. I helped him out of a situation. I did not know that he would be inside."

"I don't believe you," said Isabel.

"You don't need to," Liam retorted.

Before Isabel could ask any more questions, Mary entered. "Here, dear, please have some lemonade. It's hot as Hades already today."

"Thank you," Isabel said, accepting the cold beverage.

"Why don't you get settled in and come to the main house whenever you are ready," Liam suggested.

Mary, eager to please, added, "Please take your time."

The pair left the small cottage to allow Isabel to get acquainted with her new surroundings. She looked around and was pleased with the space. She went through the living room and out the back door to find a large deck overlooking a wooded area.

It wasn't her front porch, but this would certainly do.

Maybe this was a good career move after all, she thought. The pay was higher, the work was less, and the living arrangements were far nicer than she could ever provide for herself.

Isabel had spent many years surviving. Perhaps it was time for a slower pace that offered financial security. She opened the refrigerator, hoping to find any morsel of food since she hadn't eaten, and the Kaats had already stocked it with fresh fruit and a pitcher filled with sweet tea. She poured herself a tall glass and went out the back door to the deck. She sprawled out on the oversized couch and soaked in the hot sun. After a short while, she went back inside, only now noticing the display of fresh-cut flowers in a large vase on the kitchen table.

By the time she reached the main house, it was about time to start supper. She let herself in through the back door that led to the kitchen, hesitating momentarily as she entered, overwhelmed by its grand features. She first noticed the high ceilings and two large stoves.

Large pans hung from the wall, and granite countertops covered a vast island in the middle.

The space was massive and filled with every luxury a chef could imagine. The walk-in pantry was half the size of the kitchen and held another large refrigerator.

She heard Liam's footsteps approach as she ran her fingers across the stainless-steel appliances.

"Impressive, huh?" said Liam.

"I'd say so. This is something," Isabel said as she walked around the room, observing its enormity. "This is a better equipped kitchen than any restaurant I have worked at."

She spoke in wonderment.

"I'm glad you're pleased. I love this estate. We have done some renovations, but it's been in our family for centuries."

"Lucky you," said Isabel.

"Don't let old money fool you. It comes with its share of problems," Liam offered.

"I wouldn't mind some of those problems," said Isabel, laughing.

"Trust me, I wouldn't mind life a bit more mundane." Liam was pensive as he watched Isabel take in what he took advantage of. "The truth is, there are so many expectations and responsibilities from being born into the family. It almost feels like I never chose my life. It chose me. It gets exhausting."

Isabel's eyes widened with this admission.

She hadn't taken Liam for a man who shared his feelings. A lot about him surprised her; he was more sensitive and vulnerable than she expected. She was still uneasy about his behavior and his part in the fire, so she stayed guarded. She didn't want to be made a fool of again.

"I can see that. People assume that money fixes problems, but sometimes, it causes them."

"Exactly. That's why I took such an interest in you."

Isabel felt her face flush.

Liam continued, "You could have been like so many other women around here, fixin' to find a husband to care for them. They were giving up themselves for status, money, and power. But you chose your own path. Certainly, an unconventional one."

Liam was staring at Isabel with desire. "I admire that," he added.

"I never really thought about it that way. When Mama was alive, she would tell me there was a fire in my eyes and never to let a man put it out. I was young when she passed, so I didn't know what she meant by it." Isabel paused, embarrassed by her rambling. She barely knew Liam except for the brief exchanges through the years and a strange attraction. She felt her shoulders stiffen. She knew men like Liam who played on a woman's emotions to cross them later.

The police were still investigating the fire and Johnny's death, and she didn't want to get too comfortable. However, in reality, she knew that, despite Liam's part, there would never be charges against him; he was too powerful, and the law didn't apply to those with money.

Isabel's voice tightened. "Anyway, I've been alone for a long time. So, I ain't looking for a man or anyone to save me. Which leads me to my next question."

"And what is that?" asked Liam.

"What was it with you and Johnny? And why did you insist I work for you? What's in it for you?" Isabel's questions came spitting out like fire, one after another, without receding. She expected Liam to get annoyed by her aggressive inquisition, but he didn't. Instead, he lowered his eyes and shook his head. She watched his shoulder slump as he let out a sigh.

"It's more complicated than I have privy to divulge. There is still an investigation, and it wouldn't be right for me to spread rumors."

"I wouldn't tell anyone," insisted Isabel. "I cared for Johnny. He mentored me, and I can't imagine what could have gone so wrong in his life that he needed to end it."

"He had more problems than you can shake a stick at. He was simply good at hiding them from everyone."

Isabel found this hard to believe. Johnny had never indicated that he was struggling financially or that he was depressed. The week before the fire, he'd been excited about the specials and adding more items to the menu, even considering offering discounts on weekday nights. It seemed bizarre to Isabel that his mood would shift dramatically and suddenly.

Liam swiftly changed the subject. "I almost forgot," he said, guiding Isabel down a long hall leading to the garden. "This is my favorite space of the entire estate."

The floral aroma permeated Isabel's senses while the bright blooms dazzled her eyes. "This is incredible," she gushed.

"We spoke about it," Liam noted.

"I remember," said Isabel softly.

"Isn't it, though? My great-great-grandfather planted all of these magnolias himself," Liam said proudly. The rows of colors went on for as far as the eye could see. Looking to the left, Isabel noticed a line of sabal palm trees. "I planted those myself last season. I thought it could use a little tropical feel back here."

"It is certainly impressive. I have never seen so much color and so many blooms in one spot. Then again, I spend most of my time inside a kitchen," Isabel said, laughing. "Liam, I need you to tell me about the fire."

Liam shot her a glance, and she watched his eyes grow cold.

"Isabel, you work for me. This is a working relationship, and I am your boss. Speaking of which, I'm sure you have much to do, and I must get to work."

Isabel stepped back from Liam, aware that she needed to stay guarded.

She fixed her hair in a bun and asked, "Is there something special you want me to prepare for you and your wife this evening?"

Liam thought. "Actually, yes. I have been fixin' for some collard greens, hush puppies with that rich, creamy butter on the side, and your famous fried chicken."

"Perfect." Isabel returned to the kitchen, taking one last look at the garden before leaving. She noticed Liam staring off at the magnolia trees in deep thought.

Once inside, she eased into her new working conditions, reorganizing some pots to make the kitchen more efficient. The estate was impressive, but Isabel was most surprised by Liam.

He seemed troubled by the fire, and he was certainly hiding something.

What Isabel couldn't figure out was what it was.

As Isabel was preparing the collard greens, Mrs. Kaats came in carrying a bag of vegetables.

"Hi, darling. I'm sorry to bother you. On my way home from the salon, I just went to this wonderful farmers' market."

Isabel noticed Mary's welcoming and joyful voice.

She, too, surprised Isabel with her kindness. Isabel assumed Mary would have help with the shopping, but instead, Mary unloaded the hefty packages herself, admiring the fresh peaches.

"Want one?" Mary said as the juice dripped from her chin. The Kaats seemed like real people, not from the Southern prestige Isabel had formerly imagined.

"I will enjoy one of these later. Thank you very much. Right now, I'm preparing supper. Mr. Kaats requested my famous fried chicken this evening."

"Great choice. Where is Liam anyway? I wanted to talk to him about a fundraiser in town later this month."

"I believe he's out back. The garden is magnificent," Isabel added.

"It sure is. Liam spends a lot of time alone out there. Says a man needs his quiet time."

Mary took her half-eaten peach in search of her husband as Isabel continued preparing.

Isabel smiled in gratitude for this opportunity that she initially had resented. However, she was still confused by the earlier conversation with Liam about Johnny. The entire situation felt off, but she had no way of knowing what had really transpired, now just grateful that Liam had insisted she come to work for him right before the fire, though, a distinct attitude change in her.

Life has a way of working itself out, now, doesn't it? She thought as she chopped the greens and put them into the sizzling pan.

CHAPTER NINE

ISABEL, OF COURSE, HAD no way of knowing that Liam Kaats was pining for her in any way.

Despite their past, Isabel had built a wall around her and kept everything professional, even calling him Mr. Kaats. She was too busy to pay attention to his long stares or when he carelessly brushed his arm across her back as he passed by during breakfast.

In fact, Isabel didn't think much about Liam. She worked for him, doing something she loved, got paid generously, and immensely enjoyed his wife, Mary. Her goal was eventually to find a way out of this arrangement, save money, and maybe even find Gary in Myrtle Beach.

The Kaats family was a wealthy banking name, and Mary indulged in the finer things. However, she was not unkind and was quite likable. She had a natural beauty that was intimidating for people who didn't know her, but her warm demeanor made her all the more attractive.

Liam was charming but quiet and had an air of arrogance and shyness.

He stood over six feet tall with big green eyes, blonde wavy hair, and a dashing smile.

The pair was unable to have children, but Liam, too proud to admit it, blamed the poor state of the economy for their lack of offspring. The war had ended, and the country was still feeling the effects of the financial burden. Luckily for the Kaats, the finance business was booming, and bankers were making much money even in these adverse times. Still, the couple had a sweet connection, though Mary doted on Liam while he seemed too preoccupied to notice.

"My, you look handsome, my lovely husband," Mary would say sweetly.

Her voice was almost a song that was pleasant to the ear.

Liam grumbled as he hurried out of the house, kissing her quickly on the cheek.

Isabel would try not to eavesdrop and focus on preparing the night's dinner.

She noticed Liam staring at her as Mary droned about the week's social calendar. Despite Liam's best efforts, she quickly looked away to ensure their eyes never met.

"Now, don't forget we have dinner with the Ellisons on Wednesday. And Friday night, we have tickets to the opera," she added.

Liam, who was barely listening, watched as Isabel was elbow-deep in flour.

Her hair was tied in a messy bun, and her apron was stained from weeks of preparing dishes without washing it. She had meant to throw the apron in the wash, but with her busy schedule, she barely had enough time to shower. She was fortunate to have manageable hair that didn't need much fuss or washing either, while her lean legs from standing had grown accustomed to the long hours, but her arms would still become tired from the constant stirring.

Her arms were naturally toned, though her midsection was wider than she would have liked. Fettuccine Alfredo was her favorite dish, and though she tried to go light on the cream sauce, the homemade bread dipped in butter did not help her weight but satisfied her senses.

When Isabel noticed Liam's gaze, she smiled softly and returned to work.

She had no idea that her boss was infatuated with her or that he had any other feelings for her than a fondness for her cuisine. It would never have occurred to her that a successful banker married to a beautiful once-beauty pageant contestant would pay any mind to a woman who barely had a high school education.

Lately, he had been mulling around the kitchen more than usual, and Isabel suspected he needed a little time away from Mary's doting.

"Whatcha making today, Ms. Isabel?" Liam said as he poked his head inside the oven.

"With the downpour today, I reckoned we should have some comfort food."

"Indeed. The weather has been terrible all week. I also hear the rain won't be letting up until the day after tomorrow. Most preposterous if you ask me."

Liam stared out the kitchen window, overlooking the big wrap-around porch.

During nice weather, he would sit outside sipping bourbon and listening to the birds greet one another. Isabel wondered what it would be like to have the time to sit on an old porch and soak in the atmosphere. She probably would never know, as every hour seemed to be about work.

Her days started at four in the morning, and it wasn't until half-past ten that she would collapse into her bed with exhaustion. Even if she had the time to relax, she lacked the energy. Even sitting upright in a chair and sipping on a mug of sweetened tea required a certain zest.

Instead, after work these days, her body begged for peace and to be lain prostrate in clean sheets, giving way to slumber. She had not an ounce of energy to stay upright. It was strange since if the Kaats ever asked her to work late for a social event or soiree, she managed it without a grumble. It was only when the work hours ended that her joints and back moaned and groaned.

Granted, this work was easier than being in a restaurant, but the hours were just as long.

"I was thinkin' that some shrimp and grits with collard greens and fried okra are just what this rainy day calls for, and for dessert, some warm pecan pie," she offered to a morose-faced Liam.

"That. Sounds. Delectable," he said. "I'll be looking forward to your delicious meal all day."

Isabel smiled. "I am glad to hear that, Mr. Kaats."

"Please, Isabel, I have told you before. It's Liam."

"Okay, Liam," Isabel said curtly. "But as you have mentioned on many an occasion, I must remember I work for you." Isabel's face flushed. "You go on and have yourself a nice day."

"Isabel, I am trying to gain your trust. I know you have a lot of questions, but as I have stated, I'm not at liberty to—"

Isabel cut him off. "Enjoy your day, *Liam.*"

Liam left the kitchen with a weak wave, mumbling something under his breath.

Isabel continued to prepare the evening meal.

She prepared the shrimp stock with care. Fortunately, the South Carolina Lowcountry was rich with whole shrimp, which added flavor to the stock. Mount Pleasant had the freshest shrimp, and the Kaats gave Isabel full rein on the meal budget, which allowed her plenty of options for high-quality head-on shrimp. She would drive to Mount Pleasant once a week to pick up seafood, which was always their favorite meal on the menu.

Last week, Mary had been most grateful for the array of seafood. "My goodness, this shrimp tastes as though it just came from the creek," she'd commented. "So fresh. So alive!"

Except you wanted it killed, Isabel thought, giggling. *And I can't blame you! So did I!*

"It has just come from the creek, pretty much," Isabel said in a buoyant reply. "The shrimp is sweeter here in South Carolina, so the flavors really stand out. One of my favorite dishes."

In a large skillet, she added the shrimp stock, some sausage, and country ham she had bought at the market and stirred in the fresh shrimp and chopped tomatoes for a quick and lively sauté.

Once it was ready, she added garlic, green onion, and a tablespoon of butter to enrich the flavors. The aroma filled the house with an array of scents.

Isabel was happy to provide food for the pair while practicing her cooking techniques, which she later hoped to use in her own restaurant. She knew it was a long shot, especially now.

Still, she dreamed of having a small upscale establishment that featured only the finest ingredients and honored South Carolina's cuisine. There was pride in Southern cooking, and Isabel was excited to show off her passion. She just needed the opportunity to do so.

Isabel also rather enjoyed cooking for the Kaats when they had polite company.

They were of a different class than most people she knew, and she relished impressing people of a higher echelon. She searched a heap of random cards for the recipe card for her Aunt Peggy's cheesy meatloaf. The Kaats often invited friends and business associates over for dinner, people who would openly gush about the hostess' more than delightful and opulent cooking.

Except, of course, it was not the hostess who prepared with love any of it. It was all Isabel.

"Isabel, you must tell me your secret sometime," Cathy Crate would inquire.

"Listen, y'all, you want my recipe. You all are going to have to kill me," Isabel teased.

Isabel had learned from her Aunt Peggy to put slices of bread at the bottom of the pan and sprinkle oats to ensure the grease got absorbed. Of course, she would not share that information with the others as she loved being known as the best cook in town, with amazing, unique recipes.

Often, with permission from the Kaats, other people in the community sought her out to make dishes for parties and weddings. The Kaats paid her well, but Isabel saved any extra money in a hidden box so that she could make a downpayment for her restaurant someday.

She also loved the attention she received for her ability to make even the most mundane recipe pop with flavor. For example, she used cinnamon and mustard to help caramelize the top of her meatloaf, which surprised the crowd with its glossy color and unique taste.

Isabel believed that cooking was a love language. Admittedly, she still missed working at the restaurant; a big part of her missed the rush of the crowd and the exhilaration from the stress.

"C'mon, Isabel. You are the best cook in town. Give us one of your little secrets," Cathy continued.

With a whisper, Isabel leaned in and said, "You all want to know my secret?"

She had complete command of the crowd, who eagerly listened. "The secret is …" Isabel said slowly. "You should hire me for your next party to wow all your friends."

The room erupted into laughter, and Cathy took a long sip of her white wine. Holding his belly in laughter, her husband Keith pointed at Isabel. "Oh, Isabel, you are something!"

Isabel, who had no lack of confidence despite the vast difference in social strata between them, gave a wink as she exited the dining area and returned to the kitchen. She knew that between her delicious concoctions and personality, she'd ensured at least three more catering bookings this month. After a moment of laughter subsided, she peeked around the corner to watch the company toast in celebration. She waited another moment and delighted in the success of the evening before saying, "Just wait for dessert. It is going to knock your socks off!"

People rushed to the table excitedly, speculating what treasure Isabel would present next.

"I hope it is her seven-layer coconut pie," Mary said.

"Oh, I would love her peanut butter pie," said Keith.

"Perhaps an apple turnover," added Mary excitedly.

"I'm so full from dinner y'all, but some peach cobbler does sound good," Cathy said.

Liam smiled graciously at the joy Isabel brought. He proudly looked over toward the kitchen, knowing he was already in love with the most talented person in the South Carolina Lowcountry.

Chapter Ten

THE SUMMER HEAT GAVE way to the relief of cooler weather. The humidity subsided, too, as the leaves changed colors late into October. Isabel settled into her duties and most enjoyed when the Kaats had dinner parties. At least four times a week, people would gather at the estate for wine, company, and—of course—Isabel's finest cuisine. The Kaats loved the attention they received for having access to the freshest ingredients and a chef who would prepare exquisite dinners.

Isabel still thought about Johnny often, wondering if she had missed the signs.

However, when thoughts of him crept in, she quickly distracted herself with the Kaats. Working at the Dig-In Diner had been one of Isabel's greatest joys.

However, there was something more intimate and elegant to be found in working for just one family—one of high prestige—who were also gracious and appreciative of her services.

The Kaats knew Isabel could go elsewhere to find work in the city at one of the new hotels. She could even work in Hilton Head with one of the McHowlands, the wealthiest family in the South. The McHowlands were far more affluent than the Kaats and had come looking to inquire about Isabel. One of their mutual friends had raved about her services while visiting with the Kaats, and Mack McHowland had inquired if Isabel would consider working for them instead.

"Now, Now," Liam said with a laugh. "While I, too, believe Isabel is irreplaceable, there must be someone along the coast who could fill your needs. Isabel is too valuable for me to allow her to leave. Especially to you." He snickered.

"I thought you'd say that, but you can't blame a man for trying. After all, you poached her."

Mack was a short man with a large belly, and his facial features always made him appear to be smiling. His deep laugh lines and a twinkle in his eyes charmed even Liam.

Isabel was flattered that two of the wealthiest families in the South admired her enough to share bourbon and cigars to determine who would win her.

However, they didn't consider that Isabel was of her own free will and would reject both employment opportunities if she only had sufficient money saved to open her own place.

She still dreamt of the day she could say she had enough money to start a restaurant.

She spent many late nights graphing out a business plan, a kitchen design, and her best recipes for the menu. More than anything, that was her dream.

It would be difficult to achieve such high aspirations as an unmarried woman in this part of the country, but she still hoped. There was never any harm in that, was there?

Isabel even considered finding a husband for the convenience of monetary advancements.

But even after much consideration, she shunned the idea, knowing the only thing a husband would bring her were headaches and babies, and no time to run her restaurant—a fate worse than death to someone so enamored with the notion of someday running her own establishment.

Whenever she wasn't cooking or planning, which was relatively rare, Isabel would go into town and join the locals at the pub. She recognized familiar faces from the Dig-In Diner, who always came over to comment on how much they were still missing her divine cooking.

"C'mon, Isabel, when will you return and feed the locals here?" one gruff, corpulent man asked. He slurred his words and held onto the bar's edge. "Remember me, Isabel? I have been a loyal customer to you for years. Kevin Hall," he said as he reached out his hand.

Isabel gave a weak handshake back, unsure where this odd conversation was headed.

"We heard you work for some fuddy-duddy now and think you are too sophisticated for us townies. Don't you forget where you came from, little lady! We townies got you recognized so that you could work at a cushy estate sipping wine with the elite. We are the ones who paved the way for you, so don't you go forgetting us."

Is this what people think of me now? Isabel wondered. She hadn't even considered that anyone could have missed her once the restaurant had burned down.

Isabel felt attacked by the accusations, becoming defensive.

She stood from the barstool to face Kevin.

"Pardon me. Let me start by saying that what I do with my life is of no concern to you."

Kevin's eyes widened. How dare some trumped-up little woman speak to him like that!

Before he could comment, she continued, "Next, while I very much enjoyed my time at Dig-In Diner, life changes, and you need to go with the flow. I am grateful for the opportunities provided to me by Johnny, but make no mistake, my hard work has gotten me to where I am, nothing else. And it most definitely has nothing to do with anyone but me, and it most certainly had nothing to do with you," she added.

If she could have poked him in the chest, she would have done, but his voluminous belly prevented access to it.

Before she finished, she added, "To be clear, I am where I am not because of you or any other man. I am here because of my abilities and tenacity." Isabel took a long swig of her whisky before she put down the empty glass, signaling to the bartender that she would like another.

Right now.

"You're kinda of an oddity around here," Kevin said, his voice softer.

"I can't say I mind that," said Isabel. "If that is the worst thing, I get called …"

Of course, with company like Kevin's, she knew it was not likely to be the worst thing she got called. But she was not going to care when more insults came. Men like him were common, and she just shrugged them off and gave back as much cheek as they gave to her.

Kevin was interrupted when some of his buddies came rushing in from the gun club. "If you will excuse me, Isabel."

"Of course," she said as he walked off. Hearing this most polite ending to their conversation, anyone listening in would have deemed them good friends or colleagues. But they were not.

The conversation had been unexpected and peculiar in the extreme. Isabel hadn't considered what people had thought once she'd left to work for an affluent family.

Often, wealthier families looked down upon the locals who helped keep the town running. Isabel didn't realize this was equally true of the many good folks who worked hard to sustain the small town. One of the greatest assets and also the downfalls of the South was people's talk.

If they loved you, they would give the shirt off their back for you, but if you crossed or embarrassed them, you would be cast out quicker than fish on a hook.

Isabel considered this as she again mulled over her future plans to open a business.

If the community accepted her as one of their own, she would fare better than if they viewed her as a traitor who had gone to work for the elite. Isabel made a note that she would spend more time in the town and play down how much she enjoyed working for the Kaats.

After all, in reality, this hadn't really been her choice. She had been left with few options. Now, with the failing economy, there weren't as many opportunities as there once had been, so Isabel was grateful to be employed despite the fact there was still a part of her that longed for her old life. She would still spend some nights at her house just to remind herself of how things had been before Johnny had taken his life. Indeed, she was now also believing that was the case.

Being back where she felt most comfortable was always a good reprieve.

She would sit on her porch on the swing, listening to the night sounds, cracking open a beer.

The life she had lived there was far different than the one the Kaats enjoyed, and of which she was now a part, albeit still sitting on a different social level. They involved her in a lifestyle she otherwise would not have seen and experienced. But it was important to keep a perspective of her roots so that when the time came, she could return to doing what she loved most.

As the months passed, Isabel became content with the luxuries of the estate but longed more and more to advance her career elsewhere. She wanted to talk to Mary about taking less of a role in their home. If anyone would understand, it would be her; she was a sweetheart, Isabel thought.

Isabel intended to explain how much she missed working in a busy restaurant. Although she was grateful for this opportunity, she felt she wanted to grow as a chef in new environments.

Yet she tried to speak frankly with Mary on multiple occasions but found her oddly distracted and uneasy. There was something different in the way she looked.

Her eyes were often glazed over as if lost in her thoughts. One rainy afternoon, Isabel watched as Mary spoke to the trees swaying in the wind from the window.

"Hello, Ms. Mary. That's some wind we have here today, isn't it?"

It took Mary a few moments to realize Isabel was speaking to her, but then she said, "You come and sit down and take some sweet tea with me."

"Well, maybe just for a minute. I have some grits cooking and don't want them to overcook. They get nasty if they're overdone."

"Don't you worry about grits! Relax for a minute." Mary stretched out her feet on the patio, kicking off her sandals. "Let me ask you, does Liam seem a bit distant lately to you?"

Isabel hesitated to answer. Despite their close relationship, she didn't want to overstep any obvious boundaries. It was an awkward question to answer, too. But yes, she did notice that he spent more time away and often came home with a strong smell of booze.

"Hmm, I haven't taken much notice," said Isabel, her cheeks flushing as she spoke.

"Between us girls, we haven't been intimate in months, and he sleeps in the guest room." Knowing she had overshared with Isabel, Mary's face turned three shades of red.

Isabel attempted not to be alarmed by this admission.

"Really?" This surprised her. She hadn't realized things were that bad between the couple. She assumed Liam was playing golf with his buddies and maybe enjoying the drink too much.

"Well, whatever it is, I am sure it will work out. Maybe something is happening with work, and he needs a little space," Mary opined in a way that suggested she needed to believe it.

"Could be. I don't know much about men, but I do know that when stressed, they tend to go inward," suggested Isabel.

"I'm sure you're right. I just find it odd. A woman has her feelings, ya know?" Mary stared at the magnolia trees in the distance. In deep thought, she said, "Come to think of it, I haven't seen Liam in this garden in months either. He used to spend his time out here tending to the bushes, and I don't think he has set foot in the garden for ages."

Isabel hadn't seen him taking his usual roam around the estate either.

He'd been spending much of his time out of the house lately, and when he was home, he locked himself in the study. He was quieter than usual and had dark circles under his eyes.

Isabel noticed all of it just as much as Mary did, but she didn't tell Mary so.

Instead, she listened politely and said, "I sure do hope Liam sorts out whatever is happening. I'll make some banana pudding tonight to brighten the mood."

"Thanks, Isabel. You are a good friend," said Mary.

Isabel knew that Mary thought warmly of her, but this was the first time she had referred to her as a friend. "I better get back to those grits," she said as she patted Mary on the shoulder. As she was walking away, Isabel could have sworn she heard Mary mumbling to herself about being a little kid wanting a lollipop. Before she could ask, Liam walked in with his arms folded and eyebrows furrowed. "Isabel, I think it's time to check on those grits."

Liam, threatened by Isabel's friendship with Mary, intentionally kept the pair apart.

Their friendship intimidated him, causing him to resent allowing them to become close in the first place.

As the months passed, Isabel rarely saw Mary from now on.

Liam had tucked her away in the west wing of the house, insisting Mary be left alone.

This arrangement often left Liam and Isabel alone downstairs in the house, but Isabel was careful to return to the guest house when she suspected Liam had been drinking. She could always tell if he was drunk by how he drove up the driveway and the sound of the gravel.

It had been years since Isabel had first met Mary, and the decline in her health was apparent. Isabel knew something had drastically changed with the sweet woman.

Her memory loss had become more frequent, and she was no longer the bright, bubbly woman she had met years ago. When she'd met Mary years prior, she had been quick-witted and warm, but now, there was a dullness residing that Isabel couldn't quite figure out.

Just a few weeks prior, Mary had left the house and not returned for hours.

The sheriff had brought her home, and Mary admitted she didn't know what had happened.

"I don't know how I ended up over an hour away. I was just going to the farmers' market to get strawberries."

Isabel wondered if this was a medical situation and suggested seeing her doctor.

In private, Mary revealed to Isabel that she was frightened something was wrong but afraid Liam would leave if he found out.

"Now, I don't think that is possible. He loves you, Mary."

"I don't know. He's becoming more distant and downright mean at times."

"Give it time. Sometimes, men go through things."

"Isabel, I am not saying this to be hurtful. But sometimes, I feel as if Liam regrets marrying me. That I'm not the one he would choose if asked about it now. It's so very frightening."

"Oh, that can't be. Really, Mary, I'm sure he doesn't think that way."

"No, really. When we're out, he gushes over you. He talks about your cooking, beauty, and personality—he speaks of you the way a man should talk about his wife, not..." Mary hesitated. "Not about help."

Isabel was flattered by this omission but felt awfully sorry for Mary.

"I wouldn't pay much mind to it. I think Liam admires my work, nothing more."

Isabel hadn't thought much about the conversation since but noticed the way he looked at her when he didn't think she was watching. Admittedly, she was intrigued by Liam and found him attractive. She suppressed her feelings, knowing that crossing the line could only lead to trouble.

With Mary's health declining and Isabel keeping her distance, Liam's mood became more sullen. Isabel watched from the window as he came stumbling up the driveway.

When he reached the front doorsteps, he straightened his jacket, ran his fingers through his thick hair, and walked inside. Isabel was preparing an apricot cobbler for the following evening when he entered the kitchen. "Hello, Isabel," he slurred.

"Good evening. You are home later than usual."

Liam glared at Isabel before looking down at his shoes.

"Many things are happening right now. Things you cannot understand." He put his hands in his pockets. "I'm starving. Are there any leftovers, by chance?"

"I prepared a plate for you. I thought you might be hungry when you got home," said Isabel, reaching into the stove.

"What would I do without you?" asked Liam.

His voice was sweet as he inched his way closer.

"Well, tonight, you might go to bed hungry," Isabel chuckled.

Liam removed the tinfoil from the plate and inhaled a big bite of the roasted chicken. "How do you do it? This chicken is so tender and flavorful."

Before Isabel could explain how she cooked the chicken slowly and on a low heat, Liam reached into his suit pocket and removed a flask. He took a long swig from it before placing it down. "Takes the edge off in stressful times."

Isabel turned away, unsure what to say.

She busied herself with the crust of the cobbler as he continued drinking and eating, occasionally making sounds of approval. "The best thing I ever did was hire you," he revealed.

"Did you hire me, or was I forced out of a job because of a dangerous rivalry between you and your brother?"

"Half-brother," corrected Liam.

Isabel always wondered what had happened between him and Johnny, and it had been years since they'd spoken about it—until now. She had tried to tell herself Johnny's death was suicide.

"You never did explain to me what happened between the two of you."

"The mess my brother left when he killed himself has taken me years to unravel."

Isabel adjusted her apron. "I have stayed quiet now for longer than I should. You owe me an explanation of some sort."

Liam shifted uncomfortably. "I didn't want to get you involved, Isabel. I was protecting you."

"Now, why would you do such a thing? We barely knew each other. Despite what you may think, you were one of my many customers."

"You know we were more than that. You had to have felt the connection between us."

"Even if that were true, you were and are married, and to a most wonderful, lovely woman too. And any attraction we may have felt is long gone, Liam."

"Maybe so, Isabel. But my feelings were real toward you."

Isabel turned away. She truthfully had long forgotten her feelings for him and now viewed him as nothing more than her boss.

"My half-brother was extorting me," Liam blurted out.

Isabel, surprised by the revelation, turned to face him.

"Extort? Johnny? Why would he do that? He seemed to have everything together. It just doesn't seem like his nature."

"Johnny had a gambling problem and had gotten himself in some trouble with dangerous folk."

Isabel tried not to act surprised by this information.

Liam walked closer to her, making the closeness uncomfortable.

"Isabel, the truth is, if I hadn't insisted on hiring you, what you don't know is those thugs were threatening Johnny that they'd cut off your fingers as retribution."

Isabel dropped the mixing cup onto the counter. "What? They did what?"

"I don't know what Johnny's told you, but his finances were a mess. He blamed me for his mother's affair with my father. I tried to help him in the past, but that man had too many demons for me to deal with. In the end, it was between him and God."

Isabel could not believe what she was hearing. She had heard rumors that Liam and Johnny were having issues, but she had no idea the depth of it. Even when Johnny had discussed their friction, he'd insisted that Liam was the dangerous one wrapped up in shady business deals.

Isabel's head was still swirling around the fact she'd been in danger because of Johnny's debts, and if it hadn't been for Liam, she would be missing limbs or, even worse, dead.

"Liam, are you sure it was me they were going to hold to ransom for his debts?"

"I'm very sure. Johnny's restaurant was the hottest ticket in town. Everyone knew he was making money, yet he wouldn't pay his debts, claiming he was broke. They gave him ample chances to make things right, and I wouldn't pay another debt for him. That man never learned."

Liam shook his head. "I tell you, Isabel, God didn't bless him with common sense."

Isabel felt a rush of adrenaline running through her veins.

"Am I still in danger? Did his debts ever get taken care of?"

"I took care of all of it. I made sure I paid off each hefty debt acquired by Johnny and hired you to work here so I could keep them away. I didn't want your blood to be on my conscience. You seem like a good woman, and I am a God-fearing man."

"Thank you for saving me. I had no idea," Isabel's voice trailed off.

"I had nothing to do with the fire or his death, though I didn't stop it. He did it all himself. He couldn't have me taking over the restaurant, and that's what would have happened. The damn fool would rather have burned it down than for me to help. His pride killed him in the end."

"I considered him a friend. Didn't think he'd lie to me about this or take his life," said Isabel.

"You just don't know what people are capable of, I suppose."

"Well, thank you again. I feel like that isn't enough," Isabel said sheepishly, having doubted Liam for so long over this. "I'm going to finish up the cobbler. You should get some sleep."

Isabel watched as Liam stumbled side to side back down the hall, taking sips from his flask along the way. When he was out of sight,

Isabel leaned against the refrigerator, holding the counter with shaky hands. She was breathing deeply and felt tears sting her eyes. She also felt betrayed by Johnny and wondered how she had never picked up on the signs.

That night, she couldn't sleep, recounting the conversation with Liam.

It was disturbing how little she had known about Johnny and how much she had trusted him. She recalled her conversations with him about Liam, yet something still didn't feel right.

Johnny had said Liam was a pathological liar and deranged, but Liam had just revealed disturbing information. The fact Johnny had burnt down his own restaurant and was in deep debt, so Liam had to help, didn't make sense. She just didn't know who to believe.

She did know she didn't want any part of that drama and was happy it was in the past.

By this time, she had been working for the Kaats for years, and even though Liam was moody, she hadn't faced any direct issues. Everything had gone better than she had ever hoped.

CHAPTER ELEVEN

As she lay awake, Isabel recounted a conversation that had occurred late one night after closing. Johnny confided that he didn't want any more trouble from Liam and was a man not to be reckoned with. It was an embarrassment to Liam's family to have a bastard brother, he'd said, but she'd never thought that Johnny had been the one with the problems.

"Liam is a mean son of a bitch, and I tell you—my mother's blood may run through his veins, but certainly, there's nothing of her soul in him." The words had spat out of his mouth with vengeance and disgust, and Isabel had believed everything he had said that night.

"Wow, I'm sorry. I didn't know things between you two were this hostile. He always seemed polite when he came in," Isabel had said at the time.

"He may come off as charming, but make no mistake, he has no loyalty to anyone but himself." Johnny had reached for a bottle of bourbon, pouring it over a glass of ice cubes.

Isabel had only stood awkwardly at the door, observing his eyes grow dark.

After a quick swig, he'd placed the glass down, thinking.

"I think something is wrong in his head. He goes from warm and friendly to dark and mean in minutes. I've seen him doing it with others, too. That man will turn on you in a hot minute."

Isabel had tried to offer advice, but she'd had none. Johnny continued, "I tried to put the past behind us and establish a relationship with the family. They made things so difficult for my mama. She was a good soul despite her terrible taste in men." Johnny looked at a framed picture of his mother, her hair in a messy bun, hugging him tightly and smiling at the camera.

"Eventually, we were run out of town by the insults and threats. My mama finally had enough when they spray painted "UNWED MOTHER" in black across her front door; that's when she knew it was time for both of us to start over somewhere else."

Johnny had tears forming, but his fists were clenched as he recalled that time of his life.

"We moved to the upstate and enjoyed more open space. I missed Lowcountry and begged her to move back, but she wouldn't." Johnny shook his head in disappointment. "My mama would say, 'We don't belong there anymore, son. Let it go.'"

"It made me mad, ya know, seeing her so broken over a man. Don't get me wrong. I spent some good years upstate, where I enjoyed the outdoors. A young boy can learn much by fishing and hiking with friends."

Isabel had allowed Johnny to continue his drunken ramble, nodding in agreement and encouraging him to tell her more. So, that was what he did.

"I came home after a long day of fishing to find my mother dead. They say it was a brain aneurysm." He wiped a tear from his eye. "My mama went so quick, I never had a chance to say goodbye. She was here one minute and gone the next. Despite everything, my mama was a good woman. I don't care who she took to bed or why, but she was a good woman and didn't deserve to be treated poorly by that family. I want retribution for the damage they did to us."

"Pardon my bluntness, Johnny, but can't you just let it go? What good will it do now? You have your own business despite them. You should be proud of your accomplishments without their money and influence."

"Why can't I let it go? Because there's more, Isabel," he'd said thoughtfully. "When I returned to town and demanded I get my rightful piece of inheritance, they were shocked."

"I can imagine," commented Isabel. "Well, after all these years, did you? Did you get your inheritance?"

Johnny slammed his fists on his desk. "No, not yet. But one way or another, I will."

He'd grabbed his keys and left Isabel standing there in the dark.

He had never mentioned it again, and Isabel had never asked either.

Isabel lay in the dark, more confused about the facts from the past. She felt uneasy about her conversation with Liam and decided to leave the past where it belonged.

Liam's drinking and agitation had increased after that night, and Isabel noticed a coolness in his demeanor. Mary occasionally appeared downstairs for a meal. Her eyes were glazed over, and she looked disheveled. The woman who had once worn custom blouses with her hair neatly pinned up now appeared in a house dress, unwashed. Her hair, now almost entirely gray, hung limply from her head; her face was pale, and her body was weak and thin. This all alarmed Isabel. Liam's dismissive and often cruel behavior towards Mary, along with his constant criticism, did not help her mental state. "Woman, how many times have I told you I don't like my collars starched? Are you daft or what?"

"I'm sorry, Liam. I will be more careful."

"You had better. I could replace you in a heartbeat. Do you know how many women would love to be in your shoes?"

Mary's head hung as she rushed off. Liam poured another drink as Isabel stood nervously in the den. She looked out the window, noticing birds gathering near the feeder, hoping it would distract Liam's foul mood.

"Not everyone can be like you, Isabel," he commented.

"Ahh, I make plenty of mistakes myself. Don't be so hard on Mary. She is a kind woman who loves you very much." The birds pecked at the berries hanging on the tree.

Isabel pointed it out to Liam, who ignored her observation.

"Sit, Isabel."

Liam patted the seat next to him as he made himself comfortable on the leather couch.

Isabel motioned toward the window again. "Aren't birds interesting? I love watching them from this room. They are truly one of nature's best delights."

"I love how you appreciate the small treasures in this godforsaken life," Liam commented.

"I think we all should," Isabel noted, unwilling to turn the conversation so negative.

Isabel walked toward the open bourbon bottle, picked it up, offering it to Liam.

"I would love one," said Liam.

"I've been helping Mary clean out the attic. You do know she is trying to please you."

Liam stiffened. "Well, too bad. Mary doesn't know how to please me anymore. Something isn't right with her." Liam looked out to find a cardinal fluttering about. "She is forgetful, even a bit irresponsible these days, if the truth be known."

Isabel had noticed some changes in both Mr. and Mrs. Kaats.

Mary walked around confused and in a trance, and Liam was always angry.

It wasn't for Isabel to comment but living with either of them had been challenging lately. They had stopped having dinner parties and were rarely spending time together.

Isabel sat down with her own glass of bourbon.

Liam raised his glass to clink hers. "Cheers to late-night talks," he said. After a brief silence, he said, "Isabel, you're an easy person to talk to. I mean it when I say having you here for the past years has been a joy. I look forward to our chats, wisdom, and cooking."

He smiled.

"Thanks, Liam. I, too, have enjoyed working for you both. I'll admit, at first, I was worried. I thought working for just one family would stunt my culinary creativity and that I would miss the restaurant. However, both you and Mary have grown to be like family."

"Mary," he huffed.

Isabel ignored the irritation in his voice. She didn't want to partake in talking poorly about Mary. She had always been kind to her, but Mary and Liam had done nothing but quarrel lately.

She noticed the lines that formed around Liam's eyes, which showed maturity and appeal. He treated Isabel with respect and gave her the attention she craved.

The pair talked as time passed faster than either had realized. The drinks went down quickly, and both felt the spinning room take control. Isabel had not intended to have more than one drink. She had missed dinner, and it had been hours since she'd last eaten anything at all.

An urge of want welled up inside her as she opened another bottle.

Their eyes met as he pulled her in for a kiss.

"Liam, no, this can't happen," Isabel said breathlessly. "What about Mary ..."

"Isabel don't try to deny this. We have both felt this since your time at the diner."

"C'mon, Liam, that was just some innocent flirting many years ago," said Isabel, trying to keep control.

"I think we both know this has been much more between us." Liam inched his way even closer. She could feel his breath on her skin and the wetness between her legs.

"But Mary. What about Mary?" said Isabel again, allowing his lips to touch her neck.

Liam pulled away gently. "Don't pretend you haven't noticed. Her memory is failing her, and she is only getting worse."

"Still, it wouldn't be right."

"This is right, Isabel."

The alcohol fogged her senses, and Isabel allowed Liam to pull down her pants, caressing her body. She unzipped his pants, too, feeling the hardness press up against her groin.

He thrust himself inside of her until they both moaned in pleasure.

The two were deep in entanglement before Isabel lost control. Afterward, she drifted to sleep as he held her tight on the hardwood floor. When Isabel woke, her head was foggy, and her vision blurred. She looked over to see Liam sleeping soundly. She jolted up and began shaking regretfully. "What did we just do? Liam, no ..." Her voice trailed off.

She gathered her clothes, leaving Liam in the den and rushing off to the guest house.

CHAPTER TWELVE

THE NEXT DAY, SHE avoided Liam and busied herself with odd jobs around the house. Her head felt heavy, and when flashes of the night before raced through her mind, she touched her heart, which pounded nervously inside.

In an effort to avoid Liam, Isabel would leave plates of food for the couple and make excuses about tending to a sick aunt out of town. If Mary grew suspicious, she didn't say a word about it, but the guilt was eating away at Isabel. She noticed Mary becoming more confused, only making her feel more guilt-ridden about her feelings for Liam. Perhaps her lack of intimacy made her desire Liam, but her moral compass conflicted with her.

Despite her avoidance, Liam intentionally tried to steal moments away with Isabel.

This only made Isabel feel worse about their transgression. She would quickly race away, making excuses for her absence, only to be faced with Liam's increasing impatience. In return, Liam would ask Isabel to assist in additional chores, insulted by her all too frequent rejection.

"Ms. Isabel, please be sure to make pecan pie, coconut pie, and apple cobbler this evening. I just can't decide which I fancy this evening."

Isabel's eyes pleaded with him, hoping he would stop the unnecessary tasks. Each pie took hours to make and would put Isabel behind with her other duties. During dinner that night, he pushed his plate away, claiming the collard greens were too bitter and demanding she make it again. By then, the rest of the entree was cold, and he refused to eat any of it. Not one mouthful. In short, he was beginning to treat Isabel the same way he treated his wife.

"What has gotten into you?" demanded Mary.

"You shut your face, woman," he said as he gulped another shot of bourbon from the bottle.

Mary got up from the table and disappeared upstairs. When Isabel next appeared to remove the plates, she noticed the uneaten greens. "Were the greens not good?"

"That would be an understatement," he retorted to her.

"Liam, look, I know you are upset. I'm not sure what you want me to do, though."

He spat back, "I want you to make edible food. That's all. Now get back to work."

Liam's sudden cruelty surprised Isabel. Had it been there all along, or did the rejection spark an upset so deep that he had lost all sense of humanity?

As the weeks passed, the drinking became worse, and Liam could be heard in his office slamming things against the wall. Both Mary and Isabel avoided him, intimidated by his rage and scared of the consequences of his behavior. Isabel heard Mary yelp from the upstairs bedroom, where her head was being pounded against the wall. Isabel crouched under the counter, waiting for the screams to subside as the guilt of her nonaction took hold of her consciousness.

Hours later, when Mary emerged from upstairs, her lip bulged, and the dried blood was still on her chin. Without provocation, she said, "I keep forgetting things, he says. He's right. I'm such a nuisance. I don't know how he stands me." Before Isabel could console her, she walked back up the stairs and closed the door, not returning for the rest of the night.

It was raining like the dickens late one night when Isabel thought Liam had gone to bed. The raindrops pelted the windows, and the sound of the splashing puddles could be heard over the teapot kettle. Isabel was sorting through the mail when, unbeknownst, Liam was out in the garden with a bottle of bourbon and a cigar, watching through the window, drenched from head to toe. When Isabel noticed, she waved quickly and hurried back to work. Liam entered the kitchen, and his soaked clothes left a puddle under his feet. He could barely stand as his wet hair covered his eyes. He was intoxicated more than Isabel had ever witnessed before. "Liam, dear Lord, what have you done?" His eyes were bloodshot, and his voice was cold.

"Isabel. Are you here to tell me what a bad man I am? Did I hire you to hear this nonsense?"

"Liam, no," she said softly. "You need to get out of these clothes."

"I was hoping you'd say that," he said and smirked.

"No, Liam, here, take this towel and dry off."

Liam approached Isabel with more aggression.

Isabel retreated two steps back. "We both know this can't happen. It was a mistake that can't happen again."

"So, I'm a mistake now, am I?" he growled.

Liam's shoulders straightened as he raised a hand toward her. Isabel thought he would strike her, but he stroked his hair, brushing it away from his face. She hadn't noticed how much weight he had gained. His cheeks puffed out, and his breath smelled of rancid liquor and stale cigars.

Liam's eyes narrowed. "I'm not a man who accepts rejection." He said the words slowly, gritting his teeth as he enunciated each syllable. "Listen here, I saved you. I think you know where your loyalties lie. I am a powerful man, and I ain't going to have some woman servant reject me." His voice was cold, and his eyes turned to ice.

As he staggered even closer, his pupils enlarged, letting Isabel feel the impending danger. She felt her stomach turn as Johnny's voice echoed in her head. "He will turn on you in a minute."

Hadn't Johnny warned her many moons ago? She should have heeded his warning.

Frightened, Isabel replied, "Yes, sir," as her voice trembled.

"That's a good girl," Liam said slowly. "Now, why don't you make some fried green tomatoes and pour me a drink? I'll be in my study." His voice was softer now.

Isabel nodded.

When she'd finished preparing his meal, she brought it into his dark study, where the only light emanated from a small window above his desk.

"Liam, I brought you some fried green tomatoes and okara."

"Shut the door behind you."

"Liam, you need to eat—"

"Don't tell me what to do. You work for me," he snapped. "Did you bring me another drink?" Liam was standing now, facing her and looking through her.

He looked possessed, and Isabel carefully did what she was told.

"Right here," she said, handing him the drink. Her hands shook as she watched Liam finish the glass in one long gulp.

Isabel took three steps back, but before she could react, he grabbed her and pushed her up against the edge of the desk.

"Liam, what are you doing?" Isabel said nervously. "You're hurting me."

"Just getting repayment for my good services."

Liam paused, his heavy breath illuminating her senses. "I have been trying to hide my feelings for you, Isabel. Don't tell me you don't feel the energy between us. It has been there since your diner days." He looked desperate. "Now, you reject me? How fucking dare you be disrespectful? I've had real feelings for you for years. That's why I brought you here. I demand what's mine."

"Liam," she started. She still was hoping to give him the benefit of the doubt, blaming his abhorrent behavior on the demon drink.

This is not the real Liam, she wanted to believe.

"It's Mr. Kaats to you."

"Mr. Kaats, I didn't mean to disrespect you. I care about you, and I know you care about me." Isabel trembled. "Sir, you are a married man, and I am your employee."

"You know you are so much more than that, Isabel. I feel closer to you than I ever have to my wife."

"I respect your wife. In fact, I even consider her a friend. And what's more, I have been riddled with guilt since it happened between you and me. We both drank too much that night, so please, Liam, be reasonable. Please. We have to let this go, for everyone's sake."

Liam hesitated for a moment. Then, gulping bourbon, he said, "Then get out. Pack your stuff now. I want you out by morning."

"But, but …"

"You heard what I said. I want you gone by morning, or what happened to Johnny will seem mild compared to what will happen to you."

Isabel ran out of the house through the pouring rain, all the way down the brick path, until she reached the guest house. Once inside, she locked the doors, breathing heavily and trembling as she took the suitcase from under her bed. She quickly began to stuff it with whatever she could find. She wouldn't have time to say goodbye to Mary and worried for the good woman's safety.

She knew she needed to leave quickly before Liam came looking for her, so she grabbed her kitchen knife and kept it close as she gathered more belongings.

Isabel went to the back of her closet, where she had hidden the money she had saved to open her restaurant. She found the silver box beneath an old comforter and opened it.

Her heart sank. The money was gone, and in its place was a note saying, "It's never smart to cross a man with influence and power. It will leave you with nothing. Such as you are."

"Bastard," she hollered. All this time, Johnny had been right about Liam.

She should have listened to his warnings; now, it was too late.

She rummaged through her purse, relieved to find enough money that she had yet to put with the rest of her savings. There was just enough to fill her gas tank up, get out of town, and, if careful, she would have enough funds to scrape by for the next few months.

She was grateful to have the little money to escape but felt a rage that her life savings had been stolen by a man who had enough money and power to destroy everything she had built.

By the time Isabel had finished gathering the rest of her belongings and packing them into her car, it was almost midnight. She started her engine and looked at the estate she'd once called home. She saw Liam peer out, watching from the top window.

She pulled away down the gravel driveway, going slowly, hoping to creep out unnoticed.

Isabel drove back toward the house on Cradle Street, where she had once lived before Liam forced her to move to his estate. Slowly, she drove through the winding roads, noticing the scenery she had missed in the years she had been gone. She walked up the steps and glanced around the porch, which was filled with debris from storms and neglect.

When she entered the house, she was reminded of the familiar feeling of the home.

She had spent years on a beautiful estate enjoying the comforts of the Kaats', but being back in her little house gave a welcomed sense of familiarity and peace.

Isabel locked all the doors and windows and slept with the sharpest knife she owned beside her bed. She didn't know what Liam was capable of and was afraid of what he would do next.

She had hoped when he awoke from his drunken stupor that he would feel shame.

But she didn't trust him and knew she would never step foot back on that estate again.

CHAPTER THIRTEEN

IT TOOK THREE WEEKS for Isabel to regain her home and feel a sense of normalcy again. With all she had been through, she was traumatized by the events and needed time to heal.

She busied herself cleaning and organizing, even applying a fresh coat of paint to the living room and kitchen. After airing out the musty scent, scrubbing the floors, and cleaning the counters, Isabel sat for a while on her porch. It was an ongoing process to remove the smell of mold from the house after so many years of being left vacant.

However, the distraction was how she coped with the uneasiness of Liam's final betrayal.

She poured herself some sweet tea, noticing she was more tired than usual. Making the tea that way also made her think of Mary; sweet tea had been what Mary often offered whenever the two were together or when Mary was down and needed someone to lean upon and talk to.

She dozed off in the Southern sun and awoke to a feeling of nausea rushing through her body. She leaned over the porch's side and vomited into the bushes, then wiped her mouth with her sleeve and returned to the house for some water. She made it two steps into the kitchen when a wave of nausea again occurred, and she leaned into the sink to vomit once more.

Must be some sort of bug I caught, she thought. Isabel fell into her bed and slept through the night, only to awaken again the following morning feeling just as ill, maybe more so.

Isabel spent another full day in bed, drained, barely able to lift her head. The overwhelming sense of exhaustion plagued her, rendering her useless. Three days had passed, and Isabel still felt no relief. She made an appointment with the town doctor for the following day.

After some routine testing, Dr. Griffin left the room and reappeared shortly afterward. He glanced down at Isabel's left hand, rolling his eyes before sternly glaring.

"There is nothing wrong with you but poor morals."

Isabel was confused. "I'm sorry. I don't understand."

"You heard me. You are not sick. You are pregnant."

He slammed her file down on the counter next to her.

"Take some prenatal vitamins and come back in three months for a check-up."

Isabel's jaw was agape; she could not believe the words spoken.

Her head spun, and her stomach curled.

"Is there a daddy to this baby?" asked Dr. Griffin as his eyes narrowed.

Isabel knew better than to mention Liam Kaats' name.

Despite the supposed confidentiality, there was no way the doctor would keep it a secret. In fact, Isabel had seen Doctor Griffin months prior at the Kaats' house for a dinner party. He had commented on her homemade dinner rolls but, luckily, hadn't recognized her today.

Isabel's silence indicated to Dr. Griffin what he had suspected. "I figured as much. I suggest you figure out your situation soon because you are already past your first trimester." He handed her a pamphlet of local adoption agencies, scribbled some notes on a pad, and walked out.

Isabel was stunned by the news and frightened about bringing a child into the world.

She could barely take care of herself, and now, to take care of a baby as an unwed mother was too much to consider. If anyone found out that Liam was the baby's father, history would repeat itself. She had held way too many conversations with Liam about his daddy bringing a bastard child into the world, and she sure as hell didn't want her baby to endure the same shame as poor Johnny.

The months flew by, and Isabel worked at small establishments, earning extra money while still concealing her pregnancy under oversized, baggy cotton shirts. The town would ask too many questions, and having an unwed mother working would look bad for business.

She needed to save enough money to care for her baby before she decided what to do next. She thumbed through the pamphlet she had received about adoption, feeling a sudden ache in her heart. She would be left with no choice if she didn't find a way to support them both soon. Anxious and infuriated, Isabel slammed the cabinet door.

Liam, taking her savings, had well and truly ruined any chance she had of opening the restaurant. However, she was determined to rise above and take control.

Still, at night, she lay awake worrying, rousing too early in the mornings, and experiencing heart palpitations and the familiar morning sickness.

―――――――

By her final weeks of pregnancy, Isabel could barely move. It had been discovered she was pregnant weeks prior, and her employer had encouraged her to stay home and get rest until after the baby was born. It was clear why she'd been released early, but Isabel took the advice and spent her days preparing for the baby, who would soon arrive.

As she poured herself a tall glass of sweet tea, she flipped through a pile of unopened mail. There was a white envelope with her name and no return address.

Inside was a stack of hundred-dollar bills.

Isabel knew this was from Liam, but how could he have found out about the pregnancy?

She had been careful to avoid people who indulged in gossip and was mindful to wear clothes that concealed her baby bump. Yet even so, Liam had a way of finding out what he needed to know about her, and Isabel was sure he must be worried that she'd reveal him as the father.

He would vehemently deny it, of course, but just the insinuation that he'd fathered a child to the hired help while being married would tarnish his reputation. Her pregnancy needed to be kept secret for as long as possible, or at least until she figured out a plan.

Liam's "gift" of the money was to keep her silent, she assumed. It still went nowhere near the sum she had lost to him when his greedy, immoral hands had taken all her hard-earned savings.

Gone were all the thoughts of giving the baby up for adoption, however. Now, Liam knew about it, and she did not know whether he would see adoption as a wrong move or a right one.

If she made a wrong move, she would dearly pay the price for it again.

Anyway, Isabel felt a strong connection to the baby inside her. "I feel you, baby. I'm here, and together, we are going to be okay," she said, dozing off to slumber.

On a hot, late summer's day, the pain of labor invaded Isabel's body. It took six hours of pain as the midwife encouraged her that the baby would arrive soon.

Isabel was unprepared for the pain and loneliness of it all, the agony of enduring hours of contractions and the overwhelming feeling that there was no one to help her with this.

She had never imagined she would find herself in this situation. This abysmal scenario was for other women, careless ones, not ones with intellect and a strategy to build a viable business.

This was for women devoid of any ambition, and she was far from being one of them.

As the pain intensified, so did her anxiety about giving birth. She screamed wildly and pushed as she felt the baby's head begin to crown. Finally, dripping with sweat, Isabel pushed one last time to deliver a baby girl. Caralyn screamed her way into the world just after midnight, and despite her exhaustion, Isabel fell deeply in love with the child from the moment she was placed in her arms.

Before long, Isabel embraced motherhood naturally, nurturing her baby with immense care.

The money never stopped coming each month, and while they were not rich by any means, it allowed Isabel to stay home for a while to care for her new daughter.

At first, she hadn't missed working as much as she would have thought.

Eventually, she became eager to return to the kitchen and no longer wanted to rely on Liam's money alone to care for her baby. She knew that he could stop sending money at any time of his choosing or, even worse, come for her daughter.

She had to stay vigilant and be prepared for anything.

An older woman from church named Ruth offered to watch Caralyn for a small weekly fee, which no doubt was sent by Liam yet again.

Isabel considered allowing Ruth to watch Caralyn but worried that Liam would come to take her baby while she was gone, that his magnanimity was yet again a ruse.

When it became apparent that was not the case, Isabel confidently began leaving for short shifts at different restaurants. She took on odd jobs and small catering jobs at first.

However, once she started cooking again, Isabel was reminded of her love for cooking and began to dazzle the community with her skills.

These accolades were addictive for Isabel; the more compliments she received, the more she yearned to be in the kitchen full-time. The hours were long, and she missed seeing her daughter, but she trusted that Ruth would keep her safe and well.

It occurred to Isabel that Ruth had come out of nowhere to offer her services. "I was wondering how you knew I had a baby when you knocked on my door, Ruth," she said.

Ruth fidgeted in her seat. "I am a Christian woman and really hate lying. Can you just trust that the Lord sent me to you and your God-given child?"

Without inquiring further, she knew for sure Liam had sent her.

She still worried he would stake a claim on their child but reconsidered, knowing that the revelation of this secret would ruin his life. "Ruth, I need you to promise me you will help protect Caralyn like she's your own. No matter what is offered to you, I need you to swear you will never allow someone to take her away from me."

Isabel's eyes were pleading, and Ruth took her hand.

"Child, no one will take her from you. I can promise you that, dear."

While Isabel was grateful for Liam's generosity, she wondered what had changed.

The last time she had set eyes on him, he had been cruel and vengeful, violent and a bully, verbally and physically. Liam was a complicated man with polar opposite personalities.

In short, was he not exactly what Johnny had claimed?

Yes! He was kind and compassionate one minute, cold and calculated the next.

She thought about him often, especially since the birth of Caralyn, but the shame of deceiving Mary and having unholy thoughts about a callous married man stung her to her core.

She wondered if Liam still thought about her or their child.

Yes, he thought of her sufficiently to remember to send money each month. But that did not indicate either fondness or care; it only said he did not want his secret getting out.

But did he ever care for them beyond that?

As she got lost in her thoughts, she heard Caralyn fussing in her crib. She held her baby's downy soft skin against hers, hoping she had made the right choice of trusting Ruth.

But there were very few options for childcare, and with Mary still living, Isabel doubted Liam would want a scandal attached to his name.

For now, she felt safe with Ruth and had to believe her intentions were good.

Three years later, Isabel was startled when she noticed a car hidden behind a bush. She and Caralyn were out playing tag in the yard. Caralyn laughed in delight and twirled when Isabel noticed movement only feet away. Without hesitation, she quickly scooped up the small girl and hurried into the house. Her blood ran cold when the car urgently drove away.

"What's the matter, Mommy?" said Caralyn.

"Oh, nothing, sweetie. Mommy just got a little tired. Let's have some lunch and bake cookies. You can help mix the batter."

"Can we use the yellow bowl? It's so pretty."

"Absolutely, sweetie."

Isabel continued to peer out the window, feeling unsettled. Could Liam know about Caralyn?

Was he watching them? Isabel couldn't be sure, but the constant stress of this awful possibility left Isabel on constant alert.

Three months passed, and there was no other sighting of Liam or the mysterious car.

Isabel wondered if it had been a coincidence and concluded that the mysterious car was just a passerby pulled over on the side of the road. Still, she considered leaving South Carolina to start over because this was no way to live, not really. There was no future here.

She worried about whether Liam would come for her and what that would mean for Caralyn.

But in moving, the challenge would be finding childcare for Caralyn and, worse, a job.

Ruth was aging, and eventually, her services would no longer be available. In the meantime, though, their arrangement was viable, and Isabel needed to keep life as normal as possible.

After much careful consideration, she realized her effort would be futile since Liam could find her wherever she went, so she decided to stay in the house, where she loved doing the job she adored most. She knew it came with risk, but losing Ruth or her blooming career could alter their lifestyles. Anyway, she didn't want Liam to gain control over her decisions.

Although the threat was always in her mind, Isabel chose to stay and raise Caralyn, hoping against hope that Liam would stay happy with their silent arrangement and never come looking.

Chapter Fourteen

By the time Caralyn was school-age, Isabel's career was in full force. Society had changed, and more women were now employed in hotels and restaurants. The town had built up more than anyone had anticipated. Large hotels, shops, and restaurants occupied the streets.

Visitors from all over the East Coast would visit to enjoy the warm waters of the Atlantic Ocean and experience the famed Southern hospitality.

Isabel still heard others' sneers about having a child out of wedlock.

Because Isabel had already established a reputation as different and ambitious, however, it was not as shocking as it would have been years prior.

Being a single mother in the South certainly raised eyebrows, but Isabel Loring had never been the type of woman to follow protocol, had she? Although respected for her talent and rich flavors in the kitchen, however, most stayed far away from her because of her unusual lifestyle.

While most women were preparing food for their families in the kitchen, she was drumming up business to expand her own wallet.

What's more, she made no apologies for it, unlike some local seamstresses who would proclaim they did it to help out in their free time. Isabel worked because she wanted to pursue her talents. Women in the South were born and bred to be wives, but not Isabel.

She was happy to be a mother and didn't need a man to be a good parent.

She celebrated her independence and, as she put it, "Other people's opinion of me is none of my business. They can curse me all day for all I care."

As Caralyn got older, she asked more questions about her father.

Caralyn was starting to develop. Her once flat chest was blossoming, and a sudden change in her figure began to appear. It was then that Isabel realized her little girl was growing up and would become infinitely more curious about her past.

"Do I have a father?"

"You do. But he died in an accident a long time ago," Isabel lied.

"What was his name?"

"Carl. I named you Caralyn because it sounded similar."

Caralyn fidgeted in her chair. She wanted to know more, but Isabel was visibly uncomfortable whenever her father was mentioned.

"Mom, I think I want to be called Cara from now on." She met her mother's gaze with a willful stare. "To give respect to my father." Caralyn played with her hair nervously as silence filled the air. "Anyway, Caralyn is a bit old-fashioned."

Isabel was hurt by the suggestion but listened intently as Caralyn continued, "Did Carl have any other family? It seems odd that no one's come looking for me, wanting to know how I am."

"Your father was an only child, and his parents died when he was a child. We both connected because we had no family and became kindred spirits," Isabel lied again.

The lies became more embellished, although Isabel was careful to stay as close to the truth as possible without giving the game away.

"Where did you meet him?" asked Cara.

"We worked in a kitchen together in town. He was much older than me, but he had the kindest heart. You have his spirit, Caralyn. I mean Cara."

"I wish he didn't die. I always have a strange sense that he's around me. Like someone's watching me, you know?" The statement was innocent enough but yes, Isabel did know what her daughter meant. She knew how it was to be watched like that. The statement sent frissons of shivers through her. Cara continued, "Just the other day, I felt like someone was following me, but when I glanced behind me, no one was there."

Isabel nervously clasped her hands together.

Had Liam been keeping tabs on Cara all along? She figured he had become busy with new business deals and forgotten everything about them. She had heard he owned the latest hotel right outside of town, and the state was giving him grief over outstanding filing fees.

She assumed he was too preoccupied with his businesses to pay mind to personal matters.

She had already witnessed for herself how fickle his mood and emotions could be and didn't want to take any chances.

Isabel kept to herself except for work, though she expanded her customers to Charleston, who would hire her on weekends for weddings. Weddings were becoming bigger events in the inner cities, and Isabel was more than happy to reap the financial benefits of her services.

Despite earning a decent living, the money from Liam continued to arrive as it had for over a decade. Isabel was even able to save a little each month, still hoping to eventually open her restaurant in the town center. She hadn't given up on her dream, but her priorities had shifted. Being a mother often does that; being a single mother forces it.

As Isabel was headed for her car one night after hours, she felt the presence of another person. The crime rate had increased, and Isabel was aware of her surroundings. She nervously fumbled with her keys before Liam came out of the shadows.

"Isabel," he said breathlessly.

"Liam. What are you doing here?"

Liam had grown older now. He was thinner than Isabel remembered, and his face looked worn from worry.

"I know. I have a lot to explain."

Isabel stood stiffly as Liam approached her slowly.

"What do you want?" asked Isabel.

"I want to apologize for how I treated you all those years ago. I was under a lot of pressure. I was an absolute mess, and I'm ashamed of myself." He looked down at his shoes and kicked a rock. "Drinking too much and acting a fool. Johnny had caused me more trouble than I'd ever let on, and I feared that in time, all of his sins would become mine."

Isabel considered this but remained silent, allowing Liam to continue.

"I know that girl is mine. She has my eyes and smile. I want to be part of her life. For as long as I can," he added.

"What is that supposed to mean?" Isabel said with annoyance. How dare this man show up now, on a whim, when the girl had been brought up singlehandedly and was doing well!

"Doctors say if I don't watch my drinking, I could be a dead man quite soon. I've been trying to cut back, but we both know how I feel about someone telling me what to do."

He shook his head.

Before he could continue, Isabel interrupted.

"Cara is not your child," she spat. "I met a man around the same time I worked for you. His name was Carl, and he died in a horrible car accident."

Isabel's voice was shaking, but she forced herself to speak confidently.

"Is that why you have been sending me money each month? You thought this child was yours?" Isabel scoffed for theatrics and feigned that she had never considered this before now.

After all, if Liam thought she had accepted the money from him all along while knowing he sent it only because he assumed the child was his own ...

Then, things could turn ugly in a heartbeat.

She took a step back, securing her safety before saying, "All this time, I thought you'd gained a conscience and were trying to repay me the money you'd stolen from the box in my closet."

Liam looked at her, puzzled.

"I don't know what you are talking about, but I do know that child is mine," insisted Liam.

"Liar," Isabel scoffed.

Liam observed her pointedly, waiting for her to crack.

"Listen, I am coming now for her because Mary's dementia has advanced, and she has now been put in a home. The poor thing no longer even knows who she is."

A wave of sadness came across his face if such an emotion were possible for one so hardnosed. "As I mentioned, I have my own health troubles," he said, putting his hands in his pockets. Isabel didn't feel empathy for him; she felt more fear, though she could not show Liam her emotions. Instead, she became outraged, even a bit unhinged. It was also quite possible he was only showing up now because he was hoping to claim their daughter as his live-in help.

Isabel was fuming, and her voice became louder. "You listen to me now, Mr. Kaats. I have already told you that the child's daddy died long ago, and I ain't looking for a replacement. Do you really think one drunk-infused night would produce a child? You are a dang fool, Liam Kaats; look at you spending all these years pining for a child who isn't even yours."

Isabel shook her head for effect before saying, "Now get on and leave us be."

Her voice was steady and agitated, knowing this would be her only chance to stand her ground. If Liam even suspected she was lying, she knew firsthand he would take his daughter in the middle of the night. Isabel couldn't take that chance and forcibly swatted Liam away.

"Now, if you'll excuse me, I need to get home to *my* daughter."

She started the engine.

Once Liam was out of sight, Isabel let out a scream, feeling the shake of her hands and the beat of her heart. "I have to get out of here before he learns the truth. He will take her away from me, and then who knows what will happen?"

She replayed all the scenarios, trying to figure out the best route.

By the time she was pulling up the gravel driveway, she knew she would again abandon the home she loved. It pained her to give up everything she had worked for in her career.

Cara would also hold this against her, never understanding the sudden move away from everything she had known. There was nothing else she could do, however.

And she needed to leave quickly.

As soon as she walked into the house, she reached for the phone and began to make calls. There was no time to waste.

The following morning, Isabel awoke to her head spinning as she frantically packed the house. She left most of their belongings behind and only took what they could fit in their four-door sedan. Though they had been living a modest life, their home was quaint and welcoming.

Tall ceilings welcomed guests into a large foyer with house plants and herbs from their garden in the kitchen. The wood floor creaked when you walked through the hallways to enter the living room, but floor-to-ceiling windows occupied the room once there, offering blinding sunlight. Between the smell of Southern cuisine and the house's openness, she loved her home.

In the evenings, she would sit on their wrap-around porch, drinking sweet tea and savoring biscuits as they listened to the crickets chirping in their own language.

"Mom, what's going on?" demanded Cara. "Why all this packing?"

"Honey, listen, I know you will not understand this, but we must leave today."

"Leave to where?" questioned Cara.

Cara was puzzled as to why they were leaving their beautiful home and the town she loved so much, and Isabel gave only the vaguest explanation about a job opportunity.

"But why do we have to leave? You have a fantastic job here. There's a waitlist for your cooking services, and you worked hard to reach this point."

Cara's tone was snarky and on the verge of disrespectful.

Isabel let it slide but was losing patience with her teenage daughter. She didn't answer her daughters' questions, grabbing anything worthwhile and shoving it into the large green suitcase.

"Mom, what's happening? Why do we have to leave? This is our home. You're so selfish!"

Isabel slammed the cabinet door and forcefully stuffed her favorite mug into a box.

"This is not our home anymore," Isabel snapped. "And I am not selfish. You'll see someday."

She softened when she saw the confusion and fury in Cara's eyes.

"Honey, look, it's time for a fresh start: you and me, SugarBear. There are many more opportunities up North, and the summers won't be so dreadfully hot. This is a good opportunity for me."

Cara looked at her mother, hoping for more information.

"C'mon. Let's give it a try. It will be a new adventure for both of us."

"No, Mom. I don't want to go."

"I wish we had another choice, but we don't," said Isabel, turning away so Cara couldn't see her tears.

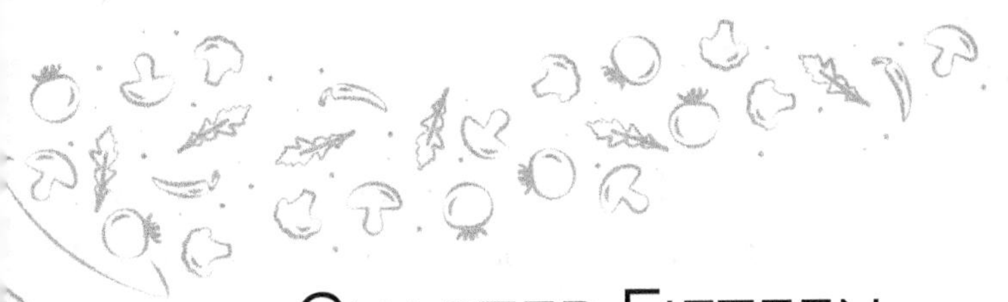

Chapter Fifteen

When the car was packed with as much as they could fit, Isabel looked around. There was still furniture and items shrewd about, but she knew the people of the town would take the rest of her belongings to give to people in need. She couldn't show Cara that she, too, was grieving, but she was left with no other choice. Her life was on the line, and Cara would never forgive her if she found out the truth at this stage of her young life. The only way to avoid it was to leave quickly.

She grabbed her handbag off the little bench below a shelf.

A picture frame caught her eye, one that she had forgotten to pack in her haste.

It was one of the homemade spaghetti picture frames that Cara had made one year at summer camp. She saw that some pieces of the spaghetti were missing and cracked as she reached for it.

Smiling back was a photo of Cara baking in their kitchen.

The same yellow bowl had been carefully packed away just hours ago on the table.

In the image, Cara cheerfully smiled at the camera, never knowing what had passed or what would still come to them in the form of life's unavoidable turmoil.

Isabel's cheeks became wet as she held the frame close to her chest, glancing around the house for one last time. Cara interrupted her as she stomped back with arms crossed, pouting, demanding once more why they even needed to move from this beautiful place called home.

"This is so unfair," she stammered.

"I know, sweetie," Isabel said in a cracked voice. "But we got to go. Get in the car."

Cara's eyes showed desperation as she glanced at the photo Isabel held tightly in her hands.

"We have so many happy memories here. I love South Carolina. It's our home."

Isabel herself was close to tears as she took a breath, wrapping her arms around her daughter for a quick squeeze, and said, "C'mon, SugarBear, let's go bake the next batch of memories."

It rained the entire journey as they drove for the last time through the winding roads.

Cara stared out the window, taking in every large tree as each creek they passed became smaller. She loved the South Carolina landscape, and the thought of leaving it behind was devastating. Cara cried bitter tears throughout the car ride, and though her mother never mentioned it, she, too, was distraught over the move.

At that time, a woman owning her own small business was unheard of, so this only caused Cara more anger toward her mother for throwing it away and leaving a place where they were both cherished. She sat with her arms crossed and her head leaning against the window, watching other cars pass by, silently raging at her mother. After two hours, Isabel finally broke the silence.

"Don't you want to know where we're going?"

"Not really. If it isn't our house, I don't care," Cara said glumly.

'Well, I'm going to tell you anyway. It is our house, but a different one. That's life, SugarBear. Times change, and we can change things for the better, even if you don't think so right now. Anyway, we are going to Maryland, a small town outside of Baltimore. There are tons to do in North Baltimore, and I hoped we could catch a baseball game. The Orioles are playing the New York team, and I was hoping to get tickets for us. Memorial Stadium is supposed to be a great place to watch a game."

Cara shrugged. She didn't share Isabel's love for baseball, but at least Isabel tried anything to entice her daughter to try something new. "Oh, and we won't be too far from Washington, D.C. We could see the White House!" Isabel said.

Cara had always enjoyed history in school, and Isabel hoped that learning that they were only a short drive from the nation's capital would excite her.

Still, nothing interested her, especially not thoughts of moving away.

"Also, they have hiking trails we can explore. One of the biggest tourist attractions is Fells Point. There are also many historic sites we can visit in Federal Hill and Fort McHenry. It's where the Star-Spangled Banner was written," said Isabel, hopeful for any positive reaction.

Isabel was becoming increasingly desperate to elicit some reaction from Cara. Instead, Cara kept her gaze fixed outside the window, listening but not responding to her mother's suggestions.

Isabel tried again. "And Baltimore ... It's known for its blue crabs, like Mount Pleasant is known for its sweet-tasting shrimp."

"I'm going to miss that," Cara said as she turned her body toward the window, shutting her eyes for the rest of the trip, deliberate in shutting her mother out.

The long drive provided Isabel time to reflect. She had warmed up to the idea of moving and suddenly felt excited about starting anew. Although Isabel loved South Carolina, people up North were different; however, so was Isabel. She welcomed the change, especially after the last few weeks filled with her constant fear that Liam would return and destroy her life.

She was feeling the confines of overly powerful men of the South and didn't want to be trapped. However, she would have difficulty convincing her daughter to have the same belief.

She made a conscious decision that, while she would sympathize with Cara and the abruptness of this move, she wouldn't allow either of them to drown in it.

Hours later, when they pulled up to their quaint house in Fulton, Maryland, Isabel was relieved to find that it had a front porch. She called one of her produce vendors to tell him about their sudden move, and he suggested she contact his cousin Ronny, who was renting out a small cottage.

The homes surrounding her were more prominent in size and rather grand, but Isabel loved the charming feel of the smaller quarters.

They felt more like what she was used to in South Carolina. There wasn't much land, but the streets were lined with trees, and the neighbors kept their homes tidy. There were vibrant baskets of potted flowers on almost every porch and many lawn decorations with the word "Welcome."

Isabel smiled at a woman who passed by as she strolled her baby in a carriage. She had hoped there were kids Cara's age to help make the adjustment more manageable.

Not that seeing a baby meant there would be kids of Cara's age group, but still, it was a good sign.

"We're here," Isabel said cheerfully.

Cara yawned, opening her eyes for a moment. She looked around briefly and turned away from her mother, who was standing with a hopeful smile.

A moment later, she reluctantly rubbed the sleep from her eyes and looked around. She didn't appear impressed with the area but didn't scowl either. Isabel took that as a win.

The home was comfortable and inviting. The walls were painted soft ivory, making the space seem more expansive, and the big floorboards throughout the house were a deep walnut color. They emptied their belongings from the car as Cara remained silent.

Thankfully, the home came fully furnished, so Isabel didn't need to do much decorating. She placed the spaghetti-framed picture on the living room coffee table.

Cara rolled her eyes as she walked past it to what was her bedroom, slamming the door shut.

Isabel huffed, "When will this end?" and unpacked the last boxes.

Luckily, she had a job lined up and would start in three days, giving them space.

Until now, she and Cara had enjoyed a close relationship, but after discovering the sudden move, Cara became unbearable to be around. Isabel had enough to worry about aside from her daughter's reluctance and teenage angst. Cara still had no clue what was at stake, and Isabel had no intention of ever telling her the truth about her father. She had more things to consider, such as how she would manage her new role working for a hotel chain.

She wasn't used to working for a corporate hotel chain and worried if she was qualified.

With no professional culinary training behind her and having learned many techniques through trial and error, she was only given a chance because she could pull some strings through connections she had made and the miraculous opportunity that had appeared to come out of nowhere.

Chapter Sixteen

Isabel became concerned and impatient with her daughter, recognizing that her decision to leave had likely saved her life. She continuously reminded herself that Cara was unaware of the circumstances.

Isabel had to be patient and hope that she would eventually come around.

Of course, it was natural that the move was far more difficult for her soon-approaching teenage daughter. Cara was the new girl, and by the time the school year began, almost everyone was in a clique already, leaving Cara to spend much time alone.

It was a lonely time, and she often felt outraged that her mother couldn't just leave well enough alone in South Carolina. To Cara, it always seemed her mother was never satisfied.

"Didn't you work for a prominent family in town?" Cara grumbled. "Can't we move back, and you can return to working for them?"

Isabel froze at the mention of their name. She ignored the questioning, but Cara continued the badgering. "I know you did well working as a caterer, too. Why can't you do that? Why did we move here? You don't even have a job you're qualified for here!"

Cara was incredulous and wouldn't let up.

It was true that Isabel had abandoned South Carolina when her business had been really taking off. She had been building a clientele when they'd abruptly moved.

Most of the clients she received were because she provided the parishioners at church with samples of her latest creations. When people tasted her cooking, they were so impressed that she got requests for baby showers, special birthdays, graduations, and weddings.

"It was time for a new adventure, that's all," Isabel reasoned.

Cara was puzzled by her mother's sudden departure from their small hometown to live in a city. "You always want the next best thing. You're always looking for more," she snarled.

Isabel felt rage run through her veins, but she stood up, glaring at her daughter before walking out and slamming the door. Isabel's sobs could be heard from where Cara stood.

Her mother had never shown much emotion, and hearing her cry behind closed doors caused Cara to reflect on her behavior.

From that point on, Cara rarely mentioned South Carolina in front of Isabel, even though she still longed to return.

It had been nearly six months since they'd settled in Maryland. Cara walked into the kitchen for juice, still raging from the move, when she saw her mother carefully whisking egg whites.

"Mom, the bowl?" She said excitedly. "You brought it with us!"

"Of course I did, SugarBear. Did you think I could ever leave this behind? This here is one of my most prized possessions."

Isabel gently kissed the top of her daughter's head as she watched her examine the bowl.

She touched it, saying, "I hope you take this bowl and make your own recipes someday."

Isabel watched as she noticed Cara's shoulders relax, her heart softening.

It must have shown that Isabel hadn't forgotten their past. The mixing bowl had so many memories; they were just as important to her as they were to Cara.

This moment was the beginning of their mutual healing and forgiving. As time passed, they became more comfortable in her new surroundings, even trying new recipes together.

Isabel would mix ingredients in the large yellow bowl, experimenting with different flavors and textures and ultimately throwing the concoction away and starting again.

She needed it to be perfect to impress the many businessmen who came through Baltimore Harbor. Cara contributed by helping her mother wash bowls, measure flour, and tenderize meat.

It gave her something to do, and her mother enjoyed the company.

Cooking together grew into their connection and something they both cherished.

PART II

Focaccia Bread

Ingredients

- 4 cups all-purpose flour
- 2 teaspoons kosher salt
- 1 packet instant yeast
- 2 cups warm water
- 4 tablespoons olive oil divided
- Italian seasoning
- Sea salt

Directions

Prepare the dough

In medium bowl combine flour, salt, and yeast. Stir well. Add warm water. Mix well until the flour is incorporated. Cover bowl with plastic wrap and put in the fridge for at least 8 hours up to 24 hours.

Lightly grease 2 – 9" cake pans. Line with parchment paper. Pour 1 tablespoon of olive oil into each pan. Divide dough in half, place one ball in each pan, turning to coat with oil. Tuck edges of dough underneath to form a rough ball. Cover each pan tightly with plastic wrap and allow dough to rest for 2 hours. The dough should cover most of the pan.

Preheat oven to 450 with rack in the middle of oven.

Drizzle another tablespoon of olive oil over each pan of dough. With oiled fingers using both hands, press straight down creating dimples like deep holes through the dough. Stretch the dough through this process to fill the pan.

Sprinkle both with Italian seasoning and salt.

Reduce heat in the oven to 425. Bake 23–27 minutes until golden brown. Remove from oven to baking rack.

Recipe provided by Judy Smith,
Summers Corner, Summerville, S. C.

CHAPTER SEVENTEEN

It took Cara a long while to adjust to the busier streets and the more bustling city. She missed her friends and how people knew her by name. Here, people passed by without even a proper hello.

Her school was much larger than in South Carolina, too, and the kids were often unkind.

Because of all this mess and upheaval, it took weeks for Cara to fully start warming up to her mother again. Until then, she would only answer questions with yes and no answers and speak only when spoken to. After all, what was there to say about any of it?

A cooler climate replaced the intense heat of the southern summer, and Cara longed for the soft sounds of nature and open land. She grew impatient with Isabel's presence, never feeling at home in her new surroundings; sure, she admired her mom's tenacity but wondered why she hadn't considered her feelings about the move. It had all seemed rushed and unnecessary, and Cara resented her mother for hastily leaving. It appeared that they'd had it all in Grover Creek.

The sudden move had made the girl uneasy and left her feeling insecure.

Their life in Maryland had also become quieter than in South Carolina.

Cara enjoyed her mother's local notoriety and felt proud of her accolades. She had pushed societal boundaries, and their life in their tiny town had always been exciting.

Now, she was just another person without a history or connection to the people around her.

Since there weren't family or friends around this place, things were different.

They only knew Ted, a man to whom her mother had introduced her during the early months of their arrival. He had a son around her age named Nathan, who visited only during summer vacations. Nathan lived with his mother in Florida for most of the year but was always excited when he returned to Maryland to spend time with his father.

It seemed peculiar how quickly Ted and Isabel's friendship blossomed and how they seemed to have a mysterious connection. When she inquired about their relationship, her mother told her they had met at a specialty grocery store up the street from their apartment that Ted owned.

They had become fast friends over a cup of coffee and their passion for baking. Still, the connection between the two always struck Cara as odd.

Ted was always kind and friendly to Cara and took a particular interest in her life. However, she would often find him staring at her, which made her uncomfortable.

When he noticed her discomfort, he quickly apologized.

"I'm so embarrassed. I didn't mean to stare at you. It's just that you remind me so much of someone I used to know." When Cara pressed for more information, Ted only offered, "It was a long time ago. Childhood seems like another lifetime."

Before she could ask again, Ted changed the subject and excused himself soon after.

Ted also didn't have much family around, so over time, the three of them became a family of sorts. Cara wondered if Isabel had romantic feelings toward Ted since she often heard them whispering beyond earshot. One afternoon, when they were alone, Cara confronted her mom.

"Mom, it's okay if you want to date Ted."

Cara could tell Isabel was startled by her comment but kept her eyes focused on the batter she was mixing.

"Me and Ted? Oh, Cara, no, we are just friends."

Distracted, Isabel mindlessly added too much salt to the batter.

"Dang it. I'll have to start over," said Isabel as she poured the batter into the trash. Her hands shook slightly at the discussion, though she mustered the calmest face possible.

"Mom, really. It might be nice for you to have a companion," Cara pressed.

"I don't have time for that right now. Honestly, Ted and I are good friends who enjoy spending time together. Ted misses his son tremendously, so we kind of take his place until summer break when he gets to spend time with Nathan. He is just a bit younger than you, but when he comes up next time for a visit, it would be nice to show him around."

Cara knew her mother meant it would be nice for Cara to act as a hostess …

Cara watched her mother as she baked.

"Okay, I suppose. No, that sounds great. Ted is a blessing, and I would love to get to know Nathan." Cara scooped a heaping batter pile and shoved it into her mouth as her mother swatted the spoon away playfully.

"That's enough, Cara; you are going to get a belly ache," she said.

Cara laughed as she reached for one more bite. "By the way, you never mentioned how you met Ted. He kind of came out of nowhere."

Isabel's eyes widened, and she spilled the measured flour on the floor.

"What's wrong with me today? I need to focus on the recipe, or I'll never get the crust right." Isabel felt her voice rise but quickly regained her composure before laughing.

Cara waited for a response as Isabel wiped the counter.

"I told you, Cara. We met at his shop. What more can I say? Are you trying to catch me out? Ted and I are just two lonely people—friends—who find comfort in each other."

It was clear Isabel was distracted and didn't want to talk further about Ted. Cara noticed her mother's discomfort and tried to soften her questions. "It seems like Ted is lonely and attached to us. I like him, Mom, and if you do too, don't let me stop you from pursuing a relationship."

"I'll keep that in mind," Isabel said, laughing. "For now, I'm happy with being friends."

Nathan began visiting more often than just on summer vacation. He was tall and slender with a quick wit and infectious smile. He had a strong resemblance to Ted, and it was uncanny.

When Nathan was old enough to make his own decisions, he chose to live with Ted and help out at the store. He complained it was too hot in Florida and needed a change.

"Pops, the summer heat in Florida is too much for me. Anyway, I miss you."

Ted's eyes narrowed. "How is your mother handling your decision?"

Nathan considered the question. "You know Mom. She's sad and still angry as hell at you for leaving. But she knows I need a father, and right now, she's working a lot of hours, so I think she's relieved to be focusing on her career."

It was clear that Ted already felt guilty about his part in their marriage's failure and didn't want to cause any more pain. Nathan could see the worry in Ted's eyes, quickly adding, "Don't worry, Pops. I'm going to visit Mom on holidays. We will make it work."

Ted took a deep breath. "As long as your mother's fine, I'd be thrilled to have you. I just don't need another woman angry at me," he joked.

Despite his complicated relationship with Nathan's mother, Sara, Ted was ecstatic about the news. "Son, that would be great. I would love to have you here."

When Ted told Isabel and Cara the news, they were just as excited.

"Now I don't always have to be the third wheel," joked Cara.

By the end of the summer, Nathan was fully immersed in his new life and helped his father expand his store to give it a more modern feel. Nathan, who had recently graduated from Florida State University with a business degree and a minor in entrepreneurship, knew that the business his father had started years ago could expand into a much bigger operation.

Ted was wary of the change, but Nathan assured him he would take full responsibility.

They now sold a wider variety of specialty coffees and expanded from chocolates to an entire bakery and deli. The once small convenience store had developed into a place where people would gather for lunch and coffee.

An acoustic guitarist would often play in the evenings, bringing in more customers. Business was doing better than ever, and with Nathan's help, the profit margin increased substantially.

On many occasions, Nathan and Ted tried to convince Cara and Isabel to go into business with them, but they refused. "We are going to do this ourselves," stated Isabel.

Although unsure, Cara tried convincing her mother to consider the offer, saying, "Mom, Ted really means it. This could be our opportunity to start something. Or maybe we can take a loan from Ted and promise to pay him back as soon as we start making a profit."

The thought of this made Isabel nervous.

"There is just too much at stake, Cara. I can't risk having our identity attached ..." Isabel stopped speaking, realizing she had already revealed too much.

"Mom, what do you mean? Why would it matter if people knew us?"

Isabel took a long breath, quickly changing the subject. "Cara, listen to me. I have been in business with people like Ted. They're great friends and loyal allies, but to mix business and pleasure is just not something I want to consider. Trust me, I have been fooled before, and one thing about a good Southern woman is that she never makes the same mistake twice."

Cara was irritated by her mother's stubbornness, but she couldn't help but notice. "So, you still consider yourself a Southern woman—just as I thought, Mom," she said with a smirk.

Over the years, the offer continued to come up, and Isabel repeatedly rejected Ted's proposal. She insisted, "It wouldn't be right, and I don't need any handouts from a man."

She could be stubborn, and while Ted told her the offer was always on the table, he knew Isabel would never take him up on it.

Cara sensed her mother was hiding something about her relationship with Ted but decided not to pry. Like a good Southern daughter, she had been taught to mind her business and didn't press her mother on the issue.

In many ways, Isabel was a mystery to Cara.

There were things that didn't make sense. Cara couldn't quite figure out her mother. On a hot summer day, while folding laundry together, Cara made one last attempt to ask about her father.

"Mama, is he alive? Did you love him? Where did you two meet?"

"Who?" Isabel asked, perplexed.

"My father," said Cara. "Look, I'm not a child anymore. You don't need to protect me. For goodness' sake, I just graduated from college. I'm an adult!" pleaded Cara.

Isabel put down the half-folded shirt, meeting Cara's eyes.

"Mama, I deserve to know who my daddy is. Why is it so hard for you to tell me?"

"Why is this so important, Cara?" Isabel asked impatiently.

She felt a reluctant rattle in her voice, her eyes pleading for the questions to stop.

Cara felt her voice soften, sensing her mother's grief. "Mama, did he break your heart? Leave you? Maybe if he got to know me, he would want a relationship."

Isabel's sorrow quickly turned to impatience.

"Enough, Cara. We have been through this. Carl died a long time ago."

"What about his family? Do I have cousins or grandparents? Mom, I just want to know where I come from. I love and appreciate all you have done for me, but I want to know."

Isabel's heart softened. She understood her daughter's curiosity but didn't want her to carry the burden of knowing the truth.

Isabel pinched her lips tightly. "The truth is, I don't know much more than you. It was a long time ago. I was young, immature, and irresponsible." Isabel inched closer to her daughter. "I'm sorry I can't be of more help. It's also not something I'm not proud of."

Isabel met Cara's eyes. "But I am proud of you, so grateful to have had you, and the rest, well, it's in the past. And there it should lie."

Cara let the silence between them linger. "I know, Mom. I'm sorry. I love you, and I'm glad we have each other." She wanted to push for more information out of sheer curiosity, but seeing the hurt in her mother's eyes was too painful to continue the inquisition.

Isabel embraced her, holding her tightly. She hated it when Cara mentioned the past, asking questions and wanting to know more.

Cara knew in her gut there was more to the story, but each time she inquired, Isabel shut her down until, finally, she stopped asking altogether.

***

Still curious, Cara asked Nathan if his father had ever mentioned anything about her mother's past. Nathan was as clueless as she was.

"They are definitely hiding something," she said as she took a long swig from her beer.

Nathan responded, "Many years ago, I overheard my parents arguing. It was the biggest fight I ever witnessed between them. My mother was crying, saying that everything had been a lie. I never asked about it, but things between them were never the same after that day. I think whatever secret my father had was part of why my parents divorced."

Nathan fiddled with a napkin and tapped his fingers on the bar.

"What about your father? Do you keep in touch with him?"

Cara pulled her head back, letting out a laugh.

"No! According to my mother, my father died many years ago. I'm not sure I believe it, but whoever he was or is, she doesn't want either of us to have anything to do with him."

"Are you okay with that?" asked Nathan.

"Honestly, when I was younger, I wasn't," admitted Cara. "It bothered me not knowing who he was. I would wonder what he looked like or if he was a stranger on the street. After a while, I came to accept it, and with my mom always working to give me a stable life, I felt it was unfair to keep pursuing it. It just didn't feel right to go against her wishes."

Cara was quiet momentarily as she watched Nathan's eyes meet hers.

"Being raised in the South, there was a certain respect you gave your elders, so I did," she said.

She nodded, surrendering.

Then she offered, "One day, though, I will find out the truth, but probably not while my mama is still living. Whatever she's hiding, she's determined to go to the grave with it."

They clinked their drinks and motioned the bartender to bring over another round.

Their parents' secrets were theirs to keep, and for now, Nathan and Cara were content not to know more about them.

———

As Ted aged, Nathan assumed more responsibilities in managing the store, ranging from stocking inventory to offering catering options. As both young adults embarked on their careers, Cara and Nathan developed a strong friendship and considered each other like siblings.

Since both were still young, it was the closest thing she had to a brother.

She and Nathan would go to bars, try new restaurants, join a bowling league, and mingle with mutual friends. Their friendship was far more than just that of family friends, however, as they genuinely enjoyed one another. They had an unexplainable connection based on trust and knowing they would always be there for each other, no matter what.

As best friends would, Nathan knew his friend David would be the perfect match for Cara.

It was Nathan who introduced her to David one evening at an upscale restaurant.

They were celebrating Ted's retirement, and Nathan had invited David as a guest. He was tall with big brown eyes, wavy dirty blonde hair, and a dimple on the left side of his cheek.

Cara couldn't keep her eyes off him from the moment he approached the table.

"Hey there, everyone." David's teeth shined as his smile illuminated the room. "Nathan, thanks for inviting me." Nathan got up to shake his old buddy's hand, giving him a half-hug before saying, "David lived in Florida and was transferred to Baltimore last month. I thought I would show him around and introduce him to some of my friends."

David looked around the table and greeted each person with a handshake and smile.

When his eyes locked with Cara's, she could see no one else around. It felt as if time stood still, with both of them hesitant to break their gaze. After an awkward yet magical moment, David resumed his pleasantries with the other guests but soon made his way to a seat beside Cara.

The two talked for the entire evening, sharing stories of their past and laughing.

By the night's end, both knew there would never be another night without the other.

The following day, Cara raced to the shop for coffee and to talk to Nathan.

She was deciding on a breakfast item when Nathan came up from behind. "I guess you hit it off with my friend," said Nathan.

"Nathan, why didn't you introduce us sooner? He's amazing."

She was gushing about him, the words rushing from her mouth as if they had a will of their own.

"Slow down there," Nathan said jokingly. "Wow, you two must really have made some connection because first thing this morning, David called to say the exact same thing."

"Really? He called you this morning?" Cara had never felt like this before. "We have plans later this evening. He's the nicest guy I've ever met."

"Umm, excuse me?" Nathan joked.

"Okay, fine, the second nicest! But really, Nathan, thanks for introducing us. I owe you one."

Cara left the bakery section with a latte, a croissant, and the most enormous grin.

It wasn't long until the two became engaged.

David was just as smitten with Cara as she was with him. They enjoyed hiking, trying new restaurants, and going to local farmers' markets. Nathan, of course, took full credit for the romance and insisted they be forever in debt to him.

"Of course, Nathan, we thank you endlessly," David said at the engagement party.

By the following summer, David and Cara were married in an intimate ceremony at St. Paul's Church. She was dressed in a handmade white lace gown that her mother had made and carried a small bouquet of daisies. Nathan acted, of course, as both the best man and maid of honor.

As Isabel watched with pride, Ted proudly walked the blushing bride down the aisle.

Her greatest accomplishment had been raising Cara alone, especially after everything she had done to keep her true identity a secret.

After the ceremony, David and Cara set off to France, where they spent six weeks exploring.

Weeks earlier, one of Cara's former culinary professors had arranged for her to meet with an associate to train alongside her.

It was an amazing opportunity, and Cara was excited about the prospect.

The meeting at La Francine could potentially change their lives, and though nervous, Cara felt confident she had a shot to impress the well-renowned chefs. If that were to happen, Cara would have more opportunities when she returned to the States to open her own café.

Cara spent many evenings dreaming with Isabel about opening such a place. They planned the menu, decor, and even what silverware would be best. This was the chance of a lifetime.

She knew it was a long shot for the head chef and owner, Bastien Romilly, to take on an American to train. He was impressed by Cara's skill and determination and had shown interest in her when they'd met at a conference she had attended six months prior.

If chosen, Isabel would live in Paris by spring and be trained by one of the world's top French chefs. While the idea of this massive step was overwhelming, Isabel had taught her to take risks.

Without her mother's guidance, she might not have had the nerve to pursue the opportunity.

"I couldn't have done this without you, Mom."

Cara's eyes were wide with both excitement and fear.

"You go and show that fancy French chef what you are made of. And don't give a damn what he thinks," Isabel said proudly.

"I really hope he likes me. This is a once-in-a-lifetime opportunity. He only grants one American chef this opportunity, and I want it to be me!"

"One thing I've learned through the years is not to get your hopes wrapped up in one dream. Go out and catch a bunch of them. Who knows what is next for you, Cara, but keep your eyes on all opportunities."

Cara hugged Isabel, grateful for her wisdom.

She knew how to calm her nerves and encourage her dreams.

"I don't know what I'd do without you, Mom," she said.

"You would do exactly what I've taught you. Be bold, unapologetic, and show that Frenchman who is boss," Isabel said as she raised her fists in the air.

CHAPTER EIGHTEEN

CARA AND DAVID ARRIVED in Paris on a Tuesday night. During the first three weeks of their visit, they explored the city and studied French culture. Cara wanted to be prepared for her meeting with Bastien, but she was already intimidated by the prospect. She kept thinking of her mother's tenacity, knowing she, too, had it in her.

When the day arrived, she stumbled as she got dressed.

"Relax, love. You got this," said David. He smiled at her before kissing her forehead.

He always knew what to say to Cara when her nerves got the best of her.

"I can't get this darn pearl necklace to latch."

Her voice was strained as she tried the clasp again.

"Darling, let me help you. This thing always gives you a problem."

"Please be careful. My mother gave this to me years ago at my college graduation. She must have saved up for ages to afford it." Cara caressed the pearls as David secured them around her neck. "What do I do if he picks me, David?"

It was the first time she had considered possibly moving to Paris for six months.

"Let's first get you there. Let Bastien be as impressed with you as I am, and then we will worry about the details."

David knew how to keep Cara calm. He had a soothing voice and the right amount of empathy and focus to keep her from becoming unhinged. Unlike her mother, Cara had a natural nervousness about her that would often leave her riddled with anxiety. Cara paced the floor as she reviewed her notes, stopping every couple of lines to make even more jottings.

"Relax, Cara. You are going to do great," said David.

Cara stretched her arms out to receive a hug, inhaling his scent and embracing his warmth. "I know. It's just that I feel like I owe this to my mother. She sacrificed so much for me and never really fulfilled her own dreams. I feel like it's my time to do it for the both of us."

Cara spoke slowly as she reconciled her thoughts with her words.

"It sounds crazy, but I have always suspected that there are things I don't know about my mother." Cara hesitated, lost in her thoughts. "I may never know."

David looked at the clock, tapping his watch and signaling Cara it was time to go.

"Good luck," he called out as he watched his wife race down the stairs into a cab.

Three weeks later, Cara found a letter in the mailbox inviting her to study abroad for the next six months. She screamed in delight as she dialed her mother's number.

"Mama, Mama, I did it! I got the job in Paris."

Cara was talking fast as she read the letter to her mother.

"I knew you would, SugarBear," she said. "When does it start?"

"I have some time to brush up on my skills. It doesn't start until late fall, so there will be plenty of time to prepare." Cara paced the floor, excited when a wave of nausea attacked.

"Not this again," she thought.

Lately, she'd been having bouts of queasiness that would subside by late afternoon.

"Mama, listen. I've got to go. I have to tell David the great news. I wanted you to be the first to know! I love you, Mama. Thank you for everything,"

Cara hung up and nibbled on dry toast as she called David to tell him the happy news.

"That is fantastic, Cara. While I will miss you, I couldn't be prouder of you."

"Promise you'll visit, David." Cara had a weariness in her voice.

"Listen to me, Caralyn Loring. It's just six months, and then you'll come back, and we'll work on a plan to get you your café."

Cara smiled, grateful for her husband's staunch support.

"Who knows," he continued. "Maybe one day, that fancy French chef will come and work at your café!"

Cara giggled as she hung up the phone. She went into her bedroom and lay down while she reread the letter. "This is really happening," she said, hopeful as she fell asleep.

Three hours later, she awoke to the sound of David entering the apartment, startled by the time.

"Oh, my goddess, David. I must have dozed off!" she said, wiping the sleep from her eyes.

"It was an emotional day. Your adrenaline must have been on overdrive before you crashed."

"I suppose so," said Cara in agreement.

"What do you want to do for dinner?" asked David. "How about we go out to celebrate?"

"I don't know, David." She sounded so subdued and looked pallid and clammy. "My belly is a bit upset. I wonder if I ate something bad," said Cara as she splashed chilly water on her face.

"Then we'll celebrate another time," David offered. "I'll make some pasta, and you can relax on the couch."

David prepared the meal and walked into the living room with two wine glasses and a bowl of pasta. By the time he reached the couch, he noticed that Cara was breathing heavily in slumber. He placed the glasses and bowl on the coffee table and felt her head. She didn't have a fever, but he worried she might be coming down with something. He covered his wife with a blanket and quietly went into the kitchen to pack up the dinner to save it for the following day.

As the days passed, Cara still wasn't feeling herself.

In fact, she was more fatigued than she had ever remembered.

Finally, by the second week, David insisted she see a doctor.

When they arrived, it wasn't long for the doctor to figure it all out: just like her mother had been so long ago, Cara had gotten unexpectedly pregnant.

The doctor walked into the examination room with a wide grin and announced, "Congratulations, soon-to-be parents!"

Looking at David and Cara, he noticed the shock and disappointment in their expressions. He lowered his voice. "I guess this is a surprise then, huh?"

They both nodded, and Cara held back tears. "I need a minute," she said as she stormed out of the office, David chasing behind her.

On the ride home, both of them were silent, unable to formulate any emotions. It would take hours to process the information before either of them would be ready to talk.

By nightfall, David lay beside Cara as she stared at the ceiling.

"It's a shock, isn't it? I don't know what to say," he said, taking Cara's hand.

"Me either," she said quietly. "What will happen with Paris? I can't possibly go now."

A single tear fell from her eye as David squeezed her hand in agreement. "Another lost dream," Cara said, rolling over before falling asleep.

The next day she sent a regret letter back to Paris declining the offer and begrudgingly mailed it off. Tears flowed privately, though Cara tried to find solace in the new life she was carrying.

With each passing day, Cara still didn't mention her trip to France.

"Honey are we even going to talk about this?" asked David.

Cara rubbed her belly and looked up with tears. "One thing my mama taught me is to be grateful and to adjust my plans, not give up on them," she said.

David was pleased that she hadn't given up entirely but worried she was not expressing her true feelings. At times, she could be stoic when feeling pain, but he gave her the space to process her emotions in her own time.

He vowed to continue supporting his wife as she came up with another plan.

After a week, David found Cara staring blankly out the window.

"Honey, I know you're disappointed. I'm unsure what to say." He caressed her back.

"Disappointed doesn't even begin to describe how I feel, David," she said. She held onto the counter, taking a breath before turning to see the hurt in his eyes. "But, as disappointed as I am about this opportunity, this is our baby, and I'm even more excited about our blessing."

A smile swept across his face. "Me too, baby," he said, embracing his wife.

As they prepared for their baby's birth, Isabel was ecstatic at the thought of becoming a grandmother. "I'm going to spoil the bean outta that little one," she proclaimed.

Unlike Cara's birth, Maggie Mae was born in a hospital surrounded by doctors and welcomed into the world with two eager parents patiently awaiting her arrival.

There were no secrets or worries that someone would come for her in the middle of the night. Isabel watched joyfully as her new granddaughter thrived, and her parents loved her dearly.

Isabel worked less as she was becoming more fatigued by the arduous work.

The long days that she once had been able to handle became too much. She would tire easily now, and her body just couldn't keep up with the demands of the kitchen.

Additionally, she wanted to spend as much time as possible with Maggie. Isabel spent most of the week at Cara's house, watching the baby while Cara developed a plan to obtain a loan and open her café. Cara worked at a small bakery in the center of town, but the owner, who was the head chef, maintained full control of the menu. Cara bided her time, observing and learning how the business operated, but she still longed to open her own little place.

As the years passed and Maggie got older, Isabel began teaching her how to bake just as she had with her own daughter. Those small hands stirred the batter, reminding Isabel of the time she had spent in the kitchen with Cara. Time passed by too quickly, but she was grateful to spend quality time enjoying her granddaughter in ways she had not been able to with Cara.

Having a granddaughter softened Isabel as she reflected on the past.

She'd considered telling Cara the truth about her father many times through the years but wondered if the consequence of telling her would be detrimental.

For the first time in her life, Isabel felt like a coward for not being honest, but she still felt the need to protect herself and Cara. "Some things are better left unsaid," she confided in Ted.

"Honey, listen, this is your decision, but at some point, Cara does have the right to know," said Ted. An awkward silence filled the room as Isabel fiddled with the fruit basket on the counter. "It was so long ago, Ted. Does it really matter?"

Ted edged closer, taking Isabel's hands.

"It matters to me," he ventured. "And I know it would matter to Cara as well. You don't want her to feel resentful if she finds out by herself someday. She needs to hear it all from her mom."

"I'll give it some thought," said Isabel as she grabbed her coat and raced out the door, late for another doctor's appointment.

Later that day, she practiced telling her daughter about their past. She decided that today would be the day she told her secret. It was time she divulged the truth to Cara. She was nervous with anticipation and hoped her daughter would understand and maybe even manage to forgive.

She had hoped her secret would never be told, but with age and wisdom, she now understood that some secrets needed telling.

About to leave for Cara's house, she was interrupted by a phone call from her doctor.

"Yes, this is she," said Isabel.

Isabel went white as all her breath escaped from her chest.

She heard her doctor on the line say, "Are you still there?"

"Yes, I am. I don't know what to say." Her voice trailed off.

As Isabel hung up the phone, she placed her head in her hands and began to sob.

She walked around her living room, dazed at the news that she had cancer.

She only went in for a routine exam. The words terminal breast cancer kept ringing in her ears. Did she have a fighting chance?

Any hope was shattered when the latest test results revealed inoperable conditions.

Any chance of Isabel telling her daughter the truth about her father was now off the table. It seemed unimportant in the light of the overwhelming news.

"This is too much information at once, and frankly, Cara has gone this long without knowing the truth," she reasoned.

Far from it being some kind of liberation, revealing the past could cause a rift between her and Cara; she didn't want to spend her days explaining past choices and asking for forgiveness.

She wanted to enjoy her days with her family and be at peace, knowing she had always done her best given her circumstances at the time. Isabel was waiting for the right time to tell her daughter the news, but really, there was no right time. She asked to see her daughter alone at her apartment, where they could work on a new recipe she had been practicing.

When Cara arrived, she was wearing a yellow dress with prints of daisies at the bottom, along with flats and oversized hoop earrings.

Her makeup was light, complementing her big eyes and bright pink lips.

"You look lovely today," said Isabel.

"Thanks, Mom. I have a meeting later this afternoon with the bank. Our dream is right around the corner for us."

Isabel turned toward the window to hide her expression.

Before she could continue, Cara interrupted, "Mom, you haven't mentioned opening a restaurant in a while. Why is that?"

Isabel remained quiet for a long while. She shrugged as she stared out the window at a lingering bird. "Life just didn't go as planned, I guess. Sometimes, we don't get to choose."

"Well, we're so close now. I'm almost certain the bank will approve my loan. I have my degree and have been saving money so that we can finally show the world our talents."

Cara spoke so hopefully.

Isabel caressed the mixing bowl that Cara was using to practice whisking egg whites for lemon meringue pie.

"I'm tired, Cara. Despite not reaching my goals, I've done a lot in my lifetime."

"Yeah, but there is so much more," Cara said. "Mom, one of the benefits of having me young is that you still have an entire life ahead of you. We have time. And now, together, we can finally make our dream come true." Cara watched as tears formed in Isabel's eyes.

"Come here. Sit down."

Cara followed her mother into the living room and sat on the floral couch. She felt anxiety creep in as her mother looked at her with a worried expression.

It was then that Cara noticed how thin her mother had gotten.

Her bones protruded from her neck.

Her arms, once muscular from heavy kitchen work, were frail. Her skin tone was no longer pink and plum but a gray shade. Cara felt her heart race as the clues of the past six months came crashing down on her. The long naps and small appetite no longer felt mundane but problematic.

"Mom? Are you sick?" blurted out Cara.

"I didn't know how to tell you."

Isabel took Cara's hands in hers and gently rubbed her fingers.

"I have breast cancer." The oxygen in the room evaporated as streams of tears found their way down both their faces. Cara's eyes closed, taking in the information and wishing it away, as she slumped further into the couch. After a brief moment, she composed her thoughts, looking at her mother, who was staring out the window.

"It's okay, Mom. We will get you help. There are doctors in Baltimore who—"

Isabel cut her off.

"Shhh, baby, no. It's too late. I want to spend the rest of my days baking with you."

Cara got up from the couch and began pacing, her voice weak but steady.

"Does Ted know?" asked Cara. It seemed like a fair question since he was part of their family. "Ted will never allow you to give up, and neither will I," Cara said, her voice getting louder.

"Yes," Isabel said quietly. "He's been a good and loyal friend. He has protected me for so long, and I'll always be grateful to him."

Cara felt her face flush with anger for not knowing sooner.

"So, what, now, Mom? Are you just giving up? Kind of seems like you are. I feel it."

Isabel saw the pain in her daughter's eyes and stared, allowing her to reconcile the reality.

Finally, when Isabel put her hand over her mouth, Cara said, "Mom, are you dying?"

The words caught in her throat.

"Aren't we all?" said Isabel. "The goal is to live while you can, my dear daughter."

Cara wasn't sure what to say and let silence consume the room. She hadn't prepared herself for this and had many emotions to sort through.

"It isn't all lost. I still have some treatments, and there's still a little hope to extend my lifespan."

"But not a cure?" asked Cara thoughtfully.

Isabel shook her head. "I should have gone to the doctor sooner.

Cara wiped her tears and said, "So now what, Mom?"

"So now, I want to live and spend time doing what I've always loved doing and with who I love most." Isabel smiled at Cara and embraced her tightly, never wanting to let go.

"Mama, no. I can't lose you," she sobbed into her blouse.

"Baby, you ain't ever going to lose me. I will live inside your heart," Isabel said, tapping her daughter's chest.

"We were all so happy. I just don't know what we'll do without you," Cara cried.

Isabel took two steps away from Cara and looked deep into her eyes. "SugarBear, I've taught you everything you need to know. When you miss me, bake something. When you're sad, try a new recipe. But what I never want you to do is give up. There are great things ahead for you."

The two embraced as tears freely flowed.

CHAPTER NINETEEN

Isabel was a fighter, and despite her illness, she carried on as if the cells in her body were not ravishing her insides. She had cancer treatments at Johns Hopkins, one of the best hospitals in the country. The doctors were confident they could keep the cancer at bay.

Cara put the restaurant's opening on hold, knowing full well that the venture would take up all of her time. She wanted this time with her mother. They baked practically every day, and although Isabel refused to live full-time with Cara, David, and Maggie, she spent most nights at their home, where they would cook dinner and talk over dessert.

It was a special time for the family that no one took for granted. They knew Isabel's time on Earth was limited now, and rather than waste it on being sad, they enjoyed the time she had left.

At night, Cara would confide in David how hard it was to watch her mother's health deteriorate. "The truth is, love, we are all on borrowed time. I know it's hard to watch someone you love slowly die, but it's most important to watch them live."

David had a way of putting things into perspective. He never feared death but accepted it as a part of life. One of David's best qualities was his belief in the power of now.

He didn't wait to see the positive; he lived each day as if it were his last.

"I know, David. I just don't know what I will do without her," said Cara.

David hugged her tightly, smelling her hair and holding her face.

"Cara, you are without doubt one of the strongest people I know. You will do what you always do: persevere. I have no doubt you are a force to be reckoned with all on your own. Have faith that you are capable of all wonderful things because that is who you are."

Cara felt the tears fall as David kissed her soft cheeks.

"Your mother taught you so much about life. Now you can give the same gift to Maggie. The greatest blessing of life is the legacy you leave behind, and you have been blessed to share your mother with our daughter even if she isn't physically here with us."

Cara was grateful to have David always being supportive and encouraging her to see the best in all situations. She couldn't love him more and was thankful for his guidance.

She pulled him close to her, letting her head rest on his chest before climbing on top of him and slowly kissing his neck. She undressed him, feeling the warmth of his body against hers as they made love before falling asleep in each other's arms.

When they awoke to the sound of Maggie fussing from a bad dream, David kissed his wife on her lips. "I'll get her," he said.

She pulled him in for another longer, more passionate kiss before letting him go.

She then rolled over, exhausted from their night of passion, and fell asleep until the following morning.

———

Despite the heartache, Cara felt grateful for her life, no longer searching for answers to questions about the past. She found peace in remaining unaware of her mother's secrets, and although she thought about asking her again, she concluded that some things were better left unsaid.

Through all their struggles, Cara wouldn't have wanted it any other way.

Though a piece of her longed to return to South Carolina, she knew that the time to consider the move was not now. Out of curiosity, she asked, "Mom, do you miss South Carolina?"

By now, Isabel was spending most of her time in bed resting but raised her head before responding, "I regret leaving, but at the time, I didn't feel I had much of a choice."

Cara moved closer to her mother, sitting beside her bed.

"Mom, why did we leave?" she asked softly.

Before Isabel could answer, David walked in with Maggie, holding a tray of cookies. "We know we could never outdo you two, but Maggie and I have been working all morning on a special treat for you." Maggie rushed over to her grandmother, who appeared more energetic by the visit. "Now look at these," gushed Isabel.

"I made them, especially for you, Granny," said little Maggie, smiling.

Maggie nestled her head close to Isabel as they nibbled on the cookies.

The room was filled with the smell of cookies baked by the young girl. The family surrounded the bed, devouring the sweet treats.

Cara smiled. "I guess baking is in our blood," noted Cara.

Isabel said weakly, "We women have a gift and the guts to pursue it. Never forget that cooking is a love language."

Cara glanced at David, who was standing proudly at the door.

She absorbed the moment but wished Isabel had answered her questions before the interruption. After enjoying the snack, her mother became increasingly tired and asked for time to rest. Maggie gave her grandma a soft kiss on her cheek.

"I love you, Granny," she said quietly.

"And I love you more than freshly baked cookies," replied Isabel.

Before leaving, Cara went close to her mother's side. "And I also love you, Mama."

Isabel took Cara's hand. "Tomorrow, we will talk. I will answer all of your questions, SugarBear," said a weak Isabel. She held Cara's hand a little bit longer before letting go. "I love you, my sweet Caralyn."

Cara walked out, knowing the time was near. She worried about what her mother would reveal in the morning but never had a chance to find out.

Because Isabel never woke again.

CHAPTER TWENTY

THE DAYS AFTER ISABEL'S death were difficult. Cara wandered around, dazed, while Maggie, who was old enough to understand the concept of death yet young enough to hold onto her innocence, kept asking if Isabel would come back. Although she was nearly a tween, she still had a childlike perspective on death.

"No honey, Granny has gone to be with the Lord," Cara explained.

Barely able to get the words out, David offered, "Let's go bake some of your Granny's favorite sugar cookies to offer to visitors. Granny will live on through her recipes."

That seemed to satisfy Maggie as she hugged her tearful mother, sitting on the chair watching birds fluttering, skittish outside the window.

Cara held tight to her mother's apron, inhaling her senses, and tears flowed quickly.

Isabel had still been young and should have had much life to live.

Had it not been for the cancer, she could well have lived over twenty-five more years.

Now, Cara felt sorry for herself. She would never have the opportunity to watch her mother grow old. She sat for a long while, thinking bitterly of all the events her mother would miss, saddened she didn't have more time. She heard a tapping on the door and saw a tearful Ted waiting outside. Cara motioned him to come in, greeting him with a warm hug.

"Besides us, you were the closest person to her," she sobbed.

"She was certainly something special," said Ted, wiping his eyes. "We have been through quite a bit together."

Cara looked curiously at him, hoping for more information, but knowing this wasn't the time to try and find it out. Not right now. The air was thick in the room as Cara opened the window.

They watched in awe as a red cardinal fluttered close by.

"Maybe a sign from Mom," laughed Cara.

"No! I would suspect she'd be holding a piece of pastry," joked Ted.

Cara smiled at the image, chuckling at it. Ted was so sensitive, thinking of precisely the right words to make her chuckle at such a time.

"I don't know what I will do without her, Ted. She was my driving force," admitted Cara.

"She still can be," offered Ted. "I mean ... she still is. Absolutely, she is."

He looked around the room, moving toward Isabel's apron on the chair. He caressed it, smiling. "Your mother fiercely protected you all through life so you could stand on your own."

Cara nodded in agreement. "She had so much life to live though. We had so many plans." Cara's voice cracked. "I feel like I've been—and she's been—robbed of it."

Ted walked over to Cara, embracing her gently.

"No, sweet girl. Anyone who had the privilege to know your mother was blessed. Remember, most people go through their whole lives never knowing a person as good and wonderful as her."

Cara smiled, knowing that was the truth. It was a fresh perspective and exactly the kind of wholesome message her mom would have portrayed, too.

Isabel had paved the way for other young women and, in her way, changed the course of society by never allowing her gender to stop her from pursuing her career.

She had been the first woman in Grover Creek to work full-time in a predominantly male trade, paving the way for others to do the same.

Had it not been for Isabel, many other women who came after her would not have had the courage to seek employment outside the home. There was, of course, still much work to be done, and society had come a long way, but Isabel Loring was recognized as a pioneer of her time.

Cara felt proud of all Isabel had accomplished and was even more determined to follow in her mother's footsteps. Now, with her mother gone, she had more time to dedicate to following her dreams. A new lightness came over Cara, knowing her mother's legacy could be continued through her talents. She sat thoughtfully, letting quietness fill the room.

"Ted, what was it that Mother never told me about her past?" asked Cara. "Do you know?"

Ted felt blood flush to his face and pivoted from one foot to another. "Cara, you need to know that your mother loved you fiercely. When the time is right, I will tell you, but for now, let's celebrate your mother's life. She was very clear that her funeral was not to be a sad event but a celebration. Let's honor her properly. There will be plenty of time to discuss Isabel Loring's secret life." He managed a chuckle, carrying Cara along with it.

"My mother had quite a story," she lamented, her eyes glazed with tears. "But despite that, I still always knew there were other things I didn't know."

Ted neared the apron, touching it as he looked out the window at the cardinal still fluttering about. "We all have our secrets, dear girl. You shouldn't try to hold your mother to perfection."

The celebration was exactly what Isabel would have wanted. Guests wore bright colors and told stories. Cara watched with pride how people she had never met came to pay their respects and gushed over the influence Isabel had held over them.

"After my husband left me for another woman, I was heartbroken. I was making minimum wage as a dishwasher and didn't know what to do. Your mama sat me down and sternly talked sense into me. She told me my worth was never measured by a man and encouraged me to enroll in a cooking class. She even spoke to my boss about giving me more responsibility in the kitchen. Eventually, I went on to be a sous chef. Without her, I'd still be stuck in that place."

The woman was thin and middle-aged, and the lines on her face revealed a tough life. When she spoke of Isabel, her face was bright and filled with admiration.

"Thank you for sharing that," said Cara.

Many women had similar stories. It was Isabel who'd encouraged them to live independently and defy societal expectations.

More than ever, Cara couldn't be prouder of being Isabel's daughter.

As she watched guests arrive and tell stories of Isabel, she knew she had a responsibility to live out her mother's dream. It wasn't until after her death that Cara understood the magnitude of her mother's great influence, starting from her days in South Carolina, where she'd worked hard to make a name for herself while ignoring so much criticism, allowing space for other women to have the courage to make their mark outside the home. Then, during her time in Maryland, she mentored other women while working hard and raising Cara alone. Isabel had accomplished a lot in her short life, and reflecting, Cara knew she also should be doing more with her life. It was then Cara decided that she, too, would focus on her career at all costs.

She had no regrets about having cared for her mother over the past years, but it was time for Cara to pursue and achieve what Isabel hadn't had the chance to do.

When the guest left the memorial service, Cara returned outside for fresh air. The air felt good on her face, giving her time to breathe and reflect. She sat beside the large white oak tree, admiring its girth. In the distance, she heard the bustling city, the noise overwhelming her senses.

The thought of living in Maryland without Isabel was almost too much to contemplate.

But Cara needed a change, and she knew that it was time.

Time to go back home to South Carolina.

As Cara was getting ready for bed that night, she thought about the day's events.

"David, how do you feel about moving to South Carolina?"

Confused, David looked at his hopeful wife.

"Cara today has been a long day. Let's let life settle for a bit, and we can talk about this in the morning."

Eager to leave Maryland, Cara pressed, "David, I feel like that's where we belong. It would be good for Maggie. And I feel like that's where my mother always wanted to be but somehow couldn't be, for whatever reason. I don't know why, but I just have this feeling ..."

Cara's voice drifted.

"I'll make you a deal," David said, kissing his wife's cheek. "Let's get some sleep, start settling your mother's estate, and we'll talk about it then."

This seemed to satisfy Cara, though she was already planning the move as she lay awake.

Chapter Twenty-One

Although Isabel's death had been expected, it hadn't made Cara any more prepared for the void.

She was reluctant to stop renting Isabel's home. The home Cara had once resented. It would mean she would finally have to let her go, at least in a worldly sense.

When brave enough, she entered the house to feel her presence.

She carefully crept up the stairs, savoring each moment as she recalled how often she and her mother had walked on the wooden planks through the entrance. When Cara was young, she loved the swirling patterns of the wood grain, which made the space feel grand.

She looked up at the chandelier.

Cara had spent countless hours trying to count how many crystals hung from the lights.

She thought it must be over three hundred by her estimation, though she could never be sure. Thankfully, the home was under the city's rent control initiative, and Isabel's rent hadn't changed for over twenty years.

This was one of the small blessings that had helped keep her finances in order and provide for Cara through her childhood.

The rent burden had skyrocketed over the past decade, and Cara was grateful that she and her mother had never been forced to move from her home.

When she finally reached her mother's bedroom door, she turned the doorknob as her mother had done many times before. Entering, Cara could still smell the faint aroma of her mother's favorite perfume, a sweet smell of blossoms and citrus.

She had worn the same perfume for her entire life.

Cara made a note to take the half-used bottle off her vanity set in her bedroom home with her today. The faded yellow wallpaper still had an old elegance too, accentuating the thick floorboards and moldings. She walked into the living room, noticing the bay windows, which provided natural light to the spacious area. Isabel had kept the curtains open during the day to enjoy the wildlife often frequenting her windows. She loved the sound of the birds chirping by the window and kept a bird feeder full of food for her feathered friends. The house had been emptied for some time now, and Cara wondered if the birds missed her mother as much as she did.

Cara remembered a couple of items she wanted to take, reminders of her mother that she couldn't bear the thought of being put in the dumpster.

The idea of her mother's belongings being sent to thrift stores or thrown away was enough to make Cara want to crawl into her bed and hide under the sheets.

However, despite her anxieties, she knew the first item she would take out of the cupboard and put in the pile of things she would keep for herself was in the same place it had been for years. She entered the kitchen and opened the top cupboard to find it. Cara ran her fingers around the rim of the bright yellow oversized mixing bowl, noticing the distinctive chip.

She decided to leave the bowl for now, unable to remove it.

It was too painful a reminder that her mother was really gone.

Long ago, Isabel had told Cara that the bowl was originally her mother's, and the small chip was present from when it had hit the side of the sink while she'd been washing it as a child.

At the time, Isabel had worried her mother would be angry about chipping her most beloved bowl, but she'd simply said, "Now, dear, we're all a little cracked. It doesn't make us useless."

Cara continued to browse the kitchen cupboard, remembering the days of sitting at the kitchen table with her mother, complaining about teachers, gossiping about boys, and asking advice on enriching the flavors of some of the recipes she was experimenting with.

The one recipe that she had the most trouble perfecting was chocolate ganache cake. She could never correct the consistency and would often get frustrated.

"It's all in the chocolate," Isabel would advise. "You need to use high-quality ingredients, or your chocolate will break, and the consistency will be compromised."

"I finally perfected getting the cream at the right temperature before it boils. For the longest time, I'd have the temperature too high or low, and it wouldn't melt the chocolate correctly."

"As you know, baking is both a science and a craft, and it takes many tries to get it right. Don't give up."

Cara smiled.

"Remember that you will want a thinner ganache for the cake—too thick ganache is for truffles. It's a tricky balance but an important one."

Cara was going to miss the plethora of advice her mother offered, but the essence of her mother surrounded her. It was time to put the remaining items in storage until she had more time to sift through the rest of it; Cara was exhausted from the day, and the rest of her mom's belongings could wait for another time, a time she'd be more willing to let Isabel's stuff go.

Time marched on as it always would, somewhat oddly and somewhat slowly.

Cara wanted to move to South Carolina, yet David found one reason or another to change the subject each time she mentioned it.

Cara's voice rose in frustration.

"David, why won't you at least have this conversation with me?"

David, tired of the constant nagging, felt his heart pounding in his ears.

"Cara, why must everything always be on your terms? I never said I wanted to move at all, did I? That was never part of the agreement, and you know it."

The same argument became more frequent until both gave up talking.

The tension in the house escalated, and they found themselves at odds over the smallest things, hardly able to endure being in the same room as one another. "I thought you were making dinner," Cara snapped, arriving home late from work.

"I did make it last night, Cara. And in case you didn't notice, the world doesn't revolve around baked goods."

That was a low blow even for David, and Cara stormed out and didn't return home until late into the evening. The couple began spending less time together, and after almost a year, she couldn't wait any longer for David to commit to the move after so much wavering and arguing.

She knew all too well how unpredictable life was; could anyone really blame her for wanting to live while there was still time? Plus, she'd always said she hated living in Maryland.

Perhaps her arrogance or desperation led her to believe David would follow her, but she'd made her decision—she would be leaving, with or without her husband.

There were too many painful reminders in Maryland, and Cara felt the move would help heal her and allow her to reinvent her life. It was a bold move, especially after losing her mother.

They were more than just mother and daughter; they were kindred spirits who understood the importance of perseverance and pursuing their dreams. Like many mothers and daughters, they had their share of disagreements, but both held a deep respect for one another. The void left by Isabel was often overwhelming for Cara to bear. Sitting in her kitchen, she reflected on her youth and the relentless questions she had posed.

Now, it seemed silly to have barraged her mother for answers, but then, trying to find out about her father and her heritage meant everything.

Chapter Twenty-Two

Two months later, the fall air was overtaken by the threat of winter. Cara hoped that by now, David would have changed his mind. Instead, he had stayed back to finish some projects at work, believing that the time apart would do them both good. Their arguments were worsening, and Maggie was starting to notice too. Before any more damage was done, Cara had one last thing to do before leaving. She needed to finish packing the remaining items left behind in her mother's house. She dreaded this day but knew it was time to finally say goodbye.

The moving truck would soon take the remaining items to the storage unit she rented down the road.

She entered the apartment and felt the essence of her mother surrounding her. Closing her eyes, she could still hear her mother humming as she baked cornbread.

Cara felt her heartache as she walked into the kitchen, where she had spent much of her time learning from the patient, Isabel. This was the hardest thing Cara had to do, but she kept focused on the task of packing instead of drowning in grief.

It was the only way she could get through it.

As Cara finished packing the last boxes, she looked again at the empty space where her mother had once resided. She would miss coming here for the holidays. She would miss her mother's sound advice and the smells permeating the kitchen and then the whole house.

The yellow mixing bowl sat exactly where her mother had left it, on the counter next to the picture of a young Cara smiling in a pasta frame. By now, the pasta pieces were all but cracked, though her mother had still treasured the picture and the mixing bowl more than any other possessions. That bowl held so many memories and would be cherished for generations.

Cara imagined that one day, Maggie would make and share her recipes with her daughter, too. She carefully wrapped the picture frame with extra paper, careful to keep it safe.

She held the mixing bowl close to her chest, taking in the memories.

Cara realized she had been lost in her thoughts again when the third hefty knock on the door startled her. She placed the bowl on the counter and rushed to see who it was.

She was surprised to see Ted standing there, twitchy and nervous. He gave her a soft, sympathetic smile before making his way inside, looking around in amazement.

"This place sure does have a lot of memories."

Cara took his hand, knowing this day had to be just as difficult for him.

She hadn't realized how old he had gotten or the deep wrinkles and lines on his skin. She had known him for most of her life, and saying goodbye would not come easily to either of them. He was a staple in her life, there for the highs and lows of her childhood.

Thinking back, Ted had never been absent from any significant event. He had always remained thoughtful and kind, treating her and Isabel with so much love.

To say goodbye to him would be beyond difficult.

"Oh, Ted, I was heading out soon and planned to stop by to say a final farewell."

"Well, I'm glad I caught you then." A strange uneasiness was making Cara nervous.

"Is something wrong, Ted?"

"No, no, nothing is the matter." He was staring at Cara intensely, making her anxiously brush her hair from her face. "Wow, you are your mother's daughter," he commented.

Puzzled, Cara stared blankly, awaiting more clarification.

She felt her stomach turn in anticipation. Ted appeared disheveled and uneasy.

"Ted, I know this is hard for you, too," she said softly. "Are you okay?"

"Can I come in and sit down?" asked Ted unexpectedly. He'd just blurted it out.

Cara motioned to the couch, glad the movers hadn't come yet to take it away. "Are you feeling well?" she asked. "I'm sorry I can't be more hospitable but make yourself at home."

He glanced around as memories flooded back. Taking a deep breath, he said, "It's time you knew the truth, Cara."

Cara's eyes crinkled. "The truth?" She was confused. "I know my mother's death has been hard on all of us, but—"

"Please, Cara. Let me tell you. The truth is I wanted you to know for many years. Your mother wouldn't hear of it, though," he said, shaking his head. "She insisted she protected you right up until her death."

Cara was truly baffled. Now, more forcefully, she demanded, "Ted, what is this about?"

She felt the agitation rise but then softened when he wiped a tear from his cheek. "I'm sorry. It's been a long day, and I'm quite emotional," Cara said, realizing she was also more anxious than she had imagined. She looked around, gesturing at the boxes. "This has been a lot."

"I understand. But Cara, like I said, I need to tell you the truth," said Ted. "Can you just calm down and listen to me? Hear me out?"

"Ted, what are you saying? If this is about my father, I know he died long ago. My mother told me about him but didn't give me more details. And honestly, I'm over it. I don't need to know my mother's secrets."

"There's more Cara. Things you don't know. Things you should know."

Cara stared as Ted's eyes welled with tears again.

"My real name isn't Ted. It's Johnny. Johnny Kaats. I am your biological uncle."

Cara took a step back.

Johnny continued, "All these years, I watched you grow up, feeling lucky to be in your life."

"You're my uncle?" Cara said as her voice rose. "But ... but why didn't you tell me? Why was it such a secret?"

"It was a complicated time. Your mother and I were remarkably close, and she worked for me at Dig-In Diner. Her talent was unbeatable, and so was her tenacity. We were very good friends. However, things got complicated."

"Complicated how?" said Cara.

"I had some skeletons in my closet, ones she shouldn't have been involved in."

Wait, so all this time? Cara took another step back, unsure of what she was hearing. She felt her knees buckle as she leaned up against a pile of boxes.

Ted continued, "Your father, my brother... my half-brother, was a wealthy man. He was mean as the day was long, at least to me. I was an embarrassment because his mama and my daddy had an affair. It was quite the scandal back then. You understand, times were different."

Cara put her head in her trembling hands and motioned Ted to continue.

"In any event, I got myself into some financial trouble and sought out my rightful inheritance. I didn't go about it the right way," admitted Ted. "Your father, Liam, refused, and things escalated, and, well, you can say, they got out of control."

Cara felt a ringing in her ears.

Johnny stood up and moved closer to her, touching her arm.

She instantly moved away, unsure whether the man she had trusted all these years was someone she could continue to have faith in. He had suddenly lost his credibility.

"Cara, you need to understand. It was a different time back then. Liam and his family held more power and could have buried me, or worse, buried your mother. So, I faked my death, burned down my restaurant, and left town for good."

"Why would you do that?"

"Didn't I just say why?" he asked, slightly snappy. Then he calmed. "I'm sorry. Like you said, it's a lot. It's always been a lot for me too. I'm not coldhearted. I only hope you believe that."

Ted was quiet now, allowing Cara time to understand, for the truth of it all to finally sink in.

He saw the realization wash over her face.

"Wait, so you gave up everything to protect my mother?" Cara was speechless.

"If I hadn't, he would have destroyed her. Worse still, he would've taken you from her and absconded God only knows where with you, and no one would have seen you again. He was a rich and powerful man, Cara; he could always get his own way, even legally, and even the police would have turned a blind eye. I couldn't let all that happen. Your mother had so much potential, and if I'd still been in the picture, my brother would've stopped at nothing to destroy both of us."

Cara could not imagine how her life would have been without her mother.

It would have been much poorer, that much was clear. Not poorer in wealth, but in love.

She'd also taught her so much about life. Cara now melted inside, understanding her late mother in a new light and appreciating the many sacrifices she had made, though she had conflicting emotions about it all, which was only natural.

Cara felt both anger and gratitude and couldn't decipher which emotion was greater.

"In my way," Johnny continued, "I loved her. It's just that my life was complicated, and boy, your mama was somethin' to reckon with."

Cara chuckled loudly. "Oh, I know! Believe me, I've heard all the stories!"

"Yes, she sure was something. She didn't care what anyone thought of her, no matter who they were. And she had such a bright future until Liam came into the picture."

"Now I know why my mom never wanted me to know about him," Cara thoughtfully said. "All this time, she was protecting me from him. You both were."

Cara was no longer a child but felt a vulnerability she hadn't known in years.

"What happened to Liam to make him so cruel?" she asked.

"He wasn't always bad. He was well-liked. It was just that he hated me—for so many reasons. He hated that I had the community's respect and a thriving restaurant. But most of all, he hated that I had your mother, who was so loyal to me."

"This is a lot to digest," admitted Cara.

"I'm sure. Take your time with it." Johnny pulled her close, and Cara allowed him to embrace her as she had many times. "If you have any questions, I will answer them the best I can."

Cara nodded.

"Isabel was devastated when she thought I'd died, which only made him angrier. He was obsessed with your mother, you know, Cara. She was the one thing I had that he wanted, and he wouldn't let me win. He was so used to getting his way and buying everything. But this time, he had found someone who couldn't be bought, and it drove him mad."

Cara glared at Johnny, suddenly realizing how disposably women had been treated back then.

"My mother was a person. The way you men toyed around with her emotions ... Knowing her as I did, I can't imagine she would have stood for it."

"Trust me, had she known, she wouldn't have. I feared if she knew the feud between us was for her affection, she would have let us both have it. It didn't matter to Liam that your mother and I were friends. He hated that her talents made me successful and wanted what I had with her. It was honest and beautiful, but he managed to make it so damn ugly."

Johnny clenched his fists but continued, voice raised.

"He wanted me to suffer for having the same bloodline as him, for his father's affair with my mother, and for having your mother's love even if it was platonic. He didn't care about the truth; his only concern was making my life miserable."

Cara felt her knees weaken as she stood.

"Why didn't you tell her the truth? Maybe she would have left with you. Maybe you could have started over, the two of you, and opened a restaurant together. Instead, she lived her life in hiding." Isabel felt anger rise as she waited for Johnny to respond.

"That sounds simple enough, but it would never be that easy. I had no choice but to flee, no choice but to lie. He was going to have your mother killed and frame me for it. I didn't believe it at first until I saw the evidence. I couldn't have that on my conscience."

Johnny was talking fast, desperate to have Cara understand.

"It wasn't long until I found out your mama was pregnant with you. I knew it was Liam's. There was no way it couldn't have been -the timing slotted together. So, I began sending money each month to help her out, knowing she'd never want Liam to know he was your father."

"You did that for me?" Cara's eyes grew big, and she felt her chest ache from all that had been lost. "After all this time, why didn't you tell me sooner? You treated me like family throughout my childhood, and you knew all along that you were."

"Your mama didn't want to complicate things further. Your father would never let you live freely if he'd known I was in the picture. So, your mom and I chose to keep it a secret."

Johnny bowed his head, placing his hand deep in his pocket.

"I know it may be too late, but I couldn't let you leave here without knowing the truth."

"Wait. Is that why you insisted on walking me down the aisle at my wedding and being there when Maggie was born and—"

"Yes, we were family. It didn't matter about our bloodlines. We were family because I loved you and your mom."

"Johnny, were you and my mother ever intimate?"

Embarrassment washed over his face. This was the uncomfortable question he had hoped wouldn't surface, that she would be too ill at ease to ask him this.

"Not at first. But through the years, our friendship grew; I didn't know it then, but your mother was the greatest love story never told. Unlike Liam, I loved her for who she was, not out of some sick game of revenge. Liam couldn't accept that she'd chosen me over him."

Johnny paused momentarily, unsure how much more he should reveal to her. She already had so much new and shocking information to take in.

"Please, tell me," said Cara, for a moment, showing all the strength her mother had.

"I wasn't a saint myself. I got mixed up with some gambling debts and then forged Liam's signature and filtered out his accounts to pay back my debt. But once Liam got a whiff of what had transpired, he went to the authorities to have me arrested. The only thing he didn't count on was me knowing the money in his account had been embezzled from his various businesses!"

Cara's mouth widened, unable to speak, and she allowed Johnny to continue.

She couldn't imagine the man standing before her was even capable of crimes like these.

"We were both going to get bagged by the cops. To shut me up and keep me out of prison, Liam offered to give me a fresh start in Florida if I left and never came back. The caveat was for me to give up Isabel. What I didn't count on was him taking advantage of her. Your mother later told me he was forceful with her when she refused to continue with the affair. When she made her position clear, Liam just threw her out of the house there and then."

Cara sat quietly, allowing him to continue, even though she hated hearing it.

"I knew I had to find her and tell her the truth. She was, of course, angry at me for all the lies, but over time, she found forgiveness. When Liam eventually found out I was in contact and deeply in love with her, he was hellbent on finding you and snatching you away. He threatened her so much that she'd spend most nights pacing the floors, frantic. Finally, I convinced her to just get the hell out of there, to take you and leave for Maryland. She didn't want to go. It damn near broke her heart to leave South Carolina."

Cara felt a flush of regret as she recalled the harsh words she had said to her mother about the move, realizing now that her decision was not driven by ego or career ambitions but by a fear that Liam would take her away.

"What about Nathan, though? Is he my brother?"

"No, no, no, Nathan's the result of a marriage that should never have been. When his mother, Sara, found out about my past, she threw me out and filed for divorce. I think she always knew my heart belonged to Isabel and that she deserved better. She was right."

He shrugged.

"Where is my father now?" asked Cara, her voice growing colder.

"He died years ago. The drink finally took hold of his liver, and he was gone within six months of finding out about having hepatic cancer."

"And to think all this time, I could have known my father."

A sudden coldness filled the air. Cara felt rage ignite her insides.

All the lies came crashing in, and Cara could no longer suppress her emotions, outraged by the secrets. "She had no right to keep this from me, and neither did you!" She was seething. "All this time, I knew I didn't belong and that something was off. Yet everyone lied to me."

Johnny nodded in agreement.

"I'm sorry. I know this is a lot to handle, but I thought you should know now."

"What am I supposed to do with the information, Johnny? Don't you think it's a bit late?"

"I know you're upset. But you have to understand. Like I said, it was a different time."

"Well, fuck you for keeping all of this from me. And, and ... fuck my mother too," Cara said, slamming the door as she left Johnny behind.

CHAPTER TWENTY-THREE

ONCE CARA DIGESTED THE lies told to her, she felt a justifiable angst. Everything she thought she knew about herself now felt inauthentic. It would be hard to explain this to anyone, so Cara's rage was often an internal conversation that kept playing like a record.

The secrets kept all these years were what left her feeling the most anger. How dare they? This was her life, her whole future, now affected by adults keeping secrets they should have revealed long ago for her sake. Both Johnny and her mom had often said they acted this way to protect her—but Cara just saw it as selfish, especially when she'd been a grown woman, and they still had let her carry on wondering who her father was!

Her resentment was also seeping into her relationship with David these days, making her question every aspect of her life.

He felt the distance, and her mood would darken when he tried to connect with her.

"I wasn't the one who lied to you, Cara," said an exasperated David one evening after supper.

"Well, everyone else around me has lied to me, and I don't feel I can trust anyone but myself anymore," she stammered. "I'm sorry, but it's out of my control."

David's eyes welled with tears at her rage. But didn't she see he had a right to be angry too?

"You win, Cara. Just go. Move to South Carolina and start your new life." He lowered his head and slowly left the bedroom before Cara could explain.

She sat on the bed and cried that night, David never returning to sleep at her side.

She knew her anger was directed at David unfairly, but it was insurmountable. Besides, she was still missing her mother, which made it difficult to move on in a positive way.

Despite all the untruths, her mother's death had profoundly impacted her, and she was having difficulty moving past the grief. It was one of the many reasons she needed to leave Maryland and return to South Carolina. Feeling trapped, she wanted to start over with no secrets and a place where she could finally finish what her mother had begun.

———

Six months after Isabel's death, David asked, "Aren't you going to hear them out at least? Ted and Nathan have left you messages over a dozen times."

He was still referring to Johnny as Ted, a factor that was making it all the more problematic for her to accept what had happened. The more she thought about Johnny, the more David mentioned Ted again. It was beyond awkward and way too aggravating.

"David, my entire life was built on lies. I'm not even sure who my mother was anymore."

Cara raised her hands in exasperation. "Turned out I was the only one who didn't know the truth. So, I have no interest in having any discussion with either of them."

David, who had always been a reasonable voice, understood her feelings of betrayal.

"What hurts the most is that Ted—or Johnny—and my mother knew all about this, and when I asked each of them, they acted like I was crazy, as though they thought it was unfounded. But I'd known something was up all along, and they'd made me feel like I was imagining it! That is the very same thing that abusers do, narcissists. It's called gaslighting."

Cara was still so disconcerted by the conversation and had not softened about it.

David held Cara close, relishing how wonderful it felt to embrace his wife. It had been such a long time since they'd shared a moment like this, and she melted into his arms. David's voice grew softer. "Your mother's past does not define who she was to you. She did all of this to protect you; now you know the truth. Can't you find some forgiveness?"

"The truth is, I do understand, but I still feel like I'm suffocating here. I want to feel closer to my roots. I want to move back to South Carolina. Please, David. Come with me."

David let go of Cara, considering it.

"It may take a few months, but it will give you time to help Maggie settle into her new home."

"Do you mean it, David?" Cara asked. "Things between us have been so tense over the past months."

She had clearly taken his response as an agreement to relocate with her.

"Cara, I'm trying to be who you need me to be. It's a lot. Our marriage was never just the two of us. It was always about your mother first and then me."

"I know. I'm sorry for that. I will try to do better," she said. "If we can move, that will help."

David kissed the top of her head.

"I know you mean to do better, Cara, but I often wonder if you're capable of it anymore."

"And what's that supposed to mean?" snapped Cara.

The burgeoning tenderness dissipated, Cara, becoming defensive.

"Listen, the time apart will be good for us. Give us a chance to take a pause. A lot has happened, and we could use a break to refocus."

So, he was admitting that it wasn't in his plan for them to move away together. Not yet, anyway. If she went, she would be going alone. Or, alone with Maggie, anyway.

"I want us, though," said Cara in an uncharacteristically small voice. "I don't want to make the move on my own. When I said about relocating, I meant us. Both of us."

David looked around the empty space. "Cara, you packed up practically the entire house. You want what you want, and I don't want to hold you back. I don't want to be the one you look at in a decade's time while you tell me how I held you back. You have a talent. Catch those dreams. Do whatever it is you feel drawn to do. Go with my blessing."

His voice was soft, but his tone was steady and with conviction.

Cara held onto David tightly. After a long moment, he released her and kissed her on the lips.

"I will see you soon, love," he said stoically.

Cara had a strong sense that David had other plans but trusted this was only a bump in their marriage. She recalled his absence and late nights at the office over the last few years.

She hadn't paid attention to it at the time, but it seemed all the more obvious now.

David busied himself with Maggie as Cara packed most of the house in her car, leaving David with the bare essentials. She had hoped that taking most of the household goods with her would entice him to join them sooner. Even that part of her plan had backfired.

"God has a plan. I have faith that the Universe will guide me," she said to herself as she packed the last of Maggie's belongings into the back of the car.

Cara allowed the air conditioner to cool down the steamy car as she put the rest of the bags inside the trunk.

David sighed and hugged her tightly, allowing her to melt momentarily into his arms.

Before she could change her mind, she gathered her purse.

Soon, Cara and Maggie were waving goodbye. She watched David becoming smaller in her rearview mirror as the distance grew. They headed south, ready to start a new life, though reluctant to leave David behind. They hadn't been apart ever since meeting, and she was already anxious about the distance. Though neither was brave enough to admit their marriage was in serious trouble, things had been strained lately, and she wasn't sure if it was salvageable.

She drove silently for most of the ride as Maggie, thankfully, napped in the back.

The silence allowed her to think of a plan before she arrived.

She reached into her coat pocket to find the keys to her childhood home.

Johnny had mentioned it needed work, but he had paid someone throughout the years to maintain it. Nervous feelings fluttered through her with the thought of revisiting her childhood home, especially with her mother's absence. Still, she was grateful to return to South Carolina and intended to plant roots, wanting to provide Maggie with stability and the comfort of Southern hospitality, high moral pride, and unity within the community.

As she drove down the long, windy roads, she noted the open land, clean air, large overgrown trees, and large homes with porches that wrapped around most of the houses.

She couldn't wait to sit back on the old porch she used to sit on with her mother.

They had two wooden rocking chairs where they would spend time sipping sweet tea during the long, sweltering summer days. Those chairs had been long gone, but she planned on ordering three new ones so her family could sit and enjoy the porch and the evening sun.

Though she tried to quell her curiosity about her father, the questions kept swirling in her mind. There were so many answers she still needed.

She hadn't thought about her father since childhood and now had a million things to ask.

If she had known she was the illegitimate daughter of a wealthy businessman, her life would have been far different. She scolded herself for entertaining greed but couldn't help but wonder the advantages she would have had in life had things turned out differently.

How would her life have been if Johnny had admitted years ago that he was her uncle with a vendetta against her father instead of a grocery owner?

Yes, so many questions, yet so few answers. Did it matter, she wondered?

What was done was done, and she had to find a way to move on, or this could destroy her. It was already undermining the foundations of her marriage. How much further would it erode?

And would the truth honestly change a thing?

She would forever be loyal to her mother and grateful for everything she had taught her.

Though the road hadn't always been easy, she had been raised with good morals, a strong work ethic, and a mother who would have moved heaven and earth to see her smile.

She knew that. A mother's love for her daughter was unlike anything else.

As she approached town, so much had changed with the growing businesses, yet it still felt the same. What had taken her so long to return?

Why had she permitted herself to waste so much time?

When she considered it, every decision had been based on what her mother wanted. With her mom now gone, it was time to decide on her own needs and no longer compromise. This made her reflect on her marriage. Could David adapt to the Southern lifestyle? Was it unreasonable to ask him to try? Did she truly see a future with David in it?

Would their marriage survive so much upheaval after such an emotive time already?

Until her departure, things between them had become increasingly tense, and Cara hoped this uneasy time would pass when the two reunited.

The same argument kept arising about the move, with David claiming that Isabel was fulfilling her mother's dreams, not thinking about their family. However, Cara insisted that her dream had always been to return to South Carolina to finish what her mother had started.

"You don't owe your mother anything. You need to make your own decisions based on your life now. Stop chasing your mother's dreams and find your own," he had said after another heated argument. Money had been tight since Cara had rarely worked while her mother was ill.

Naturally, David was resentful that she wanted to use their savings to move and open a business while their finances and marriage were in such turmoil.

"These *are* my dreams, dammit. I have had to process a lot about my mother's life, and if you aren't going to support me, then like my mother, I can do it without a man, too."

Cara left, slamming the door, immediately regretting her words.

She wanted to return home, but if she were honest, there was a certain internal obligation to her mother—an unspoken agreement that Isabel had paved the way for Cara to have a better life than she had. Isabel had been fierce in her fight for her position at work, and Cara didn't want to squander these opportunities.

When Cara finally pulled into the driveway on Cradle Street, she parked the car and gazed at the old house. It felt surreal to be back again, and a wave of ease washed over her.

She was finally home, back in the special place of which she had been dreaming for a long time, and at last, she had arrived where she'd started, returned to where she had felt most whole.

Though it was how she remembered it, gardening and maintenance tasks desperately required attention. The light blue paint was chipping from the siding, and it wouldn't be long before a new roof was needed either. Despite the foreseeable home projects, Cara felt hot tears as she exited the car and started to look for the front door.

When she looked back, Maggie was stirring from sleep, taking off her seatbelt, and calling out, "Mom, is this the house?" Maggie's dirty blonde hair in a messy bun appeared as she stretched her growing bones. She glanced toward the rear of the house.

"Whoa, Mom, check out this backyard. It's huge," she said.

Cara smiled at her girl's enthusiasm, remembering herself at that age, kicking a soccer ball around and listening to the birds sing in the large oak trees. She would spend hours enjoying nature and soaking in the sun. She was grateful for Maggie's willingness to move and thought back to when she had been forced to leave for Maryland. She never did forgive her mother for the move, though she now understood why Isabel had been eager to leave her old life behind.

"Wait until you see the kitchen," said Cara. "It has a double oven and a massive pantry."

Maggie hurried along to join her mother as they entered the house.

The house had been abandoned for decades, and the smell of mustiness was overwhelming.

Cara began opening the windows as she set her pocketbook down on the counter.

She looked around the home as Maggie started exploring the bedrooms.

It had been a long while since Cara had allowed herself to think of this place, and now she was here, she couldn't imagine living anywhere else.

It took hours to clean the house before they could even begin unloading their belongings.

"Mom, is Dad coming soon?" Maggie asked.

"I hope so," whispered Cara. She hadn't liked how they had left things, and a part of her worried if he would join them in their new home at all—now, or in the future.

By late evening, she had brought a cold beer outside and sat on the porch steps. Once the porch was repainted, she thought, her first purchase would be those essential rocking chairs.

For the first time in years, there came a sense of peace. She looked around the porch and decided to fix it up tomorrow. This space had always been so beloved that it deserved a fresh start.

Swigging the last of her beer, she sat still, listening to the bats swooping. She laughed and thought, *South Carolina, I sure did miss you,* before getting up and walking inside.

As she entered the kitchen, Cara noticed the yellow mixing bowl beside a pile of old recipes on the counter. She thumbed through the old cards, reflecting on how many recipes the bowl had been used for. Countless times, she had stirred the mixture in it with a wooden spoon, licking the bowl of uncooked batter clean. Back then, no one worried about food poisoning.

Isabel would even leave extra batter at the bottom for Cara's happy consumption.

Many memories continued to flood Cara's mind. She stayed up all night, a cup of herbal tea in one hand and a pen and notebook in the other. She scribbled furiously every recipe recalled by heart, thinking back to when she had been a young girl, and her mother would come up with tasty treats and teach her everything she knew about baking. As much as she'd adored her mother, only after her death did she realize that she may have never known her at all.

There were so many loose ends that, while thinking back, her mother continued to avoid. Isabel lived an interesting life that had been cut short.

Because of life's circumstances, she'd never had the opportunity to ask her mother what it was like growing up without a mother of her own. Or how she had started in the restaurant business at all. Now more than ever, she wondered who her mother had been as a young lady and what had motivated her to go against the grain the way she had done. These thoughts haunted Cara, but for now, she would occupy herself with Isabel's recipes more than her personal life.

Letting go of the past and focusing on the present would be the only way to finally move on.

While Cara was unloading the rest of the car, she watched happily as neighborhood children came by to introduce themselves to Maggie.

"Hey Mom, do you think it would be alright if I check out the park with some new friends," said Maggie.

"Sounds great. Just be home before dark. And y'all come back later for some sweet tea," said Cara.

Cara was grateful to have Maggie occupied so that she could start on some projects. After going to the local hardware store to get paint, primer, brushes, and sandpaper, she returned home and went to work, deeply grateful to have a project to occupy her mind.

She had already spent too long thinking about her marriage, career, and mother. It was time to find some purpose in her day. She had never taken on home projects before, but with David inaccessible, Cara was determined to make the porch look as she remembered. Her hair was in a tight bun, and she began sanding the wood planks until they were down to the bare wood.

Once the planks resembled a smooth surface, she added a dark primer shade before applying a fresh coat of paint. It took nearly three coats to get the color to what she wanted. The humidity was not helping the drying process, so while she waited, she went back into town to purchase the yellow rocking chairs she had been eyeing earlier in the day.

She parked the car and walked nearly a half block to Harry's Hardware to place her order.

The store held an array of home decor, outdoor furniture, and home improvement items.

She had worked hard on her porch so far, giving her a feeling of accomplishment and empowerment. It had been more cumbersome than expected, but she was eager to sit on her newly renovated frontage and enjoy her much-relished cold beverage.

As she walked toward the hardware store, she noticed for the first time an abandoned building across the street. It was a large brick building with a ripped awning hanging carelessly to one side. She crossed over and peered inside. The building was in the town center and likely had been vacant for some time, though she couldn't be sure.

There had been spray paint on the side of the place, and the weeds had taken over every inch of its grounds. However, there was an elegance about the premises that could be restored with some handywork. Through dirty panes of glass, she noticed soaring ceilings, oversized windows, and ... a fully equipped kitchen! It had all the appearance of being some sort of bakery.

There was even a long counter and space for seating in the central area. She envisioned what this area could become if only she had the opportunity to transform and develop it.

Cara felt a strong urge to pursue this space as a possibility for opening her bakery.

Upon closer inspection, she wondered if it had been abandoned or just been closed for a duration of time. Perhaps this was a sign from her mother to pursue this opportunity.

She missed her mother most in times like this, wishing she had known the truth earlier. Cara still felt anger for the deception, especially since she had been an adult with a child too.

Her father could not have done anything to persuade her away from her mother, and they could have returned far earlier had she known the truth.

There was no use in lamenting the past, however, so she'd focus her energy on the future.

She jotted down the faded number on the door, a surge of excitement about this space being available, giving her hope. When she raced into the house upon arriving home, she quickly dialed the number and left several messages on the answering machine.

She tried to keep her voice even without sounding desperate, but it was hard to conceal her excitement. Wasn't this space simply meant for her?

But she needed to find a way to get to the owner to find out more.

The landowner might only check their messages now and then, so she again went back to the building and left a letter taped to the front door with her information on it in bold letters.

By the second week, she was losing hope that someone would contact her, so she did what she always did when she felt lost: she prayed.

That Sunday, she forced Maggie out of bed and headed to the ten o'clock service.

Cara hadn't been to church in ages and had missed the community of fellowship she'd once enjoyed. This would also be a way to meet people and see the faces of those she hadn't met in decades. Nerves flowed through her body at the thought of being recognized.

It had been so long ... Would anyone notice the newcomer?

Despite the pangs of anxiety, Cara was welcomed with warm smiles and friendly waves as she walked into her pew. She had chosen to attend a non-denominational church, not the one in which she had been raised, but instead, a brand-new building with new parishioners.

Cara was glad for the change and welcomed meeting people who hadn't known her mother. She was just as excited for Maggie to meet kids her age, and Maggie seemed far more willing about the move than Cara had been when she was forced to leave her hometown.

Cara was grateful for this small miracle, rewarding Maggie by allowing her to paint her room a fluorescent green.

The church was quaint but had the Southern charm one would expect. After the service, the congregation provided coffee, tea, and various bunt cakes, brownies, and cookies.

It was a place where everyone gathered to catch up on the week and offer a helping hand to each other, to anyone who needed practical assistance or companionship. One of the blessings of belonging to a congregation was the community and people's sense of pride in their faith.

Society was changing, but Cara was grateful to hold onto her faith, something she'd been missing in the past years. She needed it now more than ever, embracing the new congregation.

As Cara and Maggie grabbed a snack and some fresh lemonade, she overheard a group chatting. Feeling awkward, she looked around while Maggie started to mingle with a few young girls who invited her to go outside and sit in the garden.

It had been some time since Cara had felt the uneasiness of being the new girl, and the jittery feelings of when she'd moved to Maryland came rushing back.

As she nervously stuffed another bite-sized brownie in her mouth, the conversation among the locals grew ever louder. "C'mon now, let's help out our neighbor. Mr. Drawler's having plumbing trouble in his upstairs bathroom," a short man with a gruff voice announced.

"Yes, but that old goat complains when we do try to help," said a slender man.

A third dared venture, "All the more reason to help him, surely. His wife has passed, and he's lonely. Complaining gives him something to do. Now, let's give him a little grace."

Without hesitation, three men nodded in agreement, volunteering to visit and see if they could rectify the situation. One of the men's wives quickly added, "I'll send over a pie with one of you. Hopefully, that will lift his spirits. And if not, at least he won't moan while his mouth's full."

Everyone chuckled, but the comment was meant in good humor.

Cara observed that one of the best things about the South was the willingness to help a neighbor and to all pitch in when someone was down on their luck.

Chapter Twenty-Four

Cara returned the following week and enjoyed both the sermon and the company again. Though she smiled politely and kept to herself, she hoped it would only be a matter of time before she made friends, beginning to get lonely without any adult interaction.

"Hi there. I noticed you here last week. I meant to come over and introduce myself. My name's Melissa. My daughter Hailey was the girl your daughter was outside with last week! They seem to have gotten on quite well. So, I thought I'd say hi to you."

Cara put her coffee aside and gobbled down the last bite of the cinnamon bunt cake.

"That was really nice. I know Maggie appreciated it. Oh, and I'm Cara! Thanks for saying hi, as it's never easy being the new kid."

Melissa smiled and said, "Or the new mom. When I first came to town, I feared I'd never fit in. But everyone around here welcomed me, and before long, my social calendar started to fill up. Just you wait till people get to know you!" Melissa grabbed a piece of coffee cake. "I don't know what Mrs. Jenkins puts in this, but I can't stop eating it. This is my second piece."

Cara helped herself to a piece of cake. After the first bite, she instantly recognized the ingredient and exclaimed, "sour cream." The pair grabbed another piece, smiling as they indulged.

Melissa and Cara soon became fast friends, so Cara invited Melissa and Hailey over for dinner the following Tuesday. Afterward, while the girls went out back, Cara and Melissa enjoyed the evening on the porch together, sipping cold beers.

"You mentioned you were looking for work?" said Melissa.

"Yes. I have a culinary and hotel management degree, but I'd love to open a bakery in town."

"We sure could use one of those," said Melissa.

"Speaking of which, do you know anything about the old, abandoned building in the center of town? The big brick one."

Melissa chuckled. "Oh, that! Believe it or not, it's not abandoned. It's an old bakery. The Brownes own it. Reluctantly, I might add."

"What do you mean?" asked Cara.

"I don't think they want any part of owning a bakery. Not too sure about the details. But what I will say is that they go to our church. They are pillars of the community but will tell anyone who listens that they don't want to run a bakery. I am actually sure they'd be thrilled to get that huge place off their hands—and off their bank accounts since it must cost a fortune in repairs!"

"That would be great. Do you think you can introduce me?"

Melissa said, "I'd be delighted to. But I must warn you, whatever you do, don't call him by his first name. He's an old Southern man and wants to be addressed as Mr. Browne."

"Easy enough," Cara replied. "I daren't offend him before I get the keys to that place!"

On an overwhelmingly steamy summer morning after Sunday service, Cara met the Brownes, who were excited to learn that she was looking for a position in their failing bakery. It seemed the natural route into their good books if she first joined as a general employee rather than steaming in as a new resident and trying to offer to run the place—or to buy it!

Upon arriving at Grover Creek, she had already spent weeks looking for substantial work. However, most positions were counter-help or part-time, and there was little in the bakery field.

Of course, she'd been trained as a pastry chef and wanted to continue the same kind of work she'd had in Maryland. There, she had worked for a hotel providing decadent pastries and cakes for weddings and corporate events. Grover Creek didn't offer large hotels, just small bed and breakfasts, so she was limited. Plus, anywhere she applied, the positions were either full or the management claimed she was overqualified. She was becoming discouraged but still hoped an opportunity would soon present itself; otherwise, she would need to figure out something soon.

"Hello Melissa," said Mr. Browne, a tall, thin man with a large bald spot.

"Hi, Mr. Browne. I want to introduce you to someone," said Melissa. Sweat dripped from his head, and he removed a handkerchief from his suit pocket and quickly wiped his face.

"Mr. Browne, it's nice to meet you finally," Cara said. "My name is Cara Loring."

"Loring? Why does that name sound so familiar?" said Mr. Browne as he adjusted his collar.

"Perhaps you knew my mother. Isabel," offered Cara.

"Oh, my, I haven't heard that name in far too long." Mr. Browne sat pensively before saying, 'Where are you stayin'?'

"Mama and I had a house long ago, a few miles out of town. She recently passed away, and I've been renovating it. It's a lot of work, but I've loved that house since I was a little girl."

"Wait, do you mean the house down Cradle Street off Old Creek Road?"

"You know it?" asked Cara.

"Know it? Dang, I should have figured this out sooner. Are you *THEE* Isabel's kid? That damn woman was the best in town." Mr. Browne was smiling at the memory. "She would make a peach cobbler good enough to make a grown man cry," he offered.

"That's her, right enough. My mother was quite the talent."

"I heard she left town to work at some fancy hotel chain. Got too big for her britches if you ask me."

"Well, you know, Mom was always a dreamer," Cara said, knowing it was not the entire truth. "Sadly, she has passed now. I miss her every day," said Cara.

"I'm sorry for your loss, anyway, Miss Cara," he said, tipping his head respectfully.

"Thank you," she replied.

Just then, a short woman with bright blue eyes appeared.

"This is my wife, Elaine." The woman smiled warmly with a faint of recognition toward Cara.

"Oh, it's so nice to meet you," said Mrs. Browne with a smile. "I was hoping to cross paths. A little birdie told me you were looking for work, and as you know, we own the bakery."

She looked toward Melissa, who held up her lemonade in cheers.

"Just so happens we're looking to retire. Maybe even move out to Arizona," said Mr. Browne.

Mrs. Browne interrupted. "Truth be told, we inherited it, and we have no place even being in the bakery business," she said with a chuckle. "I like to eat pastries, but not so much make them. The mess alone drives me to distraction." She waved her hand, exasperated. "And the noise ..."

"I can understand that," Cara said with a smile. That's why there are pastry chefs and customers who consume our work," she chirped.

"You are the young lady leaving messages on our machine, correct?"

"Why, yes. My apologies for that." Cara recognized that she had made a misstep. "I thought you were permanently closed. I intended to either buy or rent the space for myself. Once more, I apologize."

"Well, unfortunately, I am not at liberty to let you buy or rent," said Mr. Browne. "That's why we never got back to you because it would have been a non-starter."

Cara's heart plummeted.

The old man went on, "I was gifted the bakery many years ago on the understanding that I'd never sell or lease it out. So now, we have the building, but the business isn't doing well."

"I can pay you a fair price," offered Cara, momentarily overlooking everything he had said.

"Let me talk to my lawyers, but as far as I know, I'm not permitted to sell it at all," huffed Mr. Browne. "I'll be stuck with that goddamn place until my dying days. Which won't be far off if I try to keep up with all its bills and upkeep." Even his negativity didn't put Cara off.

She wasn't sure whether he was serious or attempting a joke. She did not laugh, just in case.

"Such a shame," she voiced. "You want to be rid of it, and here I am, saying I'd love it …"

So, the best she could do was start working for Mr. Browne and then figure out the legal documents for buying or leasing the property later, should either be possible. If not, she could eventually find something of her own once she established a reputation in town.

Although she wanted—no, needed—this job, she also didn't want to seem too eager.

The whispers around town said that the Brownes had too much power in the locale and took advantage of others for their self-serving needs. Cara had researched the place thoroughly by now. The business had been known as Tootsie's Treat, named after the great aunt of Bill, the original owner. He had been a second cousin of Mrs. Browne.

Bill had died suddenly from a heart attack while baking bread and had no family to whom to leave the establishment except for Elaine Browne, who, of course, had little interest in it.

It was a shame, but he'd never married or had children and was an only child.

His entire existence revolved around that bakery, and now that he was gone, it would never be the same again.

The Brownes had poorly managed the establishment, and eventually, people stopped going.

Since the Brownes didn't have much interest in running the place, they would only occasionally open it when vendors brought stuff to them to sell. They didn't even bother baking on their own premises anymore, despite having what looked to be a grand commercial kitchen. For someone like Cara or Isabel, this would be their dream property, all kitted out and ready to go.

Elaine would only bake a batch of cookies here and there, and Mr. Browne would make some rice pudding when he wasn't off playing tennis, but since Billy had died, they outsourced the baking, and the quality had declined as well. But as far as Cara was concerned, all this was a crying shame; outsourcing baking was only necessary if you didn't have an onsite facility and a baker to make products fresh, the way customers loved them, the aroma luring them in.

Tootsie's Treats had been known for its jelly doughnuts and the best pies.

Celebrities had previously been reported to stop by to test the array of pastries, but the best-selling item had always been the freshly made strawberry rhubarb pie.

Mr. Browne said he would like to restore their reputation for making these delights, but he also felt that the effort required was just too much for their age and stage of life.

Cara could accommodate both challenges, couldn't she? And she was raring to tell them so.

They already had a full working kitchen, and she had studied culinary arts as a profession.

Added to this, she had grown up baking alongside her mother in their small kitchen, so she knew how to manage in tight quarters, too, and with minimal staffing.

One thing about owning a business, especially in the food industry, was that if a person's heart weren't the driving force, then their wallet would never overflow enough to make it worthwhile, especially given the long and arduous hours and early morning starts.

Running a business like this was demanding, and the Brownes had already made their fortunes long ago in any case. At their age, they didn't have it to take on such a daunting task, but at the same time, they had an obligation to upkeep a crumbling old building.

Only because of that commitment had they bothered to keep the place going at all.

"Business has been slow," Mrs. Browne admitted. "We hope it will pick back up with some innovation and the resurrection of our most famous lines."

"I am certain I'm up for the task," said Cara confidently.

Mr. Browne's eyes narrowed. He hesitated momentarily, looking over at the young girls giggling and eating cookies. Exhaling, he said, "I'll tell you what. I'll let you run the shop if you can increase sales within the next six months. Take it on and give it a try."

He paused momentarily before looking straight at Cara.

She eyed him back, her face aglow, all the blood rushing to her head.

He carried on, "Otherwise, I will have no choice but to vacate the building for good. Elaine has been bugging me to do so for years, so if this doesn't work, it will be time to let it go."

"But will you sell me the building if I can raise your profits?" Cara's voice rose in hope.

"Unfortunately, I can't answer that. As we discussed, there is a bunch of red tape attached to the arrangement. The best we can do is—"

Mrs. Browne interrupted, "—we can see if our attorney can see a way."

Cara thought for a moment.

"I'll tell *you* what," she said confidently, emphasizing her words. "I will not only increase sales, but I commit to doubling them. In exchange, I will split the profit with you fifty-fifty."

"Seventy-thirty," countered Mr. Browne aggressively.

"Let's meet halfway at sixty-forty," Elaine said confidently, though her husband scowled.

"Deal," agreed Cara before Mr. Browne could argue against his wife's better proposition.

Cara had known men like Mr. Browne and was not intimidated to stand up for herself and get what she desired. Mrs. Browne stood by, her eyes twinkling, smiling at Cara's go-getting nature.

Cara felt her shoulders pull back as she watched Mr. Browne grin at her counteroffer. He also appreciated her tenacity and ability to speak her mind. Unlike most young women, she held herself with a particular eloquence and had an assertiveness that any businessman appreciated.

After an awkward moment and a standstill of negotiations, Elaine Browne, who stood beside him, was uneasy with the conversation's lull and quickly interrupted.

"Sounds fair to me. Isn't it, Jim? Let's give this young lady and her sweet daughter a chance. That way, we can finally enjoy our retirement. I've no doubt it's the best offer we'll get."

There was an urgency in her voice, as if a genie had suddenly emerged from a bottle and was about to disappear into the air, taking all her dreams with him.

She missed her grandchildren and wanted to spend her remaining years enjoying life rather than running a venture neither of them had ever wanted. Mr. Browne, however, wanted to ensure he was getting a good deal and wasn't quite as eager to relinquish control.

Mr. Browne glanced at his wife and then locked eyes with Cara, who was outwardly confident but inwardly panicked.

Cara could have sworn she noticed a satisfied twinkle in his eye.

"You heard the missus. I guess we have a deal. But I'll warn you, South Carolinians are not easy people to win over, especially if you're a Yankee.

"I am hardly a Yankee," Cara argued. "Maryland is still south of the Dixie line."

"Around here, that doesn't matter much. You are a Damn Yankee if you are not born and bred here. Only after twenty years we will drop the damn," said Jim.

"Now, now, Jim. Let's not intimidate the newest member of our community. That wouldn't be Christian of us. After all, it's Sunday, and we are in the Lord's house."

"Don't worry, Mrs. Browne. I can handle it. And I can't wait to show you and the rest of this town how amazing my treats will be. Anyway, I'm not worried," Cara added. "You do remember who my mother was!"

"There is no way I or anyone in this town could forget," Mr. Browne said and grinned.

Maggie, listening within earshot, was suddenly tired of the conversation.

"I'm hungry," she said flatly. "Can we go, Mama?"

"Sure thing, SugarBear. How about Eve's Café for lunch? They have the best grilled cheeses in town."

"Can we get ice cream afterward? It's so hot."

"Sure! Maybe tonight, we can watch a movie and bake cookies together."

"Yay!" Maggie squealed.

Cara was grateful she shared the same baking bond with her daughter as she had enjoyed with her mother. As a child, her favorite thing had been baking together.

As Isabel's specialty had always been the delights of Southern cuisine, she'd taught Cara how to bake the most beloved treats relished in the South. From apple tart to pecan and sweet potato pie, there was little Isabel couldn't bake, and Cara's favorite had been her mother's pecan pie.

The creamy filling and butter crust had crowds begging for seconds.

Walking out of the rectory doors, Cara sighed a breath of relief. She turned to bid farewell as Maggie smiled and waved, too.

Cara strutted away, calling back, "I'll see you tomorrow morning to get the keys so I can prepare everything and do a thorough clean-down." She ran her fingers through her hair. "I'm sorry we'll need to meet so early, though; I prefer to start work before dawn."

Cara didn't stay long enough to hear Mr. Browne chuckle.

He was clearly satisfied with the arrangement.

She held her excitement until the parish was far behind them.

Once she knew she was away from listening ears, she exhaled and screamed in delight.

"This is the chance I've been waiting for," she said as she rustled Maggie's hair. "Finally, a new start and something to look forward to."

She had spent the last few years grieving and feeling discouraged about life, praying for a break in the perpetual feeling of doom. It had finally happened on a sweltering summer morning at church. Driving back to the house, she couldn't help but smile.

Maggie noticed the excitement. "It's nice to see you happy, Mom. You seem different."

"I'm so thrilled, my sweet Maggie," she said, taking her daughter's hand. "I sense a shift, a new excitement." She glanced back at the church and continued, "This could change everything for us, SugarBear. I owe it to my mother to finish what she started."

"Mom, I think Granny had a complicated life here. Do you wonder why she left?"

"I think there's a lot we don't know about my mother." Distracted by a flock of birds, Cara stared momentarily before adding, "You know what, though? I have to let her life be hers and stop walking in her shadow. I have my own goals, which I wasn't even aware of how passionate I was about. But now, I feel energized and motivated."

She spoke in wonderment.

Maggie ignored this comment, not understanding the adults' thoughts as she watched the green landscape of their new hometown from the car window.

Once they arrived home, Maggie exited the car, grabbing Cara's hand.

The two began skipping along, singing, "Bake me a cake just as fast as you ..."

"Remember how we sang this when I was little?" added Maggie.

"I'll never forget it," said Cara.

She loved how Maggie could still be silly despite her age. It was one of her best attributes. She didn't take life seriously and could go with the flow.

When she'd been Maggie's age, she had always felt intense pressure.

Had it been because her mother was a single mom? Or did the worry in her mother's eye just give Cara an inadvertent fear of losing something?

Now, she saw that much of her mother's anxieties and striving to be the best had been based more on fear than desire. As talented as Isabel was, she had never cooked for joy.

Instead, it was to either prove people wrong or survive.

Cara worried that she, too, had gained that fear-based desire for success. She certainly didn't want to pass that trait along to Maggie. And from all appearances, she hadn't. Maggie was well-adjusted, curious, and easily satisfied.

She got that from David, for sure, since he was kind and patient and didn't demand much.

That evening, Cara sat alone on her porch, missing David and wanting badly to share her happy news. She kept hoping he would drive up their driveway, glad to be reunited with his family and excited for their fresh start in South Carolina.

As the days and weeks passed, Cara started losing hope.

She had left voicemail messages on his answering machine that he had yet to return. She hadn't heard from him in weeks, and when she did call him, her calls went directly to voicemail.

She missed him and wanted to save her marriage, but did he want the same? As much as it hurt her heart to admit it, she knew the answer.

CHAPTER TWENTY-FIVE

As promised, Cara showed up before dawn to get the key. She spent the next three weeks rearranging the bakery, putting on a fresh coat of paint, and exchanging drab gray tablecloths with a more stylish Southern blue pattern.

Looking around at the newly renovated space, she felt immense pride. The following day, she began preparing the dough for bread. From there, she whipped the cream and melted butter, starting her first batch of cupcakes.

By the end of the week, she was pleased with her efforts and proud of her accomplishments.

With still no sign from David, the project was occupying her mind, leaving her too exhausted by the day's end to worry about her marriage.

In the last phone call, he had said he needed space after another heated argument.

"You didn't even consult with me or consider my feelings," he'd said during their last call.

"David, I want this. I missed out because *you* got me pregnant." She screamed into the phone before stopping herself. "And I think you did it intentionally to stunt my career."

The line went silent as Cara immediately regretted her words, aware that her pregnancy had come as a surprise to him too, just the same as it had been to her. When she decided to give up going to Paris, David supported that decision. Secretly, she'd wished he'd push her to go, but when he didn't, she felt betrayed. Years later, the resentment from missing the opportunity exploded into hurtful words—words she didn't intend to say out loud or even mean.

But it was too late. Her accusations came at David as if from a firing squad.

"David. Wait, I'm sorry," she tried.

He said, defeated, "Cara, this is too much. I need space. You don't seem to realize that I've done nothing but love and support you for ages, but it doesn't come back to me in the same way. I can't be second fiddle to your mother's ghost, Cara. What you don't appreciate is that I've spent our entire marriage as your second most important adult. Your mother was always your main concern. I can't do it anymore. I'm sorry."

Cara cradled the phone in tears, angry at her thoughtless words. She fell into bed and pulled the covers tightly over her until she was deep in sleep.

Rarely did the Brownes check in on the bakery.

They trusted that Cara would run the business while they enjoyed their grandchildren in Arizona. But she would silently criticize the pair for being unappreciative of their family gifting the bakery to them. She fantasized about having complete control over the venue, sometimes even mapping out the decor in her head. It would have long lime green curtains hanging from the large windows, with light pink bows to hold back the material to let in sunlight.

The chairs would be antique white, and the tablecloths would be lace.

The serving dishes would be colorful yet classy, portraying assorted designs and colors both warm and welcoming. Cara would extend the lunch menu to include tea sandwiches and a variety of specialty drinks. During a phone call, Cara had suggested to the Brownes these minor changes to invoke more foot traffic, but they'd brushed it off.

"Nah, who would want to come in here for lunch? Let's stick to your delicious cakes, make money, and leave it well enough alone. Our family has run this bakery for decades, and I don't want to fix what isn't broken." Cara heard agitation in his voice and didn't want to push further.

"I'm taking a red eye from Arizona and will stop in first thing in the morning," said Mr. Browne, his voice now softer.

Although deflated, Cara responded, I'm looking forward to seeing y'all."

Cara knew Mr. Browne was misguided, but she had little say in the final decisions.

If the bank kept declining her loan, she would never have the opportunity to become his competitor and prove him wrong. She didn't mean to be deceitful, but the Brownes came from a lengthy line of bankers and had little interest in the bakery. She had to go three towns south to conceal her attempt to obtain borrowings, and even then, she suspected Mr. Browne knew of her efforts and thwarted them. She didn't expect him to be surprised but most likely relieved she would be staying to run his business and build its profits.

She had hoped that one day, they would recognize her hard work and allow her to take over. For now, she intended to work hard to make a name for herself, regardless of who owned it.

The next morning, she met Mr. Browne at the shop, proudly showing him what she'd done.

"I have to admit, I'm quite impressed, young lady. It turns out you are more like your mother than I thought. Dare I say, perhaps even better."

Cara blushed. "Well, have a slice of my blueberry pie before you decide. This is Isabel's recipe, but I added a secret ingredient to bring out its freshness."

Mr. Browne took a hefty forkful of pie and melted in its delicious tartness.

"If your treats are all this incredible, this shop will be a money-making machine in no time."

"Speaking of which," Cara said, hesitant, "We should work out clearer terms of agreement. I still want this place as my own. Have you spoken to your legal team about me buying it?"

Mr. Browne looked at her sympathetically.

"I have. And, believe me, I have no business owning a bakery, but there is still a clause that I'm not quite sure we can get around. I'll tell you what, you keep baking like this and start making a profit, and we can discuss a better payout that will make us both happy."

"I don't understand," Cara said defiantly. "Why is the agreement difficult to get around? I promise I will pay you a fair market price." She hesitated momentarily, then added, "How about ten thousand above market price?" Even though Cara had yet to secure a loan and couldn't pay for the sale, the words blurted from her mouth before she could think better of it.

"I do wish I could take you up on the offer, but my hands are tied. For whatever reason, Elaine's cousin clarified the terms before bequeathing Tootsie's Treats the property."

Before there could be further discussion, a young woman tapped on the glass door, eager to be the first customer.

"Good morning. We open in about five minutes."

"I know," said the young woman brightly. "With all the talk of Isabel's daughter being the new baker in town, it has made quite a stir. I figured you might need to hire help."

Her brown eyes widened as she pointed down the street.

They watched a line forming from over two blocks away.

"By the way, my name is Katie."

Cara squinted as her mouth widened; three dozen customers were waiting for her to open the door. "You're hired," said Cara and Mr. Browne in unison.

The bakery was bustling with customers the entire morning. Curious customers greeted Cara with big smiles and promised to be back to try new pastries. By the end of the day, there was only one slice of pecan pie left. Cara sat down, exhausted from the commotion. She took a deep breath and looked around in awe at the successful grand opening.

"That sure was somethin'," Katie said as she took a long swig of sweet tea. "I heard at church last Sunday that you were opening. Many people are excited for the new business and a place where Southern charm meets sophisticated treats."

"Well, I think everyone should be pleased," Cara said.

Katie went to the kitchen to start cleaning up before they closed for the day.

"Thanks for all of your help today, Ms. Katie. You sure did work hard."

"It was truly my pleasure," shouted Katie as she carried trays of dirty dishes to the kitchen.

Cara took the final piece of pie from the display and sat by the window.

She felt a sense of accomplishment for the first time in her career.

The only thing missing was David. She wished he were here to see the lines of people waiting to experience her baking; she missed him, wanting him to join her more than anything, but she hadn't heard from him since their last phone call.

Unexpected tears fell. She was interrupted by a smiling Maggie waving at the window. Wiping her tears away, she greeted her daughter with a welcoming embrace.

"Oh my gosh, Mom, everyone's talking about this place. I wish I could have missed school for the grand opening, but I had an algebra test this morning."

"You just worry about your grades, SugarBear," said Cara.

"Mom, you are incredible, truly," said Maggie, kissing a sweaty Cara on the cheek.

"Thank you, darling. Now you head on home and begin your homework. I'll prepare us some pork shoulder, fried green tomatoes, and okra for dinner tonight."

"The way Granny used to make it?" said Maggie.

"Of course," Cara smiled.

Cara worked day and night at the bakery, unable to keep up with the volume of customers. She took dozens of orders daily for everything from sliced rye bread to peach cobbler.

The morning crowd would gather fifteen minutes before opening to ensure they received coffee cakes, donuts, and pastries to start the day.

No matter how much she baked, Cara could not keep up with the demands.

This was a good problem to have. Despite her exhaustion, she was proud to have impacted the community in the same place where her mother had once resided and made waves during a time when women hadn't been afforded the same opportunities.

Cara was doing the same, but this time with less societal resistance.

As she locked up, she smiled, knowing her mother was looking down, celebrating her achievement.

"Mama," she said. "I owe this all to you. You taught me everything I know. I hope you are all right with me coming back to South Carolina. You tried to keep me away from here, but I'm safe now. I understand why you thought it was the right decision, but I gotta tell you, I wish you hadn't run away from the life you loved. I know now that a part of you died when we moved."

Cara stared up at the sky, hoping her mother was listening from afar. "We didn't have to leave, Mama. But I do appreciate you trying to protect me."

She listened to the night wind blowing and felt a sudden chill running through her bones. "I know you hear me, Mama. Watch over us. Pray David comes home soon."

Cara felt her words catch in her throat.

She missed her husband, and Maggie missed her father, often asking when he would join them, although Cara never said so. Maggie knew there was more to the story than David tying up loose ends in Maryland. It had been four years since they'd left. Though they spent summers together, David became defensive when it was time to commit to reuniting the family.

"I'm not Southern Bell's husband, Cara. I want our life here," he argued.

"Please, David, I want to live in South Carolina," Cara pleaded.

"You've made that abundantly clear," David snapped. "But I don't," he added.

Cara dropped the subject and didn't mention it again. Instead, she focused on the bakery and the time they spent together as a family. Though there was tension between the couple, they did their best to keep the family intact for the sake of their daughter. Truth be told, they were both miserable and exhausted by the emotional strain of the situation.

Cara and Maggie made the trip back to Maryland over the holidays.

They only had two days to spend together, about which David seemed resentful.

"You can always come home with us," Cara said softly.

"*This* is our home, Cara," snapped David. "We have a life here. I'm tired of seeing you chase dreams. Worse still, I'm even more tired of chasing your mother's dreams. You need to accept that she's gone and start living your life. The life you made with me. Or have you forgotten?"

Cara knew she was getting nowhere with David and dropped the subject. She wanted to enjoy their time together, not for herself but for Maggie.

Maggie appeared downstairs from a nap. She wiped the sleep from her eyes and smiled brightly at the sight of David, who lit up when he saw her.

"My goodness, how could you have grown up so quickly?"

Maggie wasted no time replying, "When are you coming home, Dad? I love South Carolina and can't wait to show you around. Mom and I have the house waiting for you to come."

David darted a look to Cara, who waited patiently for his reply.

"It's complicated, sweetheart. When your mother decided we should move, I wasn't ready to pack up. I still have some unresolved business to take care of here."

Maggie gave a concerned look. "Don't you miss us? We're a family and should be living together." David shifted uncomfortably as he stared out the window. "Truth is, Maggie, I've accepted a job here. The pay is great, and I'm really happy doing the work I do."

Cara felt the air leave her body.

How could he not have told her sooner? And how dare he tell his daughter in this coldhearted way before they had even discussed it together? Why was it the first time she was hearing all of this now? She felt her face flush as she took a long exhale.

David said, "It's only temporary work, sweetie. It's supposed to end within the year. Then I'll look for something closer."

"Closer?" Cara thought. He didn't say in South Carolina, only *closer*.

"Maggie, why don't you get ready for dinner? I think your father and I need to have a private conversation. I'll be up in a minute to fetch you for supper."

When Maggie was out of earshot, Cara felt her rage explode. "How fucking dare you drop this bomb on me in front of our daughter?"

Before Cara could continue, David's shoulders slipped. "Cara, I know I should have told you sooner. It happened so fast. It's only a temporary position, and then I'll look for another job."

"Closer? Isn't that what you said?" Cara felt her voice rise with every syllable.

"That's not what I meant, and you know it."

But the trouble was, she did not know it. Right now, she didn't understand him at all.

"What did you really mean, David? Is our marriage over?" Cara felt her breathing become heavier as David tried to take her in his arms.

"Don't do that. Don't you dare do that," cried Cara. As she briskly left the room, she called back, "We will be gone tomorrow, David. Then you can get on with the job you love so much here and with the life that doesn't have us in it." She slammed the door behind her, leaving David with his head lowered and hands helplessly shoved in his pockets.

Cara shuddered at the thought of the last time she had seen her husband. Still, she hadn't heard from him. She considered seeking legal counsel but buried herself in work and kept growing the business. Mr. Browne was pleased with the large profit margins and began sharing them with Cara fifty-fifty, even more than they had agreed.

Cara was grateful for being recognized for her hard work, but despite all that, she still regularly pressed Mr. Browne about buying him out altogether.

"I'm sorry. No can do," he said. "And even if I could, why would I? We are both profiting from this arrangement, and you have no liability as a business owner. It seems like a win-win situation to me." It seemed as if he was changing his mind about letting go of the business he'd said he didn't enjoy. The truth was, he only disliked it when he had to be at its helm.

Watching Cara run it and build it seemed to bring him pleasure these days.

She was sure he had even ceased trying to find out about the route to a sale.

Cara despised not having complete control but decided to leave well enough alone and focus on growing her brand. As it was, most of her time was spent at the bakery or tending to Maggie. At this point, she was raising her alone and needed to focus on her daughter as well as on the day-to-day bakery demands.

This only made her resent David more.

He could live and focus on his career with no other responsibilities.

On the other hand, Cara had a house to tend to, a business, and raised her daughter alone. Even so, she would become lonely at night, hoping David would somehow find his way back. As the months went on, then years later, Cara lost all hope for a reconciliation. She knew her marriage had already ended in all ways that mattered. The only thing left was to terminate their union legally.

David would visit with Maggie every few months, always careful to come when Cara was at work. She didn't know how to mend their broken relationship. After so long, she grew tired of waiting and accepted their marriage was over. She suspected he had found someone else, but he never told her so, and she never pressed for an answer.

It would have been too painful to know the truth anyway.

Her desire to validate her worth through success had cost her the one thing she held most sacred: her marriage. She would always regret taking David for granted and wished she could turn back time to make different choices. Like her mother, she had done what she thought was best for their family at the time, without considering the feelings of those she loved most and without asking. Perhaps that was why, after a while, she could forgive her mother for doing the same. She watched her mother make countless sacrifices to achieve her goals, and she, too, shared those relentless ambitions. It was not lost on Cara that this was a double-edged sword for which women are often harshly judged.

Cara was not surprised to receive divorce papers in the mail the following year. She had not expected, though she did hope, that one day, David would be willing to give her another chance. She begged him to reconsider, but he knew better than to think she had the ability to change. "You are your mother's daughter, after all," he said before hanging up the phone.

As Maggie walked into the house, Cara put away the paper and wiped the last tear from her eye that she would shed on David. Maggie looked at her, her eyes showing pain.

"Dad called and let me know. I kinda saw it coming, but I'm still sad," she said as she poured herself sweet tea and grabbed a handful of pretzels.

"Me too," said Cara, snatching a handful of pretzels too. "He said you two grew apart. I think Dad couldn't handle a woman with big dreams who wasn't afraid to catch them."

Cara had never considered that.

She assumed it was her fault that their marriage had failed because she wanted too much out of life. Cara had blamed herself for the failure, never considering that perhaps the issues in their marriage were more deeply rooted.

Maggie was wiser than her tender age and made no apologies for seeking autonomy and success. "That's why I'm never getting married," declared Maggie. "It requires way too much sacrifice for a woman. Meanwhile, men don't have to follow the same rules."

Cara looked at her daughter curiously.

This young woman was independent and already had strong opinions.

Maggie continued, "Look at Dad. He didn't feel bad for staying behind in Maryland for his work. But he wanted to stifle your career to adapt to his needs."

Maggie's words hit Cara like a truckload of bricks.

Her daughter was right. She had spent months beating herself up for wanting to make her dream come true. She wanted this career more than anything and was tired of apologizing for it.

Cara hugged her daughter. "I'm sorry about your father. More so, I'm sorry for always being sorry. I want this, Maggie. I really want this life."

"Well, then, you're getting it, Mom. All on your own," she added. The two cried, laughed, and hugged before settling down for the evening as they sat on the porch watching the sunset.

CHAPTER TWENTY-SIX

EVEN LESS THAN IN previous years, the Brownes seldom visited the bakery. They trusted that Cara had everything under control and happily accepted their share of the profits in exchange for Cara making all business decisions. On the rare occasion that he visited, the owner still insisted on being called Mr. Browne.

"Now don't go around calling your elders by their first name," Mr. Browne lectured. He was a warm man but had clear expectations.

On the other hand, Elaine continued to treat Cara and Maggie like family and would be welcoming and warm whenever they visited.

"Please, I'm Elaine to you. I was never one for formalities. I don't know why Jim is such a stickler about those sorts of things. But pay no mind. He's just set in his ways and was raised in a strict environment. He still makes our grown children say their prayers when we visit! It drives our two sons crazy how controlling he can be, but at his age, they respect his ways, I guess."

Mr. Browne, twelve years Elaine's senior, had different expectations than she did.

Her voice trailed off as she looked out the window, distracted by the trees blowing the leaves off their limbs. Cara interrupted, "Have you tried my new twist on chocolate chip cookies?"

"No, dear. Not yet. But I hear it sells out before noon."

It was shaped like a pizza and drizzled with fudge.

Elaine took a big bite and rolled her eyes in delight. "This is spectacular. Sweetie, you really have a talent."

Cara gushed at the compliments. "Thank you so much. This is truly my passion. I can't imagine doing anything else with my life."

Elaine became pensive as she listened to Cara discuss her plans to take ownership of the bakery. "I promise I will make you proud. It would mean so much to me to have this business. I have such a connection to it."

"I would love for Jim to sell the business so we can be closer to our kids permanently."

Elaine lowered her head, hiding the small tear forming. She was short in stature and had ash-blonde hair that could be mistaken for gray. Her eyes showed signs of aging, but her bright blue eyes, hidden under red-rimmed glasses, made her appear more stylish than she intended.

"Mrs. Browne, I mean Elaine, do you think you could talk with Mr. Browne about this? You know it means such a lot to me, and I feel as if all hopes are fading away."

"Honey, believe me, I've tried. I'll tell you a secret, though; he does want to sell it to you. He said something about how it's morally yours anyway."

"What does that mean?" asked Cara.

"He wouldn't say. He quickly changed the subject."

Mr. Browne appeared moments later before Cara could inquire more about it.

Noticing the tension in the room, he said, "C'mon, dear, let me get you back to those grandkids." The pair hurried away, and Cara watched as Mr. Browne appeared agitated with Elaine once they were out of earshot.

Later that night, Cara couldn't stop thinking about her conversation with Elaine. It was peculiar how Mr. Browne felt she was the rightful owner if that was true.

The conversation was peculiar, though Cara couldn't quite put her finger on why. She brushed off the statement as though he admired all her hard work, although her gut was telling her otherwise. Cara had learned from her experience with her mother's secret that she should trust her instincts more often. However, she had no proof that Mrs. Browne misspoke when she indicated the property was "morally hers." Perhaps she felt that way because of the long hours and effort she had contributed without legal ownership.

Cara returned to work, beating the egg for her brownies.

The phone rang three times before she realized it, and she raced to answer it with anticipation. As she listened, she continued with the clattering of the whisk nervously hitting the side of the large yellow bowl. Cara had always loved that bowl.

As she leaned the whisk against the outside of the bowl, she wiped her hands on her pink apron.

Cara was pacing the linoleum tile now. "I see. Is there anything we can do?' Her voice was shaky as she looked up at the ceiling, searching for answers,

"I understand, she said softly. Her eyes furrowed as she exhaled a long, deep breath.

The disappointment of another bank loan rejection made her lose hope.

She knew that, given the opportunity, her bakery would be successful, but the feeling of rejection was palpable everywhere she turned. As she hung up the phone, Cara noticed Maggie leaning against the refrigerator, eyeing the counter with the dripping batter.

"Ahh, there is my baby girl," Cara said excitedly.

"Did Mrs. Browne talk to you?" asked Maggie. "I asked her to beg Mr. Browne to sell you the bakery." Maggie was well-intentioned but misguided.

Cara gasped in embarrassment.

"At least they should give you a raise because of all the customers you bring in."

"Now, Maggie," Cara said sternly, "I already warned you about talking to Mrs. Browne about her business."

Maggie lowered her head for just a moment. Her teenage boldness was well-intentioned, but there was still a line of respect that was not crossed when speaking to their elders.

She then raised it again, this time more confidently. "Mom, you've taught me to be assertive. So, why aren't you assertive about this, of all things?"

Cara was surprised by Maggie's display of rebellion.

She almost corrected her daughter's tone but realized she was right.

What was it about the Brownes that made her uncomfortable? Perhaps it was the feeling that they knew something about her mother that she didn't. Or maybe it was because they were an older couple from the South who felt the need to show respect. Either way, Maggie was right. She needed to do what her mother had taught her: get what she wanted at all costs.

Chapter Twenty-Seven

WHEN THE HOUSE WAS quiet in the evenings, Cara sat on the porch, gazing up at the night sky. Only then would she release her worries and despair into the stillness of the night. Like most mothers, the weight of insecurity and grief often lay hidden beneath the hard exterior of a mother's shoulders. Once alone, in the safe space to reveal her vulnerabilities, Cara allowed herself to feel the emotions she had kept hidden throughout the day. "Mama," she would whisper late into the night air. "If you can hear me, help me get that loan. Help make our dreams come true."

When silence surrounded her, she cursed the dark sky, taking a long breath before bowing her head between her legs, letting out wild sobs into her hand.

"Why is this happening, Lord? Have I not been through enough?"

As the night air offered no explanations, Cara crept back into the house, passing her daughter's bedroom, and peered into the doorway to find Maggie fast asleep. She watched for a moment as her daughter lay in peaceful slumber. It wouldn't be long before Maggie would head off to college, chasing her own dreams. Cara wished to hold onto these moments for as long as she could. Time was slipping away, and a wave of sadness washed over Cara.

"Goodnight, SugarBear. I love you so very much."

Since obtaining a loan seemed impossible, Cara spent several more years serving the community, even extending her efforts to North Carolina and Georgia for special events. She was featured in local newspapers and enjoyed a comfortable yet quiet life with Maggie.

As many times as she considered leaving Mr. Browne's shop to open her own, many obstacles stood in her way. The bakery was in the hottest spot in town, had plentiful parking, and was in the oldest section of the popular town.

It was an ideal spot, and the threat of losing her customers wasn't a risk worth taking. She would be a darn fool to leave the place she loved and start anew.

After a while, Cara grew tired of convincing Mr. Browne to sell to her. She was making enough money to sustain a comfortable lifestyle and provide for herself and Maggie.

The strain of kitchen work began to wear on Cara too.

Her body began to ache, and she slowed down as she became more fatigued. She couldn't put her finger on it, but something felt off. She was having trouble sleeping, and her body was weak.

"Mom, you really need to see the doctor," Maggie pleaded one night after dinner.

Cara had barely eaten anything and could hardly stay awake past the evening hours.

"I will as soon as the holidays are over," promised Cara. "I have more orders than I know what to do with, and I don't want to disappoint our loyal customers.

"Mom, I mean it. Right after the holidays, you must make an appointment and figure out what's happening."

"I promise, SugarBear," said Cara as she softly kissed her daughter's forehead.

Cara went to bed that night with a bad feeling. That night, she prayed for the first time in years.

"Mama, if you can hear me, please let me be okay. Watch over me and Maggie."

Within minutes, she fell asleep, exhausted from the day's work.

She dreamt of her mother for the first time since she'd passed. She was beautiful even in the afterlife. Isabel tried to tell her something, but Cara couldn't hear.

She saw Isabel's mouth move in her dream but couldn't understand. Just as Isabel was coming close to whisper in her ear, a loud crack of thunder awoke her, followed by heavy rain crashing in on the windows. Cara sat upright, sweat dripping down her head.

Her voice called out for her mother as she searched the room's darkness. It had been a dream. Startled, she entered the kitchen to make herself a cup of tea. She sat on the couch, noticing the large raindrops making puddles in the driveway. She looked around, seeing how much history she had here, this home being where she felt happiest. Despite her unnerving feelings, she felt a warm sense of peace come over her, knowing she was living the life she had imagined, even despite not opening her own bakery. She had put the dream of her bakery to rest, knowing she was making a significant impact in the community by running the Browne's spot.

Chapter Twenty-Eight

It was weeks before her next doctor's appointment, and Cara was becoming discouraged by her lack of energy.

Her health wasn't improving, and she was starting to feel pain in her shoulder. She recalled her mother, remembering when she, too, had similar complaints. Even before receiving the results, Cara suspected a breast cancer diagnosis.

Her mother had battled the vicious disease for years, and she was aware of the genetic risk.

"I'm sorry to give you this news," said her oncologist as she left the room.

Cara sat breathless for a few moments before deciding what to do next. She settled on taking a walk by the river and watching the birds frolicking in a puddle, carelessly splashing about.

She thought about how far treatments had advanced but still not enough to save her life. Since her mother's diagnosis, there had been much advancement in treating the disease, but still, her prognosis was daunting. It had been caught early enough to treat her but was sadly advanced enough that she would need to shut down the bakery while she recovered. She contemplated not telling anyone her prognosis but, in the end, chose to tell Mr. Browne her predicament.

The phone call to the Brownes was not easy. When she explained her situation, she could have sworn she heard Mr. Browne gasp.

"Oh honey, this is terrible news," he said.

He suggested hiring a new baker temporarily, but Cara insisted on maintaining the integrity of her work to meet the community's expected standards.

"Please do what you need to do, sweetheart," added Mrs. Browne. We will help in any way we can." Two days later, the Brownes flew back from Arizona to visit Cara. She was touched by their efforts and thanked them warmly.

Cara took some time off, and the bakery reduced its hours. Since the Brownes didn't depend on the income and Cara had saved a considerable amount, she was able to manage.

Additionally, to ease the burden, the Brownes generously provided a severance until she was well enough to return to work, and they also promised to assist with any further financial plans.

"I feel like we're family," gushed Elaine. Mr. Browne, stoic, looked on, unable to speak but patting her hand before leaving the hospital room.

In the meantime, Maggie helped a lot and showed interest in following in the footsteps of her mother and grandmother. It was the first time Cara noticed how much Maggie knew about baking. She listened intently as Mr. Browne explained the business side to her. Although the situation was stressful, Cara observed Maggie's enthusiasm grow from spending time learning the business from Mr. Browne. It was a good distraction for both Maggie and Cara. Before she could thank Mr. Browne for his time with Maggie, he raised a hand, gave her a wink, and blew her a kiss before leaving.

While Cara received treatments, an outpouring of love touched her. People volunteered shifts to help with cleaning and bringing food.

The community loved Cara and showed enormous empathy while she recovered. Melissa, Hailey, Kate, and Maggie all worked part-time to keep the bakery running, even if it was open part-time.

It wasn't the same quality, but it helped keep the doors temporarily open. Since the tight-knit community knew why Cara wasn't working, they made a special effort to always give the bakery five-star reviews and send referrals their way. They also ordered sweet treats for birthdays and holidays. It felt as though, secretly, the entire community willed Cara on, buying there as frequently as they could and always asking after Cara's welfare.

During that time, Maggie continued to learn about business and recipes and showed great prospects in her own right. By the time Cara was ready to return, Maggie had gained a lot of experience and knowledge, and she was determined to pursue the career of the woman who had come before her.

Within six months, Cara returned to work full-time, and the community threw a welcome-back party. The town united to wish her health and happiness, and business flourished even more.

For years, Cara was content with life and proud that she was pursuing her dream with the help of those who loved her most.

246

CHAPTER TWENTY-NINE

TWO DECADES EVAPORATED AS time often does. Cara settled back into the bakery, this time returning to an empty home after a long day. Maggie had moved out and started her career in hotel management in Charleston. By now, the city had become popular with tourists seeking the convenience of modern vacations blended with Southern charm.

When Cara received the call of Mr. Browne's passing at the ripe old age of ninety-six, she was saddened though grateful for all the years and the wisdom bestowed upon her.

Despite her efforts after Mr. Browne's passing, Cara could never obtain the rights to the property. As a result, she was ultimately forced out of Tootsie's Treats, leaving the building vacant. This broke her heart and the hearts of the entire community, but Cara was too exhausted to continue fighting.

By now, she herself was older, and ownership didn't seem quite as important. She had given up by that time but was grateful to have served her community for so long.

Cara's gray hair was loosely in a bun, and she continued to bake part-time at a local restaurant since she had no legal right to the property, and she had witnessed it being shut down in probate.

After spending thousands of dollars fighting probate court, Cara gave up under the advice of her lawyer, George Stalin. "Whoever Mr. Browne inherited the property from, they wanted to stay anonymous, and it will take years to uncover the mystery."

Cara shook her head in disappointment.

George added, "Not to mention the money it would take to buy it out would be enormous. Especially with the interest rates through the roof. My humble advice is to work part-time for someone else and enjoy your retirement, Ms. Loring."

Cara was close to retirement age, though she hadn't considered it possible.

She still enjoyed preparing the goods each day, though her arthritic fingers would give her trouble now and again. When she looked back on her life, she regretted two things most.

First was the failure of her marriage.

David, by now, was older, and the animosity between the two had dissipated. Once again, they grew a friendship and admiration for one another.

On his last visit, he'd stopped by to bring a beautiful bouquet of daisies.

"It is always a pleasure to see you," he said, handing off the bouquet. "I just had lunch with Maggie and thought I would stop by to say hello."

Cara noticed how his hair had thinned, though he still had the most genuine smile. "I'm glad you did. Would you like to sit on the porch with me and have some sweet tea?"

Without hesitation, he responded, "That would be great."

Of course, Cara wished things had worked out differently. Sitting with him now felt right. Cara was tired from the day, and David noticed for the first time how frail she had become.

"I will always love you. Our marriage didn't work out, but it was for the best. I would have held you back if I'd been in the picture. I'm proud of you," he said.

Initially, Cara didn't reply but took his hand and gently placed it against her face.

"Look, David, I want to apologize for what I said all those years ago. I don't blame you—" David held his hand in interruption. "At our age, Cara, it's too late for regrets. I'm happy to be here now with you, and I'm glad we're at a place where we can appreciate the now."

Cara looked out to the yard, noticing a cardinal eating from the bird feeder.

"That brings me to the next thing," Cara said slowly. "The cancer is back. This time, it's more advanced. I haven't told Maggie yet, but I wanted you to know first."

David looked a long time into his ex-wife's eyes. A spark initiated as it had done decades prior. "I'm the first person you told?" he asked.

"Why yes, I couldn't think of anyone else I wanted to share the worst news of my life with," Cara said with a chuckle.

David took her hand and held it close. He kissed her cheek as he brushed her brittle hair from her face. "I have always loved you, Caralyn Loring. "You, my dear, are more tenacious than your mother. I am proud of all you accomplished." He put his arms around her fragile body.

The two held one another as they had done many moons ago.

It felt good to have closure with David. When he left, she waved goodbye, knowing this would be the last she would see of her first and last love.

PART III

Crisp Chocolate Chip bars

Ingredients

- 1 cup butter
- 1 cup granulated white sugar
- 1 teaspoon vanilla
- 2 cups all purpose flour
- 1 teaspoon salt
- 1 cup mini chocolate chips

Directions

Preheat oven to 350 degrees. Cream butter, white sugar, and vanilla until creamy and well blended.

Stir in flour and salt into the creamed mixture until just blended. Stir in mini chocolate chips.

Press mixture into lightly greased 15 1/2" X 10" sheet pan.

Bake for 25 minutes. Cut into squares

Recipe provided by Peggy Kolbas,
Summers Corner, Summerville, S.C.

CHAPTER THIRTY

MAGGIE ADORED THE AUTUMN weather in South Carolina. It was warm enough to savor the outdoors yet cool enough for the pesky mosquitoes to be gone. The air had turned cooler, and the fall breeze flowed through the house, causing the curtains to sway.

Something about the fall heat reminded her of the long hours spent baking with her mother.

Autumn always reminded Maggie of Cara, who passed away peacefully on a cool October day. Her absence often left Maggie breathless.

She'd cherished her time caring for Cara, and though her mom had battled cancer in the past, they had both known this time she would succumb to the disease.

Maggie was thankful she hadn't endured much and was grateful to have spent the years caring for the mother who had spent years caring for her. Though death is never easy, Maggie was comforted that her mother was at peace. Cara's battle had been long and hard.

During the long nights spent with her mother, listening to her cries of pain, Maggie had desired nothing more than for her mother to finally find peace.

There'd been far too many nights of agony Maggie had to watch, so when the time came that Cara was actively dying, Maggie felt relief.

Cara was fortunate to have lived most of her life cancer-free. However, her body had become too old and weak to continue to fight once the cancer spread. Perhaps after years of watching her fight it, Maggie had time to process that the end was inescapable.

When it happened, Maggie was at peace, knowing her mother was no longer suffering.

At first, she rejected the idea of moving back to Cradle Street but soon realized that being close to where they once lived helped to heal the void of her mother.

It had been three years since Maggie had decided to move back into her mother's house.

She had spent Cara's last years caring for her and had grown accustomed to the solitude that the house always provided. While living in Charleston, she hadn't realized how much she missed the quiet of the country and small-town charm.

———

Maggie kept the bakery keys hanging where her mother had left them in the foyer.

Staring at them from the kitchen, she smiled softly.

Her mother was all around her, bringing a sense of peace.

Maggie leaned against the counter, staring at the yellow mixing bowl filled with many stories. She missed how her mother's hair fell on her face and how her nose wrinkled when she was experimenting with different spices. Her curly hair brushed across her face as she looked up at her mother, who was concentrating on the flour measurements.

The home had always smelled sweet, even when Cara was not baking. It had been decades since Maggie was barely tall enough to reach the table to help. Memories of her youth were still etched in her mind, memories she would forever cherish.

Maggie walked to the porch and nuzzled up on the old yellow rocking chair, wrapping her mother's soft blanket around her shoulders. The air was getting cooler now.

Maggie leaned back in her rocking chair, remembering days gone by. It felt like only a moment ago that she had been a wide-eyed child looking to her mother for comfort.

"Mama, is it time to add the chocolate chips?" Maggie said sweetly.

"Not yet, SugarBear. I want to perfect this recipe once and for all. There's a good chance mine will be featured in the county's newsletter this summer."

"Why do you always call me SugarBear?" Maggie said, giggling.

"It reminds me of my mama. She taught me everything I know. To this day, I want to make her proud."

"Do I make you proud?" asked Maggie.

Cara scooped up Maggie, snuggling her soft skin against her cheek. "Every day, sugar. Mamas and daughters have a special bond."

When she was finally released from her mother's embrace, Maggie sat back down happily and slowly gathered the extra chocolate chips into her hand.

Hoping her mother wouldn't notice, she began sneaking chocolate chips into her mouth. One by one, she placed the morsels on her tongue until she heard Isabel scold, "I see you!"

Her mother smiled. "I think that's enough, or your belly will hurt."

"Just one more," pleaded Maggie, who already had three more in her mouth.

Maggie closed her eyes, absorbing that memory into her soul.

Now, she glanced across the yard, holding back tears. Maggie thought of that day fondly. Cara had taught Maggie what Isabel had taught Cara. Somehow, Maggie felt the presence of both Cara and Isabel in the same kitchen where they once had both baked.

Although Maggie could have continued her work in Charleston, there was something magical about this small town. There was so much history, and she felt an enormous connection to the women who had come before. For one thing, she was touched by how much Cara's passing saddened customers. For months, people would pay tribute out front to the baker who had changed the landscape of their small town. There were flower arrangements in the shape of cupcakes, balloons, and kind notes that Maggie took home and read at night.

Cara had helped shape this town from being a rural part of South Carolina to an up-and-coming spot for tourists and locals alike to gather.

Since managing Tootsie's Treats, other businesses had popped up, making the once-small town a bustling area. She had been there for happy occasions, providing birthday cakes and a bakery for sad events, where people would gather with a cup of coffee and a pastry to grieve.

Maggie hadn't forgotten her mother's dream of opening a bakery. She remained determined to find a way to open the bakery in town. At first, Maggie was hesitant, but the more she considered it, the more appealing the prospect became. Maggie began researching properties, knowing there had to be someone with answers.

After making numerous phone calls, she finally called in a favor from a friend who was a prominent real estate agent. With her mother's close ties to the establishment and strong relationship with the Brownes, she had an advantage.

After pulling strings, he arranged for Maggie to reopen the shop and pay a hefty rent until they could determine who the rightful owner was and how to secure a lease.

Apparently, the papers filed long ago had gone missing, and the current owner was a mystery. This had been the problem all along.

Maggie was confused by this information because her mother had always lamented the Browne's claim to the property. However, this new revelation gave Maggie hope that she would eventually have the opportunity to claim a stake in it. She had already been preapproved for a loan and had handsome savings in investments that she could use to purchase the property. However, first, she needed to figure out who the owner actually was, if not the Brownes.

In the meantime, Maggie rented the space, renovated the shop, and added items to the menu.

She understood that it was crucial to keep pace with evolving customer needs. Specialty coffees and gluten-free products were in high demand, and Maggie was knowledgeable about the latest trends. Although the rent was higher than she preferred, Maggie could cover the cost with her savings and the inheritance from Cara.

She was busy taking inventory when she noticed a short, plump woman sitting by the window enjoying a coffee and raspberry tart. When Maggie noticed tears streaming from her eyes, she approached, gently saying, "Good morning. I just wanted to see if I could get you anything else."

The woman's green eyes grew big. "You must be Maggie," she said as her voice cracked. "You look so much like your mother."

Maggie smiled, gesturing that she was welcome to sit down.

"Of course," said the lady, visibly shaken. "I'm Jane. Your mother was so kind to me. When my son passed away many years ago, I couldn't stay in my house because the memories were too difficult. I would walk miles by the marsh just to avoid being home alone. I always found myself enjoying a sweet treat and refreshing lemonade hereafter. Your mom made it fresh, and the tartness gave me a jolt of energy."

"That is kind of you. My mom loved how much her customers confided in her. She cared about the people in this town."

"She did more than that. She would sit with me long after closing and listen to stories about my boy Frankie. I could tell she was exhausted from the day, but she never told me it was time to go. She would listen until I was finished and sneak a cookie into my hand to have in the evening. I will never forget her kindness."

Maggie placed her hands on her heart. "Nor will I."

She came to learn more about her mother after her passing than she had done during her life.

The years without Cara had been filled with so much grief that the only respite Maggie had was in the kitchen, baking. The feel of the dough pressing against her hands as she kneaded it into the shape of a loaf of bread or pie helped Maggie stay focused on something other than her heartbreak. When she was done with the dough and the bread was baking in the oven, Maggie would sit at the table, taking in the sweet smell of whatever treat illuminated the oven door.

She was grateful that her mother had shared her passion for baking with her, and even now, as an adult, she wanted to make her proud.

Maggie understood that she came from an extensive line of strong women.

Even her grandmother Isabel had been known for saying, "Baking is in our blood, sweetheart. It is who we are." Maggie fantasized about life, having both her mother and grandmother around to absorb the magnitude of their efforts.

She still had so many unanswered questions for the pair.

Understanding the struggles faced by those described as feisty, independent women, she wondered what stories they would share with her now. She wanted to learn more about leaving South Carolina and why they had chosen Maryland. Maggie did remember asking Cara why she had moved away from South Carolina. At the time, Cara had said she didn't know.

Later, she admitted, "Moving back here was the best decision I made. I was angry for a long time about our move to Maryland. After some time, though, I knew I had to let it go. Honestly, if it hadn't been for that move, I don't know if I'd have taken such an interest in baking. I was bored and lonely, so I watched my mother create new recipes. As lonely as I was back then, it also helped me realize I wanted to follow in her footsteps."

Maggie was frustrated now, not asking more questions about it.

At the time, Cara had mentioned it casually, but Maggie didn't see it as significant. Now, Maggie walked in her mother's footsteps, not out of loneliness or a need to prove herself.

She loved the business end of baking as much as she enjoyed baking itself.

She had recently received her master's degree in business and planned to open a franchise of bakeries across South Carolina. However, now that Tootsie's Treats was rentable, Maggie reconsidered her plan. She wanted to wait to find out about the establishment's owner and continue her mother's fight to eventually buy it as her own.

The call came in as the sun set while Maggie sat on the porch writing a business proposal. On the other end was Nathan. She hadn't spoken to him since Cara's passing.

When she'd passed away, Nathan had been the first to call Maggie and offer his condolences.

She could tell by his voice that he had been crying.

The only thing he could mutter was, "Oh, Maggie. I am so sorry. I will miss her."

"Me too," said Maggie, holding back tears.

"I'm really glad your mother reconciled with me and my pops before she passed away. They actually spent a lot of time together toward the end." Nathan's voice cracked before he continued, "Did you know she even came here several times to visit right before Pops died? We had dinner and everything. She told me the past was the past."

"I'm glad, Nathan. I never got the full story out of her about the fallout between them."

"Will you come and visit me? I would really love to see you," pleaded Nathan.

Without hesitation, Maggie said, "I would love to. My mother has a storage unit I need to empty. She must have forgotten about a pile of unpaid bills for the unit. I need to go there to clean it out. When I come to Maryland, I'll be sure to settle those unpaid debts as well."

Chapter Thirty-One

Two weeks later, Maggie was returning to Maryland. When she arrived at his grocery shop, which was now massive, she was taken aback by how much had changed,

As she walked in, Maggie smelled the bold aroma of coffee.

Her taste buds soared as she approached the chocolate display, and her eyes lit up at the various chocolate selections. Maggie would have difficulty deciding between creamy caramel, pecan-infused fillings, and unlimited truffle flavors.

"There she is!" called out Nathan, who appeared shorter than Maggie had remembered.

His glasses hung off his nose as his gray hair receded past his forehead.

"Nathan Hanover! Hello! I was hoping you'd still be here so late in the day," Maggie said, leaning into his arms that were wide open.

"Well, I don't go far now, nowadays. You will usually find me here stocking shelves or making a fresh pot of coffee."

"It smells amazing in here," said Maggie.

"Well, you can choose whatever you want—we have a delicious new pistachio-flavored chocolate, and it's on the house."

Maggie smiled warmly, knowing that it was indeed his pleasure.

Before Maggie could protest, Nathan interrupted, "And don't give me no lip about it. It's the least I can do. Our family goes way back from your grandmother and my father, God rest their souls." Maggie saw a flash of sadness rush through his eyes.

"I'm sorry about your dad," she said.

Nathan took a breath. "Me too," he said with a sigh. "So, how are you making out? I know these last months have been tough with, well …" His voice trailed off.

Maggie looked down at her feet, noticing she needed new sneakers, and in an attempt to focus on anything other than the tears forming.

"Yeah. The dreaded last step," she said, inhaling deeply. "Clearing out my mom's storage unit. It's strange that she rented a storage space when she moved from Maryland."

"Maybe she thought she and your dad would reconcile, and he would bring down the rest of her stuff when he came."

I guess," said Maggie. "I didn't even know about it until a bill came in the mail about three months ago. I've only now been able to get here to empty the contents. I asked my father about it, but he has no recollection of it, only saying that my mother was always spontaneous."

"Listen, kiddo, I can help you."

"No," Maggie said more firmly than intended. She caught herself and softened her voice. "It's something I have to do on my own. But thank you."

"I understand. But if you need anything, you know where to find me."

"Thank you," Maggie said as she chose three flavors of chocolates she had never tried: one pistachio, as recommended; a caramel nut; and a nougat-filled truffle. She gathered her extra-large mocha latte and bag of treats before heading toward the door.

Nathan came around the counter, embracing her with a tight squeeze.

"Both you and your mother will always hold a special place in my heart."

"I know," Maggie said, giving a soft smile.

As Maggie released his embrace, Nathan looked at her, saying, "Your mother was so proud of you, Maggie. She would brag to anyone who would listen about how you would open your bakery someday. Don't give up on your dream, sweetie. She never did."

Maggie embraced Nathan one last time and briskly left to the warm sun.

Once outside, she took a deep breath, and her heart hurt. Realizing this trip would be more emotional than anticipated, she asked God for some grace.

"Lord, today is a grueling day. Grant me the strength to do right by Mama one last time."

She headed back down the block and slowly entered the large storage unit two blocks from her grandmother's old place. She couldn't help but walk past the old building.

She remembered visiting as a child, watching her mother and grandmother bake and bicker for hours. Her mind raced with memories of the old brick building. It was on the corner of an intersection. The sidewalk was lined with trees, and large, colorful plants hung from the lampposts. It was a welcoming neighborhood.

She smiled up at the window where her grandmother had once displayed a bird feeder.

She continued down the block toward the storage unit lined with numbers displaying the units. Before entering storage number 628, Maggie sat on the stoop.

She sipped her latte, which had finally cooled down enough for consumption.

She couldn't remember the last time she had slept through the night or the last time she'd been a day without feeling the void. "When will the pain go away?" she wondered. "Maybe never. Maybe grieving is the price of loving." After a few more minutes, she gathered the strength to walk through the doors and finish the final steps of her mother's life.

———

Maggie was relieved that the donation company had already removed most of the furniture from the unit. She had arranged weeks prior for them to dispose of some of the larger items.

The last items that needed sorting were Cara's personal things.

This was it—the final farewell of Caralyn Loring.

Sorting through her belongings felt like a betrayal. Maggie felt as if she was gaining an intimate view of her mother's personal life, one she had known very little about. Even though it had been decades since she had touched these items, Maggie sensed her mother all around.

She was feeling a pull toward her mother's old life, wanting to hold onto any last piece.

Maggie again brushed her hands over a box of random clothing items.

"Ahh, Mama, I miss you. I wish we could have opened that shop the way we spent so many nights dreaming about it." Maggie was wiping away her tears as she spoke aloud to her mother's belongings, hoping her mama was listening somehow. "You taught me everything I know. One day, the world will know your recipes and enjoy the amazing treats you taught me to bake." The tears flowed down Maggie's cheeks as she caressed an old photo of her parents' wedding day.

This was more difficult than she'd thought.

She opened the door to the storage unit to get some air. It was stifling in the small space.

On her way out, she grabbed a tissue from her pocket and dried her wet cheeks as a bird fluttered by a nearby tree. Maggie stood still, watching as the bird stared back.

Moments later, the small bird took flight as Maggie smiled. She knew her mother was watching over her, ensuring that all was well from beyond. She went back inside with a renewed sense of peace.

Chapter Thirty-Two

Maggie sifted through papers in the small chest hidden in the back of the storage unit, noticing a metal box beneath a pile of documents. She hadn't realized it was there, and it only caught her attention as she was about to move on to another section of the unit. Maggie opened the silver box and quickly thumbed through the papers inside until she reached the bottom.

There, she found a large manila envelope with Cara's name on it.

Maggie opened the envelope, careful not to rip the brittle papers. Inside was a note from Isabel to Cara, which appeared to have never been opened.

She studied the note for a moment, wondering why her mother had never opened the envelope. The writing on it said "URGENT" in block letters.

Memories came rushing back to the last time Nathan had visited their home in Maryland before they'd left for South Carolina. Maggie remembered how Nathan had come to the door nervously, asking to see Cara, but she'd refused. Since Cara wouldn't see him, he gave the envelope to Maggie, saying. "My father gave me strict instructions that Cara receive this. He told me it was especially important and was sent to him long ago." Nathan's eyes looked desperate. "Please, Maggie," he urged. "Make sure your mother gets this."

Cara listened to Nathan's pleas. "Tell her that her father was a good man. He made some mistakes, for sure, but in the end, he came through and kept his word."

Once Nathan left, Maggie ran to the kitchen to tell Cara what he had said.

Cara stood there, arms folded. "I heard the entire conversation. I have no interest in anything that man has to say to me. The nerve of him sending Nathan here to deliver some ridiculous note," Cara scoffed. "You can throw it with the pile of papers in my lockbox."

"But Mom, aren't you at least curious what's inside?" asked Maggie.

"Not one bit. It's probably love notes that he sent to my mother or maybe even something from my father. Either way, everyone lied to me."

Years later, when Nathan and Cara reunited, he asked what was in the envelope he had delivered years prior. Embarrassed, Cara admitted she'd never opened it, and when asked where it had gone, she wasn't quite sure. "Jeez, I was so angry back then, I threw it in a pile of papers and probably inadvertently threw it away."

Nathan frowned sheepishly.

"I was supposed to give it directly to you. My father insisted I put it in your hands. He told me how important it was, but I was scared to see you because of how furious you were."

Nathan looked down in embarrassment as Cara took his hand.

"I think I already know what's in there. It doesn't matter now, anyway. It was sent to me years ago, and I was too frightened to open it."

I think it had something to do with my mother," said Cara. "Time went on, as it does, and I guess we both forgot." Cara's voice grew softer.

Maggie realized that the envelope she held was from long ago and the contents could be the key to many unanswered questions.

Maggie was now nervous and carefully opened the envelope.

It was fragile, for time had passed, and the white paper was now a shade of yellow. As Maggie scanned the paper, she was surprised to discover it wasn't from Ted at all. It was a letter from her grandmother Isabel to her mother. Stunned, Maggie carefully placed the letter on her lap, grabbed a chocolate given to her by Nathan, and began to read.

My darling daughter, Caralyn,

I know there are things you don't know about our life in South Carolina. For years, I tried to protect you from learning the truth. That may have been a mistake, but I felt I had no choice at the time. I couldn't bear the thought of losing you, and it was certainly a possibility.

Long ago, I worked for a man named Johnny. He was a good man but had some dark shadows that he could never quite get a hold of. My career at Dig-In Diner is where I got my start, and I had high aspirations of one day opening up my own establishment. Things didn't go as planned when Johnny became involved in gambling debts. They threatened to hurt me if he didn't pay up, knowing I was why Johnny did so well at the restaurant.

He was forced to leave town by his half-brother Liam, who promised to employ me for life in exchange.

Johnny faked his own death, set the restaurant on fire, and was not seen for years. Until, one day, he reached out when I was in trouble. Johnny persuaded me to come to Maryland to escape from Liam's demands, and he would be able to maintain our anonymity. Johnny had opened a small store down the street under a new identity. Sweetie, Ted's real name is Johnny.

He is the brother of Liam, who is your father; your father's name is Liam Kaats.

I know I told you your father's name was Carl and that he had died in an accident. I lied to you, and I'm sorry about it. Liam threatened to take you away from me.

He was a powerful man who'd become infatuated with me. When Johnny left town, I had no choice but to work for Liam. At first, things were going well, but then, life got complicated. We had a brief affair, and the guilt ate away at me. I ended it before anyone could get hurt.

When I refused to continue the affair, he stole my life savings and kicked me out.

I was a young, scared, unmarried woman with a child who saw no other way out, so I gave up my career and took you to Maryland to start over.

Maggie put the letter down as she chewed the sweet remaining chocolate.

This information was too much to read all at once. She took another gulp of her now cool latte, wishing it were something stronger.

Her grandmother had an affair? Maggie was stunned. Even more revealing was that all those years, Ted had acted as a friend but had actually been her mother's biological uncle. She tried to wrap her head around this information, aware that there were more secrets to uncover.

She wondered if Nathan knew any of this information or if he, too, was in the dark.

It saddened Maggie to learn such personal details about her mother.

Had Cara ever found out the truth? If she had, she'd never said. There were so many pieces of this still missing pieces she hoped the rest of the letter would explain.

She took another long sip of her latte and began to read some more.

When you were a child, you were curious, but I couldn't tell you the truth back then. I was too afraid something might happen, and well, honestly, I thought the truth would hurt you too much.

I hope you can find it in your heart to forgive me for all the secrets kept. Know that I loved you deeply and once you were born, my priorities shifted to being a mother.

I had to give up some of my dreams, but I hope one day, you will fulfill yours.

Enclosed is some money your father once stole from me. He wanted to control me but didn't realize that I, too, could be scrupulous. He found us many years after he threw me out, claiming he wanted you back. I couldn't let him take you and decided to take back what was mine.

His wife had just passed away, and while Liam was tending to the final arrangements for her funeral, I slipped into his house through the side gate, petrified of getting caught, but I had to get out of town and needed the money to do so.

I had been friends with his wife, Mary, a good woman, though too eager to please a man.

She knew about our affair. It hadn't been Liam's first. Back then, wives had little control over their husband's straying eyes, and there was little she could do to stop it. There had been an attraction between us at first, but later, I realized he only wanted to control me. His control became an obsession, and his obsession became deranged and often fueled by alcohol.

Mary knew how demanding Liam could be and understood that he'd pursued me relentlessly and pressured me into the situation until I had no choice but to surrender.

If I hadn't relented, he would have made my life miserable. Still, I should have been stronger. There are many things I should have done differently, and I live daily regretting those mistakes.

In any event, Mary knew he'd taken all of my earnings from me the day I'd left to keep me indebted to him, so when he was in a drunken stupor, she stole the money back and hid it for me.

This was, of course, before her dementia set in, so I was fortunate she had done so when she was still capable.

She wrote me a letter and told me where to find it when it was safe to retrieve it. I am grateful for Mary, who, although unable to stand up to her husband, indirectly stood up for me.

The best thing that came out of that time was you, my sweet daughter, the best surprise of my life. When I left town, I made my amends to start over and put your needs first.

I worked hard to establish myself, as you have too, and I want to make life a little easier. I hope I have answered all of your questions. Listen carefully to my advice.

Secrets are dangerous because they eventually have a way of being found out.

I hope you take this money with love, knowing you have always been my top priority.

I want you to live a life in which you know your value and worth without the help of a man but live tenderly enough to love fully.

I have seen you with Maggie and am confident you have achieved both.

So now, I want you to have it. Go open your bakery and live, my sweet daughter.

I love you forever,

Love,

Mama.

Tears stung Maggie's eyes as she finished reading the letter. She folded it carefully and put it back into the envelope. Counting the heaping pile of a hundred-dollar bills took her over an hour. She was surprised to find there was more than enough for a downpayment on the bakery.

Now, she needed to find out more about who owned the property.

After going through the rest of Cara's belongings, she loaded the car and headed back South. Anxiety plagued her with the information she had learned, along with knowing she was traveling with more money than she had ever seen in her life before.

After the long drive home, she showered and called Rick, her real estate friend, and George Stalin, her attorney. With the extra funds she had, she was eager to start this project.

It took nearly a year to uncover the property's ownership, but it was not without turmoil.

Maggie grew increasingly tense as the months passed, and little additional information was provided.

"George, it's Maggie. What is the status of the case?"

Her voice was tight with anticipation.

"Maggie, hi. We're still working on it. This Browne character did everything he could to conceal the paperwork that would reveal the ownership."

Maggie was confused.

"But he passed years ago. Surely, there has to be some sort of a paper trail."

"I've called in a favor, and I'm awaiting a call back from a private investigator. I'll be in touch soon."

The phone went dead, leaving Maggie more frustrated than before.

She had worked hard to get the bakery back in running order. Profits were soaring, and the local television station would feature her in a story in the coming weeks. She hoped that by then, she could proudly take legal ownership of the bakery.

It meant everything to her to finally tell the story of her grandmother and mother. She knew it would inspire generations to come and wanted to give hope to other women. The world needed more positive storylines about how women in the South persevered despite challenges.

Chapter Thirty-Three

Three days later, George called Maggie late in the evening. She was fixing some dinner and about to settle in to enjoy her grandmother's recipe of pork shoulder.

George spoke fast as he explained, "When Mr. Browne passed, his assets went through probate. Upon discovery, it was found that he'd anonymously held the deed to the property, information he had never revealed prior. Mr. Browne claimed he'd been gifted the property and had never held the deed. That wasn't true. We are headed to court the day after tomorrow to finally change the deed to the rightful owner. The judge has already approved the motion."

Maggie was silent as she listened to the information. As she processed what George said, he interrupted, "Maggie, it's you. You are the rightful owner."

With her mind still racing, Maggie remembered her mother's mention that Mr. Browne had always been vague about the arrangement, never disclosing too much information when asked about selling her the property. It all began to make sense now.

"Oh, my goodness," exclaimed Maggie. "I've been waiting for this day for so long. I was starting to think it would never come."

A week later, she found herself in court. Butterflies ravaged her stomach as she listened to the judge give his final ruling. During the proceedings, Maggie discovered that Elaine Browne's distant cousin was, in fact, her maternal grandfather, Liam Kaats.

He didn't want Isabel to gain access to the property, so he set a long-term limit on ownership until he knew she would be long gone.

What he hadn't accounted for was that his only child, Cara, would succumb to the same disease that had taken Isabel and have a child of her own. Liam intended to give the property to Cara to run, fully aware that she, too, would follow in her mother's footsteps.

After a court battle lasting over a year, Maggie finally proved that she was the rightful owner of the property since she was Liam Kaats' next of kin.

Maggie was finally granted access to the property and awarded full ownership.

As she exited the courthouse, she heard the loud chirping of birds overhead as a light rain began to fall. Tears streamed down her face as she laughed and exclaimed, "We finally did it, Mama and Grandma Isabel. We got our bakery."

———

After a long weekend of celebrating, Maggie appeared at her lawyer's office to sign the final documents. That night, she celebrated with a glass of wine and her favorite Mexican takeout.

Once she'd filed the paperwork, she changed the bakery's name to *The Mixing Bowl Bake Shop*. Then, she gathered recipes from previous generations and started writing the menu for her new restaurant's grand opening.

Maggie redecorated using both vintage and modern items to honor the past and present. She created a display for the yellow mixing bowl that had been in her family for generations.

There were also pictures of her late grandmother, Isabel, and her mother, Cara.

She included recipes and news clippings from years gone by.

She wanted to pay homage to the women before her, the ones who had sacrificed and worked hard to fulfill the dreams of three generations of women by now. She marveled at their courage and determination and vowed to make the same impact on the community.

Like everywhere else, the South was changing, but Maggie clung to her roots, insisting that the same Southern hospitality still thrived in the small town of Grover Creek.

She thought about the generations of women before her and appreciated how it had taken three generations to forge a path to her success. "Strong women produce strong women," she stated to a local news reporter doing a story on The Mixing Bowl. Maggie raised her glass in thanks to her mother and grandma, saying, "I promise to make them proud."

A story was featured in the local magazines about the three generational bakers with a massive zest for life, the grit for success, and a wholesome set of values.

Copies flew off the shelves, attracting more tourists to The Mixing Bowl who wanted to catch a glimpse of the granddaughter of the woman who started it all.

Maggie stood proudly as she was awarded The Citizens Award on behalf of the town.

"Had it not been for the women before me, I would not be here today."

Just then, two birds fluttered nearby in a tree, making noise and singing a glorious tune. Maggie couldn't help but laugh, knowing that both Isabel and Cara were celebrating alongside.

Acknowledgments

The Mixing Bowl is a tribute to generations of strong women who keep family traditions close. I am fortunate enough to be surrounded by family who have shaped me into the woman I have become.

From my grandmothers, aunts, sisters, cousins, and my beloved mother, I hold sacred the family ties that bind us, creating a protective, strong foundation. As if that weren't enough, I have been blessed with men in my family who have also helped raise me to appreciate the value of family. This story has been motivated by the importance of family bonds.

As a result, it is one of my favorite creations, close to my heart, just like the countless family members who have driven me, encouraged me, and inspired me along the way.

I have found a home in South Carolina, where I am at peace and enjoy the beautiful atmosphere. The moment I stepped onto Hutchinson Square, I fell in love with Summerville. My immediate connection to the area was profound; it was where I was meant to land. Even so, I look forward to meeting new people, visiting new places, and connecting with yet more friends.

To my friends at Horizons, words cannot describe how fortunate I feel to have you in my life. From making me feel welcome to our chats and the love you have shown me, I look forward to more great times together. A special thank you to the Pearl Leaf Lane crew for embracing me with open arms.

To the wonderful people who helped me understand the culture of South Carolina, thank you for graciously sharing your stories and experiences, enabling me to cultivate this narrative. I truly value your perspectives and time; without you, my story would not feel as authentic. A heartfelt thank you to Sheila and Mike for allowing me to learn about their family history, sharing recipes, and showing me love and kindness.

Of course, I want to give special thanks to my mother, Franny Parisi, my first teacher in life. As a child, you read to me, sparking a lifelong love of reading. I still remember sitting nestled in your embrace, looking at books together, and hearing your warming and loving voice. The greatest gift you have ever given me is believing in me with strong convictions until I could believe in myself, too. It is because of you that I love deeper, laugh harder, and celebrate the gift of life. Mom, you are my biggest supporter and champion, as well as the epitome of what it means to be a strong woman.

Thank you, Mom, for the amazing example you have provided me and all of the love and support, which means as much to me now as it did when I was a little girl.

Thank you, Joe, for being there for my mom, all the grandkids, and all of us. You never miss a beat, and we are all so grateful for you in our lives.

Thank you to my siblings and best friends, James, Marissa, Phyllis, Andrew, Victoria, and Tim. We are so lucky to have one another, aren't we? Some of my favorite memories are of the fun times we have spent together over the years. I love you all so very much. Thank you for always being supportive and loving me fiercely.

Thank you to Suzanne, Aimee, Christine, Helen, and Judy, the strong women in my life who continue to make my days happier and so much more fun!

Gloria, how I adore you and our chats! I'm lucky to have you around me.

Jim, I am honored to be part of the family. Thanks for always making me feel welcome.

William, Sophia, Emma, Rocco, Benjamin, and Matthew—our gang! I love each of you and couldn't be prouder. I'm so excited to see what the future holds. I'll be there cheering you on, knowing you're capable of anything.

Marc Ferolito, my person, my muse, and my biggest motivator to be my most authentic self, thank you for coming into my life and opening my heart and mind to all things good and pure. You make my life fun. Thank you for knowing exactly when to listen and to simply be there for me and when to remind me to take a breath. You are the best friend and partner I could ever ask for. I am looking forward to a lifetime of love together. I already know we got the happily ever after!

About the Author

Donna Lynn Lito earned her master's degree in creative writing in May 2024. She currently produces podcasts and writes web blogs at www.donnalynnbooks.com.

In addition to her latest novel, *The Mixing Bowl,* she is also the author of *4FCKS SAKE, Securely Insecure,* and *Letting Go.*

When she's not writing, Donna Lynn enjoys spending time with her family and friends in New York while also embracing her new home and the vibrant community in South Carolina.

About the Book

A captivating, heartwarming novel about three generations of strong, capable women, each of them unapologetically forging ahead in times of strife to complete the dream of opening a South Carolina bakery.

An immersive and, at times, emotional story, The Mixing Bowl traces the paths of daughter, mother, and grandmother who are each driven to make their mark in history, not only for themselves but also for all the generations to come.

Along the way, each generation faces unique challenges and hurdles they must overcome without losing any of their values.

Isabel, from a rural town in South Carolina, finds herself surrounded by difficult men who refuse to see the place of an entrepreneurial woman in this environment.

Struggling to stay in her beloved town, Isabel faces the toughest choices about whether to remain or leave the place she cherishes. She feels torn in every direction, but must she continually surrender to societal pressures that dictate who she should be?

Giving new life to her beautiful daughter Cara, Isabel teaches her to be fearless and always hold true to her dreams, some of which are undoubtedly running through the young girl's blood.

Unbridled love and boundless encouragement bring Cara far closer to fulfilling the dream than Isabel could ever have achieved, yet even she is caught in what seems to be an endless struggle.

Will she ever get the break she craves and for which she strives so hard amidst a backdrop of society's imposed limitations? One thing is certain: Cara will fight, giving everything she has in her to push for her family's goals and aspirations!

By the time Cara's daughter Maggie is born, she is presented with opportunities that Cara and Grandma Isabel could only have dreamed of. Ultimately, Maggie uncovers hidden family secrets, completely altering the trajectory of the women's legacy and leading to an outcome no one could have ever foreseen. The Mixing Bowl reveals the beautiful intricacies and harsh complexities of human relationships. In this inspirational story, each woman capably clings to her own soul's narrative while also remaining dedicated to the goals and dreams binding together generations of strong, irrepressible, and visionary women.

www.ingramcontent.com/pod-product-compliance
Lightning Source LLC
Chambersburg PA
CBHW071410300726
48976CB00006B/2048